THE LADY'S GUIDE TO CELESTIAL MECHANICS

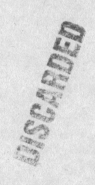

THE LADY'S GUIDE TO CELESTIAL MECHANICS

OLIVIA WAITE

AVONIMPULSE
An Imprint of HarperCollinsPublishers

THE LADY'S GUIDE TO CELESTIAL MECHANICS. Copyright © 2019 by Olivia Waite. All rights reserved. Printed in the United States of America. No part of this book may be used or reproduced in any manner whatsoever without written permission except in the case of brief quotations embodied in critical articles and reviews. For information, address HarperCollins Publishers, 195 Broadway, New York, NY 10007.

Digital Edition JUNE 2019 ISBN: 978-0-06-293178-8

Print Edition ISBN: 978-0-06-293179-5

Cover design by Patricia Barrow
Cover illustrations by Christine Ruhnke
Cover photographs © Romance Novel Covers

Avon Impulse and the Avon Impulse logo are registered trademarks of HarperCollins Publishers in the United States of America.

Avon and HarperCollins are registered trademarks of HarperCollins Publishers in the United States of America and other countries.

FIRST EDITION

19 20 21 22 23 HDC 10 9 8 7

For Caroline, Mary, Katherine, and Sally

ACKNOWLEDGMENTS

There are so many people to thank for their part in the creation of this most unlikely book. First, my gratitude goes to Cathy Pegau, whose bisexual con artist heroine in space helped me recognize a part of myself I hadn't been able to see clearly before. (Hint: it's not the con artist part.) Rose Lerner's feedback on an early draft of this manuscript was invaluable, and I stand in awe of her clarity of vision and undiluted genius for story and character fixes. My editor, Tessa Woodward, and the entire Avon Books team have been marvelously patient with an author used to flying solo. My agent, Courtney Miller-Callihan, combines steely authority with expert reassurance in the best possible balance.

My family—especially my mother, my sister, and my grandfather—have been unfailing in their love and support on what has been at times a puzzling sort of journey. I am lucky to have them and I know it.

Every writer should have so trusty a sidekick as Elwood the mini-dachshund, who is there every writing day to insist

I sit in the well-lit chair by the window and do not move for several hours, please. His selflessness is an inspiration to us all.

Lastly, and always, there is my husband, Charles: the truest soul I know, whom I am honored to share a life with, and whom I love more with every day and every new revelation.

THE LADY'S GUIDE TO CELESTIAL MECHANICS

CHAPTER ONE

1816

Miss Priscilla Carmichael made a lovely bride. Her dress of champagne satin caught all the light and haloed her, making her blond curls gleam and her eyes look as blue as a summer sky. The Honorable Harry Winlock was more than a little awestruck as he promised all his worldly goods to her endow, and grinned outright when she in turn promised to serve and obey, so long as they both should live. Their hands held sure and steady while the groom slipped the wedding band onto his bride's finger.

It was Lucy Muchelney, in the front pew, whose hands were shaking.

She hadn't wept, though. She didn't dare. If she started weeping she wasn't sure she would stop. And it wouldn't be the kind of weeping the bride's mother was doing in the pew beside her: ladylike, a-tremble, with gentle dabs of the handkerchief in the corners of her watery eyes. Mrs. Carmichael watered all through the sermon and after, while the newlyweds wrote their names in the parish register.

Lucy, dry-eyed, felt every scratch of the pen as though the point were scraping over her very soul.

One month ago, the banns announcing the match had been read out in this same church. Lucy had frozen with the shock of it, then waited until they were alone to ask Pris why. "I don't want to spend my life alone," Pris had explained. Her hands in her lap twined around one another, flexing the way they always did when she was anxious about something.

Lucy had wrapped her hands around Pris's to still them. "You aren't alone. You have me."

"I know," Pris said, "but Lucy, I can't *marry* you. My grandmother's trust only becomes mine upon marriage. I have to think about how I am going to live."

"You should think about how you're going to live with a husband—does Harry know that you don't love him?"

Pris dropped her eyes.

Lucy's mouth was a bitter twist. "Does Harry know that you love me?"

"Oh! How could I tell him?" Pris cried. "It's too cruel of you to suggest it. He couldn't possibly understand."

And then Pris had started to cry—had buried her face in Lucy's breast—had tilted her face up and kissed Lucy desperately. But later, when the buttons were rebuttoned and the petticoats smoothed back down, Pris had only said: "Harry and I will be married from Winlock House on the twenty-eighth of March." As if the past five minutes—or the past five years—had never happened at all.

Pain sent Lucy to her feet, out the door, and down the cliff path toward the sea. The rocky shores along the coast here were strewn with shells of ancient things, and the scene's steady bleakness had always offered her refuge in the past. But the cliff path looked out over the bay toward Winlock House, and the sight only drove the blade in deeper.

Now she stood on that same cliff, the lingering winter wind tugging her dark hair loose from its pins, watching carriages pull up to Harry Winlock's home in an endless stream of guests for the wedding breakfast. Even at this distance she could recognize her lover's slender shape, the green-decked bonnet bent demurely toward the tall, proud figure at her side. Pris put a hand on her husband's elbow as they walked up the stairs, and for a moment Lucy felt a phantom pressure on her own arm.

She turned her back on all such ghosts and trudged home.

Stephen was just heading out when she arrived, his paint box and canvas waiting on the table in the foyer. "So Priscilla is wed," he said. "I hope you wished her joy on both our behalves."

"I did," Lucy lied.

Stephen nodded absently, then fixed narrowed eyes upon her. "You don't have any suitors, do you?"

Lucy had to bite her lip a moment before answering. "Not a one."

"Mmm. Too bad. It's high time you were settled." His eyes flicked down to her gray mourning gown to evaluate its presentability, as though she were a landscape by an as-yet-unknown artist and Stephen had to set the opening bid at auction. "I think Peter Violet might be brought up to the mark."

The idea of marrying any man, especially one of her brother's friends, was appalling. Lucy grappled for an excuse. "Father's death—"

"Was six months ago."

"There's still so many calculations to be done—"

Stephen snorted. "What calculations? You were an able assistant to Father's astronomy work, I'll grant you, but surely you didn't think you'd be able to just pick up where he left off?" At Lucy's sullen silence, his mouth went flat. "You did think that. Well, you can stop thinking it right now. We don't have the money to indulge your self-important whims."

Lucy bristled. "The star catalogs are of enormous scientific value—"

"They were, when they had Father's name on them. And it would be different if your work was self-supporting. But we might as well sell that telescope at this point—nobody is going to employ a woman as an astronomer, are they?"

Lucy ground her teeth together to keep from saying something unladylike. It would only make things worse.

Stephen apparently took her silence for assent, because he gathered up his paints and opened the door. "I'm heading up to Yorkshire for a few weeks. We'll talk more of this when I return." For a moment, his brown eyes softened with concern. "You'll be alright on your own, won't you?"

"Aren't I always?" Lucy muttered.

Her brother's eyes gleamed. "You don't want me to send for Aunt Annabelle?"

Lucy blanched. Aunt Annabelle was loud and opinionated and cursed with five obsessively musical children. You never knew if the sound you heard was an oboe, a violin, or a protest because a sibling's hair was being pulled. "Don't you dare."

Stephen smiled ruefully at the old joke. Lucy held her

cheek out for a kiss, then waved as her brother leaped into the carriage and trundled out into the wider world.

The bands that seemed to wrap Lucy's chest loosened in relief as soon as he was out of sight. She had a few weeks' respite, then. Maybe longer, if the light was good and the wine was flowing. Stephen did have a tendency to lose track of the time when the Muse was on him.

Lucy didn't have that luxury, not when there were observations to be made and celestial bodies to be cataloged. Comets, nebulae, double stars—she'd learned their habits and mapped their arcs, calculated their distances and predicted their returns. The late Albert Muchelney might have been the name best known to the world, but it was his daughter's gift for mathematics that had fleshed out his astronomical theories with positive proof. Especially in the last few years, with his health in decline. Pris always said . . .

Lucy squashed the thought. Pris was gone. Lucy truly was alone now. Cold seeped from the stone floor through her thin slippers, as she realized that for the next two weeks she would be entirely at her own disposal.

At least with Stephen away, she would save money on food. And there would be less cleaning up for Sadie. There was no pest like a painter for leaving crumbs in the sofa cushions and stains on all the furniture. Even now, his paint box had left behind a smudge of color on the foyer table—a streak of vivid green that splashed along the polished wood and onto the letter waiting there.

Lucy recognized the handwriting and her heart skipped a beat. It was from the Countess of Moth.

The same countess who had traveled the world observing eclipses with her brilliant husband, astronomer George St. Day. Together they had set foot on six out of seven continents. The countess had thrown a twelve-course banquet in the shadow of the pyramids during a partial eclipse. She had charmed the King of Bohemia so much that he wrote her a poem every day for a year, and only stopped when his royal bride insisted. While St. Day was making observations in far-off longitudes and recording the positions of potential new stars and their arcs, the countess would copy them out meticulously column by column and send them to all the hungriest scientific minds back home.

Those minds had included Albert Muchelney—and, though nobody knew it, Lucy herself. An envelope from the countess meant a wealth of new data, ready to be converted into the star catalogs and comet charts that had been the Muchelneys' primary source of income. The smooth, elegant slope of the lady's handwriting was nearly as familiar to Lucy as her own.

Lucy snatched up the letter and hurried upstairs to the observatory.

It was far too grand a name for such a small space: two overstuffed chairs with frayed upholstery, a writing desk scarred by compasses and candle wax, and as many books as could be crammed onto the shelves without causing them to spontaneously combust from the pressure. Her father's chestnut instrument cases—violin and oboe, untouched since long before his death—were stacked coffin-like on the sheet music shelves. In the far corner, a spiral staircase led up to the slate roof, where the brass seven-foot telescope waited patiently beneath covers until its silver mirrors could gather starlight once again.

Stephen might know how expensive telescopes could be to purchase, but they could never seem to be sold for as much as one paid for them. If her brother carried out his threat and sold off her telescope, Lucy would lose the means to observe the stars on her own, and the household would be none the wealthier for it. A ribbon of bitterness at the unfairness of it all knotted tight around Lucy's gut. They would be in much better financial shape if Stephen could resist exotic paints and lengthy country visits with his artist friends. When was the last time he'd sold a painting? Did he really expect her to sacrifice her passions to support his?

She sat heavily in her usual chair and tore open the letter. George St. Day had died of a fever over a year ago, but maybe his widow had sent one final list of figures. Maybe Lucy could do another set of catalog pages before Stephen came back. If she could prove herself profitable, he might let her keep working—or at least he might see that she wasn't losing them money by what she did. It was a feeble hope, but even the smallest candle looked bright at midnight.

Alas, no sheets of data were included. In fact, the note was rather brief.

My dear Miss Muchelney,
    I was so sorry to arrive back home to hear the news concerning your father. Please allow me to offer you my most

ardent sympathies, and let me know if there is any help you need in such a trying time.

I hope that you might be able to help advise me on one particular scientific matter. One of the last things my late husband did was purchase the first book of a five-volume treatise on celestial mathematics by a French astronomer called Oléron; the work is being loudly acclaimed all over the Continent, and the Polite Science Society is very interested in producing the work in English translation for the benefit of our own learned men and scholars. I had hoped to ask your father to undertake it— the matter concerns some of the higher-level calculations he put to such use in his own work. Very rarified stuff, and a difficult project for the translator, as so few of our number ascend to those particular heights of genius.

With your father gone, do you have any recommendation for who else might best undertake such an edition? A student or a protégé, familiar with his methods? Any advice you have would be most appreciated, by myself and by the scientific world.

> *Regards,*
> *Catherine Kenwick St. Day, Countess of Moth*

Lucy set the letter on the desk and clasped her hands tight against her stomach. Thoughts of what could have been piled up inside her like storm clouds, grim and weighty with unfallen rain. M. Oléron's *Méchanique céleste* was rumored to be the most important work in the field since Newton's almost a century before. The star catalogs were very useful for other astronomers, but this? This project would have been an *illumination*. It would have let her hold up a torch to lead the way, instead of stumbling along behind the masses of scholarly, important men.

This was her one great chance, and she'd missed it. All because, as Stephen said, nobody would hire a woman astronomer. Not even one who read fluent French and had an intimate knowledge of the mathematics involved in calculating the orbits of eccentric bodies.

A student or a protégé, familiar with his methods . . . Let me know if there is any help you need . . .

The idea flowered like a bruise, with a dark and silent ache. Her father had been too isolated, his genius too eccentric to attract students or apprentices the way some natural philosophers did. His brilliance had been a kind of refinement, of taking the ore other scholars dug up and forging it into instruments learned men could use to test the world.

But it hadn't only been his work. It had been Lucy's, too. She'd been doing it for a decade, both before and after she'd gone to school at Cramlington. For the last two years she'd performed all of the computations on her own: her father had grown increasingly impatient with long lists of numbers, so she had handled all the figures while he'd worked out celestial theorems and speculated on the possibility of rain clouds on the surface of the sun. It had never occurred to Lucy to add her name as a coauthor, and now she regretted the lapse. Because having her name on even one of those catalog sheets she'd compiled would have made the chasm she was about to leap a little less vast.

Lucy was going to translate Oléron. If she could persuade the countess to agree to it.

She could probably make her case more eloquently in person. A letter could be lost, or set aside to be replied to later and forgotten about in the press of more urgent matters. A supplicant was harder to say no to. Lady Moth had always dealt with Lucy frankly, and might even appreciate a bold approach. The countess had traversed most of the globe in her life, in places both wild and wildly peopled: surely Lucy could manage one short journey through her native country, for something she wanted so desperately.

Running away to London without telling Stephen was a craven, underhanded thing to do. It would make her brother worry, it would make him angry, and, worst of all, it would make him think he was wise and she was flighty. By any reasonable metric, it was the wrong choice.

She had her bags packed within the hour.

Catherine St. Day, eighth Countess of Moth, raised the teacup to her lips. The porcelain lizard whose body formed the handle preened emerald-bright beneath the touch of her fingers. It was the same tea set her mother had always brought out for her favorite visitors to Ruche Abbey; the lizard teacups, the larger serpent-twined teapot, and the silver dessert service shaped like black currant leaves, with tiny silver ants and honeybees posed to nibble at the offered sweets.

A few other treasures remained from those days: one or two enameled snuffboxes, some heirloom porcelain, a handful of ancient cameos Catherine had loved since her childhood. But the bulk of the seventh Countess of Moth's vast collection had been sold off before George and Catherine had left on that final expedition. Thousands upon thousands of seashells, stones, corals, crystals, insects, birds, and botanical specimens, a lifetime's work of cataloging. Not to mention the zoo, the aviary, and the gardens that surrounded Ruche Abbey. Then the house and the land itself. The seventh countess had spent a fortune, had traded favors, had financed explorers and merchants and experts of all kinds to expand her holdings. She'd wanted, Mother said once, to have a specimen of every living species. She had come closer to doing so than anyone in the world.

And now it was all gone. Scattered and sold piecemeal. George had been too demanding of Catherine to leave her any time to administer such a hoard, and there was nobody else to do it if Catherine didn't. So she had arranged an auction—the catalog topped two hundred pages—sold the abbey to an eager marquess, and kept only the London house and a few items of personal significance.

Everything here was a relic. None more so than Catherine herself.

She had become the eighth countess upon her mother's death—one of those rare titles that could pass through the female line—but since her marriage to George had never been blessed with children, the earldom would now lay dormant until some offshoot scion stepped forward to claim it. So far, nobody had. Catherine doubted anybody ever would: the Kenwicks had never been particularly fruitful, each generation usually producing only a single heir or heiress. The family tree was almost entirely trunk.

She finished her tea and cut herself a second piece of cake. She might as well: there was nothing else for her to do.

The thing nobody had told her about becoming a relic was how very quiet it would be.

With George gone, there was nobody berating the parlor maids for tidying up a stack of papers that he'd been keeping specially to hand as a reference. Nobody throwing inkwells at the wall when the butler interrupted his work to announce a visitor. Nobody pacing restlessly up and down the halls at all hours and waking the cook at midnight because he'd forgotten to eat dinner, then sending footmen out at dawn for more tobacco because he couldn't think properly without a lit pipe between his teeth. Nobody raising any kind of fuss at all.

But it wasn't precisely peaceful, either. Or else Catherine had lost the knack of finding peace in silence. It reminded her too strongly of the times when George was angry and refused to speak to her for days on end.

She felt . . . rudderless. Sluggish as a ship becalmed. The long span of her future stretched out toward the horizon, a flat opaque nothingness as terrible as any sea.

At some point, she would have to find something to do with herself. She was still attending meetings and dinners with the Polite Science Society, because it was familiar, and comfortable, and they understood what she'd lost in George. A purpose, as well as a husband. But maybe there was something else out there—some cause that could be hers and hers alone. She had spent her whole life assisting others' ambitions: now she found herself at the head of a household of servants, cared for and cosseted, the freedom of her hours piling up around her like unspent coins.

She was desperately in need of occupation.

Idly, she smoothed a hand over the cushion on the sofa beside her. The vivid scarlet fans of the Tahitian myrtle blooms seemed to radiate the heat of their tropical home. It had taken her weeks aboard ship to embroider this panel. Red and pink and green shading into one another, silks shimmering against their linen background. She'd lost herself in the creation, putting in stitch after stitch, the threads a way of marking time in what had felt like an endless, eventless journey.

Just playing about with fripperies, George had always muttered when he barged into her parlor to demand her help with the latest matter of scientific urgency. An acceptable way to pass the time until there was real work to be done.

The butler entered with a gentle knock. "My lady, a visitor. A young lady, with luggage."

"Show her in, please, Brinkworth." The reply was automatic, and it was only after the butler had bowed and retreated that Catherine realized she could have declined the visit from whoever-it-was. She kept forgetting there would be no battalion of criticisms to ward off if she desired an afternoon of solitude, or if she chose to stay home rather than playing the dutiful wife at a lecture. Or a meeting. Or an expedition to the further latitudes of the earth.

Really, she was so *glad* not to have to be a wife anymore. She just wished the duties required of a widow were a little more clear-cut, that's all. It was doing her no good to linger at the crossroads. She wanted to be moving; she just didn't know which path was the correct one.

Brinkworth reappeared, his shoulders stiff and his luxuriant eyebrows held at their starchiest angle. "Miss Lucy Muchelney," he announced, and retired again.

Catherine rose from the sofa and offered up a polite smile, masking her surprise. Miss Muchelney looked younger than Catherine had expected, considering they'd been corresponding for ten years. Heavens, had the girl been answering her father's letters for him at fifteen? She must have been. She was all black hair, pale skin, and sharp angles. Her dress was a dark lavender, wrinkled with travel. But it was the gleam in her gray eyes that set off Catherine's warning bells.

"Lady Moth, I presume?" the girl said. She held out a hand, bold as you please. "Lucy Muchelney. It's a pleasure to meet you in person at last."

Catherine took the offered hand and was surprised by the firmness of the grip.

The gleam in the girl's eyes grew brighter. "I hope it wasn't too forward of me to surprise you, but when I received your most recent letter I knew I had to visit."

Letter? Oh yes, the Oléron translation. Catherine waved Lucy into a chair as the maid brought a fresh pot of tea and another plate of pastries. The girl tucked in with a good appetite. "I wonder you went to so much effort just to pass along your suggestion for a translator," the countess said as she poured. Which was the polite way of saying: *Why didn't you simply write?*

"Oh, I don't have a suggestion," Miss Muchelney said, lightly and tightly. She'd accepted a cup of tea and peered in delight at the lizard. Now she was turning the cup around and around on its saucer, the two porcelain pieces scraping together like teeth.

Catherine clenched her jaw automatically against the noise.

Miss Muchelney, unknowing, radiated a nervous enthusiasm, like a harp string just after it's plucked. "I've come hoping to undertake the work myself."

And with that, Catherine was finally able to identify that troublesome gleam: ambition. Specifically, the scientific variety.

Those two pieces of cake sank like lead in Catherine's stomach. She had seen ambition like that before. Had married it, in fact, when she thought she was marrying a man with a heart and feelings like other men. But it wasn't six months after the wedding before all George's romantic speeches and thoughtful attentiveness had vanished, to be replaced by impatience, indifference, and an obsession with his chosen field of study that swept all other passions aside. And it wasn't enough for George to pour himself into the work, oh no—his wife had to support every book, every paper, every flight of brilliance and quest for discovery. No matter what her own inclinations were, no matter what the personal cost. Catherine had been dragooned into science's service like a thoroughbred being harnessed to the plow.

It wasn't that she failed to appreciate the nobility of the endeavor. It was only that she'd wanted to put it aside sometimes to do other things. Like eat. Or sleep.

She reacted instinctively and put on her most forbidding tone of voice. "Frankly, Miss Muchelney, I was hoping to find someone with a closer working relationship to the Polite Science Society. This is not the kind of project that can be undertaken casually during the odd rainy afternoon; it will require sustained effort and consultation with other men of science—astronomers, mathematicians, natural philosophers. At least," she sighed, "that is what Mr. Hawley, the president of the Society, assures me would be ideal. He always wished your father would have visited town more, been more involved with his fellow scholars. He believes in the power of collaboration."

Miss Muchelney set her teacup down—a mercy—and leaned forward, a flush pinking her cheeks and the gleam in those gray eyes undimmed. "Would it help persuade you if I told you I was for many years my father's closest collaborator? I computed astronomical data for him and took extensive notes on his observations, as well as working the proofs his hypotheses required. There is nobody who knows his methods as well as I do—and you say Oléron's book is more abstruse than the work most Society members are doing."

Catherine pursed her lips, forced to yield on this point. "Apparently some of the mathematics are quite revolutionary. Mr. Hawley proposed inviting your father to stay with him until the work was complete." She paused. "Were you really performing all those computations you sent me, all those years?"

"Yes."

Catherine, privately, was a little staggered. She had been treating those pages as products of Arthur Muchelney's genius. With his white hair and distracted manner, it had been easy to assign him the role of a Prospero or a Merlin, pulling arcane secrets out of the very air. To imagine this slender young woman doing the same—well, it changed things. The Polite Science Society was full of wives and sisters and daughters offering support to male scholars: transcribing notes and manuscripts, compiling tables, answering letters. But as far as Catherine knew, there wasn't another woman making her own work the center of her efforts.

It made her uneasy to find one, though she couldn't say why.

Miss Muchelney sensed Catherine's hesitation and forged ahead, her hope evidently undimmed. "Perhaps Mr. Hawley would be willing to offer me the same hospitality he'd reserved for my father."

Catherine choked on her tea and had to set it aside until she stopped sputtering.

Had the girl no sense at all? Roger Hawley was a bachelor, living alone; for him to invite an unmarried girl to stay at his home would be a scandal. More so if the girl showed up and boldly invited herself. It would have been nothing in the seventh countess's day, when women of wit labored alongside their husbands and brothers to break all the laws science had held dear since Aristotle's time. But this was a more sober century: Britain had left the upending of things to the colonies and the French, and was steering a course toward the stern comfort of restraint. It was lamentable, perhaps, but one had to live in the world as it was.

Catherine had known too many scholars careless about what society thought of their behavior, but they had been grown men, not a lone young miss bereft of family or friends. She was drawing breath to say as much to her visitor, but one look at those gleaming gray eyes deflated her.

You couldn't reason with ambition. All you could do was moderate the damage it did. Try to get ahead of it, imagine problems before they started, smooth out the road for the impractical person with their gaze on the heavens.

She leaned back, succumbing to the inevitable, hands going slack as if letting the rope out and the sail unfurl before a prevailing wind. By God, she thought she'd done with being driven by the contrary whims of genius. But the girl needed guidance, and these were waters Catherine knew. "I yield, Miss Muchelney. Far better if you stay with me while you argue your case. There is a Society dinner at the end of the week—we shall see then what Mr. Hawley thinks about your qualifications for the work."

The tension in Miss Muchelney's shoulders unwound. Her response had something of a sigh in it. "Thank you, Lady Moth. I accept, most gratefully." She picked up her teacup again and took a sip, dainty as you please.

George had looked just so complacent whenever Catherine had finally given way. She swallowed her tea down to the dregs and felt she could drown in bitterness.

Apparently science was not done with her yet.

Chapter Two

Lucy looked over her meager wardrobe with an eye newly opened to despair.

None of her gowns were what Lady Moth would consider appropriate evening attire. No silks, no velvets, no satins—nothing but wool and printed muslin, most of them now dyed in mourning colors.

Only her best dress came close to elegance, with its delicate folds and floral decoration. Bright flowers crowned the puffed sleeves, and green leaves trailed the low edge of the bodice. She hadn't been able to bring herself to dye the cream and ruin the hues of the embroidery. It flattered both Lucy's figure and Lucy's coloring, and it was all she could do not to throw it on the fire and watch it burn.

She'd last worn it to Pris's wedding. Not only because it was Lucy's finest gown, but because every vivid stitch of those leaves had been worked by Pris's hands. Lucy had wanted her to see and be reminded of what they'd been to one another.

Pris hadn't noticed, muffled in the fog of nuptial congratulations. Her eyes had slid past as though Lucy weren't even there. That moment had sent Lucy hurrying home from church, instead of following the other guests to the wedding breakfast. The champagne would have burned like acid all the way down.

But tonight, Lucy would suffer twice as much pain to get that sense of invisibility back. She had a hunch that the countess was not going to overlook any of her flaws, of dress or character or temperament.

The countess was not what Lucy had expected.

She was intelligent, of course, but Lucy had known that. Sharp, too—but you'd have to be, to have survived so many sea voyages to such challenging places. The years she'd spent moving from one far-off land to another, with barely a brief pause at home in between! When she'd looked at Lucy and narrowed her eyes in that evaluating way, Lucy had gone a bit breathless. She'd felt like a book pulled down from the shelf, splayed open by a determined reader, and held firmly in place until she gave up all her secrets.

No wonder Lucy had blushed. Even now, thinking about it, she felt the heat rise to her cheeks—because what had surprised her most of all was that Lady Moth was so beautiful.

You wouldn't think, looking at the pinned-up gold of her hair and the sweet pink-and-cream plumpness of her figure, that this was the same woman who'd traversed so much of the globe, from Iceland to the Cape to the archipelagos of the Southern Seas. She'd sat in that parlor as though she'd been grown there, as immovable and domestic as a potted rosebush. Only the lines at the corners of her eyes had hinted at her three-and-a-half decades of age, so much of that spent squinting against sea and sunlight.

Those keen eyes would see Lucy's gown for what it was: a rustic trifle. And Lucy had already intruded by turning up on the lady's doorstep and all but demanding hospitality. The wild spark of hope that had caused her to leave home had burned out somewhere on the third day of stagecoach travel. At some point she would have to write to Stephen and tell him where she was. He was bound to be furious.

And then what? Head back to Lyme with her tail between her legs?

No, she had to make sure Lady Moth would not regret her invitation. Since there was nothing to be done about her attire, she would have to make up for lost ground in other ways. Docility. Gratitude. Sparkling conversation. Assuming her wits didn't scatter, pricked by those piercing eyes.

When Lucy was shown to the dining room, Lady Moth was already waiting there, gowned in deep blue satin with white embroidery like sea foam along the cuffs and collar. The long sleeves kept it less formal than it could have been, but Lucy still blushed at the contrast between the countess's grace and her own rumpled rusticity.

The chasm between them yawned a little wider.

Lucy took her seat at the table and dropped her gaze, only to find a fresh horror awaited her there.

A formal place setting. A full battalion of forks bristled on one side, and a series of spoons yawned ominously on the other. And good heavens, there was even a miniature matched pair stationed at the top of the plate, the fork's tines facing one way and the spoon the other. Like fellow soldiers pressed back to back during the last desperate stand of a siege.

Albert Muchelney had been a gentleman, but an impoverished one. Some of Stephen's artist friends had titles that stretched back into the mists of British history—but they'd prided themselves on being deliberately wild and improper, leaving the tedious business of etiquette to more commonplace minds. Lucy knew how to curtsy and comment on the weather, but this embarrassment of cutlery was beyond her experience.

Fortunately, there was an expert sitting right beside her. Lucy's gaze flew up and fixed avidly upon the countess. When the lady nodded at Brinkworth to begin, Lucy took a deep breath and gathered her fortitude.

"I expect your journey has left you with an appetite," Lady Moth said, reaching for the largest spoon in the row. Not, Lucy observed with dismay, the *first* spoon. Logic would be no guide here. "Have you traveled much, while helping your father in his work?"

The countess took a dainty sip of soup. Lucy clutched her spoon as though it were a talisman. She couldn't both eat and answer. She chose to talk first. "My father preferred to stay at home. I was sent north for schooling, and saw a bit of the country then, but afterward, Father's health took a turn and he required my help at home." She dipped the spoon in her bowl and took a quick sip—the broth was warm and salty and rich, and bolstered her courage. "Certainly, my experience pales in comparison to all the journeys you've undertaken."

Lady Moth made a polite murmur and took a drink of wine. After a beat, Lucy did, too. She licked her lips, and tried another tack. "Out of all the places you've seen, is there one in particular that you treasure most?"

The countess blinked as though surprised.

Lucy took the opportunity to spoon more soup into her mouth.

After a moment the lady replied: "On our way back from Egypt we stopped for a few days in Rome. I woke at sunrise on the second day and decided to walk in the direction of the Colosseum. There were birds singing in the trees, and all that old, weathered stone—and everything so quiet. A hidden place in the heart of a city. It felt like the ancients had built the whole thing just for me, and left it waiting there until I happened along." She blinked again, and the mask of politeness came back into place, her lips pinching in a smile that Lucy could tell was half embarrassed, and not at all sincere.

Lucy felt a ghost of loss, as though someone had blown out the brightest candle in the branch.

Her hostess reached for her wineglass again, and Lucy followed suit. The silence lengthened, as she turned over the countess's story. "Did you ever go back?"

If Lucy had hoped for more confidences, she was doomed to disappointment. Lady Moth's smile tightened still more. "George didn't care for Italy. There were too many other astronomers already there, you see."

Lucy swallowed more wine. "No wonder he went all the way to the South Seas."

"Precisely." Lady Moth spun the stem of her wineglass between her fingers, an odd light coming into her eyes. "You should have seen the look on his face when he found that the natives all knew the southern stars better than he did. With so many islands, and so much ocean between, they all grew up reading the night sky."

"A whole nation of astronomers," Lucy laughed. "I'm envious."

The countess looked up sharply, and the light in her eyes faded away.

Lucy's laughter went cold on her tongue. She set her wineglass down in silence and followed the countess's hand to the next fork.

The soup was taken away and the next course began: Lucy only recognized half the dishes set down. Brinkworth stepped forward to carve, sliding paper-thin wisps of beef onto Lucy's plate. She sent a longing glance at a platter of roast partridges, but since Lady Moth didn't take any, Lucy couldn't know and didn't dare guess which utensil to use.

She let the partridges be and took another sip of wine. "What was Mr. St. Day's favorite place in your travels?"

The countess chewed her meat a long time before answering. "None of them. He hated being abroad. Things were never English enough for him. The food was always wrong, the tea never properly brewed, the heat and the scent of the air always irked him."

Lucy shook her head. "Then why do it?"

"For science, of course," Lady Moth said. Her gaze stayed low, on her plate. She pressed the tines of her fork down until they punctured the morsel of meat, but didn't lift it to her mouth. "He wanted to be a discoverer of something. Anything. A planet, a comet, it didn't matter, so long as he could attach his name to it. Or failing that, to be first, or best, or most memorable in some field."

"He was a very accomplished astronomer," Lucy offered.

"Yes." Lady Moth's gaze flicked up, and Lucy smothered a gasp. That glance was sharp enough to cut. The countess dropped it again almost immediately and went on: "He would have been happier in an earlier age. Making that daring first voyage to Otaheite, standing beside Charles Green observing the transit of Venus. He spoke of it often, lamenting that he was born too late for that one and too soon for the next. They only come around every century, you know. If George could have boarded a ship that sailed across the years instead of the seas, I think he'd have left us all behind to try it, and thought it an excellent bargain."

"Probably easier to live until the next one, instead," Lucy offered. "Fifty years is a distance off, but at least you're already traveling the right way down the road."

Her hostess stilled, wineglass against her lips. When she spoke, her words were deliberate and her tone was wry. "I'm sure his death came as a great disappointment."

Lucy went scarlet.

Brinkworth stepped forward into the silence and refilled her glass, but Lucy didn't dare drink any more. Her tongue was clearly loose enough.

Lady Moth raised a delicate eyebrow. "I am quite taken with the decoration on your gown, Miss Muchelney. Did you embroider it yourself?"

And just like that, Lucy's mouth was full of ash. "N-no," she stammered thickly. "It was done by a friend."

"She has a very talented hand."

"Yes," Lucy all but whispered. "She did. Does." Good intentions were cast aside as she reached for the wineglass. The alcohol burned against the rawness in her throat.

Lady Moth's gaze was still on her, too keen.

Lucy cast about for something inoffensive to say. "She has lately married."

Lady Moth smiled. "I'm sure her husband's waistcoats will be the richer for it."

To her horror, Lucy felt a tear tip over the sill of her eyelid and slide headlong down the slope of her cheek. She dashed it away, humiliation scalding her from the inside out. The countess looked startled as Lucy pushed herself up from the table, chair scraping hard against the floor. "Please excuse me, my lady. I'm afraid the journey has worn me out more than I thought."

Lady Moth nodded, her golden hair bobbing in the candlelight. Her eyes were still keen, but puzzled.

Lucy, burning with shame, turned away without another word.

By the time she reached the door Brinkworth held for her, the tears were coursing down her cheeks. The butler's gaze was distant, but in one hand he held out a handkerchief. Lucy murmured an embarrassed thanks and made her escape.

By the time she reached her bedroom, the handkerchief was soaked.

Catherine's toilette was a treasury of scent pots, powders, pomades, and stray pieces of jewelry. A perfect dragon's hoard.

Catherine certainly felt like a dragon: irritable and scaly. There had been no call to be so sour to the girl at dinner last night. Apparently two years of widowhood had blunted her ability to rein in her tongue around company. She would have to polish up her manners before Mr. Hawley's dinner party later this week.

"Narayan," she said, as her maid's light brown fingers slid the last hairpin precisely into place, "will you tell me when Miss Muchelney is awake?" The girl deserved an apology, or at least an olive branch, after having been run out of dinner in tears.

"But Miss Muchelney has been up since dawn, ma'am," the maid said at once. "I brought her toast and tea, then she asked to be shown to the library."

"Oh," said Catherine, surprised. "Thank you." Narayan curtsied and departed. Catherine looked at herself in the mirror—hair pinned just so, face powder-pale, a decorous string of pearls around her neck—and made a face. "If only you were half as sweet as you looked," she muttered, then went to the library to speak to her guest.

And stopped, with her hand on the knob and her heart in her throat.

Pausing to listen at this door was second nature by now. The muffled *whap* of books being pulled from the shelves and tossed to the table, the low rumble of her husband's voice arguing with imaginary interlocutors, the sharp *thunk* of footsteps against the floor as he paced restlessly, struggling with some turn of phrase or feat of logic or mathematical formula—the symphony these made would tell her what kind of mood George was in, and how best to approach him.

Guessing wrong meant the difference between a mollified husband happy to attend a Society dinner, and one who insisted on locking himself and his wife away until the vast, slow glacier of his anger had melted away again.

But George was gone, and no matter how hard she strained her ears, all she heard from the library was a silence she had no way to interpret.

She let out the breath she was holding, then pushed the door open. There was Miss Muchelney, in a deep gray gown, perched in George's favorite armchair. Catherine looked for telltale signs of her mood—the set of her mouth, or the tension in her posture—but the girl was frustratingly relaxed. She was resting her back against one arm and had her knees pulled up tight against the other. Her hair shone black as a crow's wing in the morning sunlight, and she was biting her lip as she turned the pages of her book. Catherine recognized the mulberry leather of the cover: she'd found the Oléron, drawn directly to it like a magnet to a lodestone.

So this young woman had been the mind behind all those long strings of numbers. George had always been so thrilled whenever a new set of charts appeared, built in no small part from observations collected on his many journeys. He'd perched in this library like an ancient alchemist in his workshop, poring over the arcs of celestial objects, checking them against earlier published catalogs to see if he'd managed to find something new. Once or twice Albert Muchelney had shown George to have confirmed a nebula spotted only once before, or a star that was known in Europe but had never been observed in the Southern Hemisphere. "For all he lets his imagination get the better of him," George had said, "there's a brilliant mathematical mind in the old man yet."

But it had been the old man's daughter all along.

George would have been livid. Even now, two years after his death, Catherine felt herself wilt a little inside imagining him angry.

Miss Muchelney turned another page, completely oblivious to Catherine's scrutiny. The silence looked likely to go on forever. Catherine gave a delicate little cough.

Miss Muchelney flushed charmingly. She yanked her legs down, closed the book, and tugged her skirts into some semblance of order.

Catherine put on a smile and sat on the sofa nearby. It creaked beneath her—the springs were old and in need of replacing. "My, you are early to work today, Miss Muchelney."

Miss Muchelney blinked in apparent surprise. "But I slept quite until dawn, Lady Moth. Besides: there's nothing so rejuvenating as a new proof, eloquently laid out in clear language." Her smile was shy and self-effacing. "It's better than tea."

"I am glad to know you've had both, then." Catherine fidgeted slightly. "Please allow me to apologize for being such a poor hostess last evening."

"Apologize?" Miss Muchelney stopped fussing with her skirts and looked up, cocking her head. "What for?"

Catherine pressed her lips together and tried not to squirm with embarrassment. "Surely it's not a good thing to send a guest running from the dinner table in tears."

Miss Muchelney's head cocked a little farther. "But all you did was compliment my gown."

"I . . ." Catherine stopped, and took a breath, and groped for words. And let the breath out again in a frustrated huff.

Miss Muchelney's lips quirked in amusement. "Did you mean it as an insult?"

Now it was Catherine's turn to blush. "Of course not."

"So what is it you're saying you're sorry for?"

The words were gentle, almost laughing, but Catherine winced as though they were shards of glass. Because the truth was that she did not know—and it was mortifying to have it pointed out. She swallowed hard and tried again. "I am glad to see you are feeling better this morning."

"Oh yes." Miss Muchelney reached into her sleeve and pulled out a folded linen square. "Your butler was kind enough to loan me this last night—could I ask you to see it is returned to him?"

"Of course." Catherine took the handkerchief back, flattening the folds against her knee. Someone had embroidered it in white work: it looked plain and simple from far away, but close up her fingers could trace the hidden texture of a chevron pattern, all fierce points and lines of impeccably straight stitches.

Just seeing it made Catherine itch to escape this room and go back to her own sewing, to the vines and buds and blossoms that soothed her when she felt awkward or out of place.

But she couldn't abandon her guest so easily as that. Catherine's blush deepened, and she cast about for a change of subject. Science was a safe choice. "Do you think Oléron is going to be very difficult to translate?"

Miss Muchelney shook her head. "Oh no—the French took a little getting used to, I'll admit, but the mathematics are beautifully clear. It's a great achievement: tying together nearly fifty years' worth of work on gravitation. I can see why the Society is so interested in making it available in English." Her long fingers stroked the cover tenderly.

Catherine wondered what that touch would feel like if— but no, such thoughts were not to be entertained. She put that vision away in the same place she hid all the others, and folded her hands deliberately around Brinkworth's handkerchief. "Have you started writing out your translation yet?"

The girl shook her head. "Oh no, I'm still in the preliminaries. I worked through the table of contents, and now I'm just skimming to get a sense of the author's style. To just dive in headlong would be like trying to map a place you've never been before." She smiled, a dimple appearing at the corner of her wide mouth. "Probably not sound cartographic practice."

Catherine's smile felt a little more natural this time. "Certainly not to any mapmaker I know."

Miss Muchelney looked up again, her amusement dissolving. Her fingers twisted round and round one another. "May I ask a favor of you, my lady?"

In Catherine's experience, *favor* meant *trouble*. She braced herself. "Of course."

"Will you introduce me to the Society properly? The whole Society, I mean—not just Mr. Hawley."

Catherine frowned. "But your father was a Fellow— surely you must already be known to them as his daughter."

Miss Muchelney shifted in her seat, eyes evasive.

Catherine's puzzlement deepened and darkened. "Or did you not manage all his correspondence?"

"No." An embarrassed pink was creeping up Miss Muchelney's neck. "He had me respond to your letters specifically, since you were the one who most often sent us figures. He wrote monthly to Mr. Hawley, Mr. Chattenden, and Sir Eldon. Less frequently to a few others." Her hands were white-knuckled, wrapped so tight the grip had to be painful. "His genius was of a quicksilver, meandering variety. He could see how the calculations were to be done, but he would leave the actual working of them to me. It was mere labor at that point. He would rather spend time allowing his mind to stray into the higher regions of natural philosophy, stretching the bounds of what we presently imagine, trying to pierce the veil between our sight and the grand truths of the universe." The girl bit her lip. "Or so he liked to say."

"Yes," Catherine said slowly. "I remember Sir Eldon reading us a letter about cities on the moon. It caused a great sensation at the time; they argued about it for months afterward."

Miss Muchelney's head tilted, the briefest of flinches before she forced herself upright again. "My father loathed being joked about. But science always wounds the ones who love her."

Catherine bristled instantly. "Science does nothing of the kind," she retorted. "Science merely exists. She can't raise a hand to anyone. It's people who do all the wounding."

Miss Muchelney was staring openly now, startled by Catherine's vehemence.

Catherine was a little startled herself, and forced her tone into a gentler register. "Let me tell you about my first scientific voyage. George and I had been married two months before we departed. It seemed like such an adventure: traveling to the far side of the globe, visiting new islands in southern seas, sleeping beneath new stars. And the islanders were so very friendly, so happy to see us. At first." She found she had balled up the handkerchief, and made herself smooth it back out and fold her hands as primly as she could. "There was a terrace we found near where the ships landed—a beautiful, wide thing made of black coral, with a large central altar. The islanders would bring food there, and flowers, to honor their ancestors. They told us about this, as soon as we had picked up a little of one another's languages." Catherine took a long breath. "And then our geologist took his pickax to one corner, breaking it apart for a sample. Our botanist plucked the flowers and named them after himself. And my new husband swept aside all the offerings to the dead and set up his telescope on the altar, because the clearing was free of trees and he wanted the best vantage into the skies. When one of the islanders protested, and tried to push George away, Captain Lateshaw had the man flogged. Because order had to be maintained." She pressed her lips together, the anger and disappointment still sharp even all these years later. "The islanders weren't so friendly after that."

"I see," Miss Muchelney murmured.

"I know the men of the Society," Catherine went on. "They are devoted to knowledge, and they do not shy away from arguing with one another. They will run roughshod over maidenly feelings and reticence. They will question your assumptions, your theories, and your facts. Are you *very* sure you want to open yourself up to their attacks?"

The girl's gray eyes flashed, her mouth settling into a

mulish line, and for a moment Catherine went cold with dread of the outburst to come. George had always let loose the most vicious edge of his tongue whenever she'd doubted him, no matter how slightly. She tensed her fingers to hide the shaking of her hands and focused on breathing, out and in. A strike sometimes hurt more if you braced against it.

But when Miss Muchelney spoke, her voice was cool and quiet. "I am an astronomer, too," she said. "So long as they confine their arguments to points of theory and observation, I have nothing to fear from them, however fierce they may be. I assure you I can be just as ardent in defense of my own theories, and just as quick to point out the flaws in someone else's argument." She looked down at Oléron, and back up again. Her eyes were warm and liquid as silver. "It is kind of you to worry about me."

Catherine could only stare. That the blow hadn't come had left her dizzy. The library walls seemed to spin around her, and when her hands tightened around each other she felt the bones of her fingers grinding together. She parted her lips, trying to catch her breath.

Miss Muchelney's eyes dipped down to Catherine's mouth, and that silver gaze grew warmer still.

The countess felt heat curl tight and low in her belly.

Then Miss Muchelney looked away again, and the moment was broken. "You mentioned that there might be other candidates for the translation?" she asked. A little too diffidently.

Catherine coughed slightly, clearing unaskable questions from her throat like so many cobwebs. "Yes . . . I believe Mr. Hawley has someone in mind he knows here in town, and Sir

Eldon's younger son has expressed an interest as well. There may be one or two others brought up, as the wider membership writes in with opinions, but those are the likeliest men you would be collaborating with. The Society is taking more of an active interest in this publication than they have in the past. They hired out someone to edit Captain Lateshaw's final botanical journals two years ago, and the results were infamous: meandering poetry, expurgated passages, and none of the man's celebrated tables of species or orchid illustrations." Miss Muchelney's horror was evident. Catherine arched an eyebrow, relishing the coup de grace of this particular tale. "Apparently the editor we hired had traded the original drawings all to his local pub one by one, in exchange for glasses of gin."

Miss Muchelney sputtered most gratifyingly.

Catherine's lips tilted up again. "So you see why Mr. Hawley is keen to avoid repeating the experience."

"I should think so!" Miss Muchelney reflected a moment.

Caroline stared at where her teeth bit into that long lower lip.

The girl tapped a fingertip against Oléron, thoughtfully. "If I were to translate just the first chapter, would you read it over for me? A sort of experiment, to make sure my work is up to the Society's standards."

"I am not sure how much use I could be," Catherine demurred. "The mathematics are well beyond my reach, believe me."

"I can promise you there will be no poetry." Catherine laughed at that. Miss Muchelney offered her a rueful smile. "It makes me a little nervous, to be honest. I haven't done any translating from French since my school days—and those were short passages. Short enough that I did them two or three times, in styles varying from more to significantly less formal." Her generous mouth stretched out in an unabashed, girlish grin. "Once, we found a shocking play by Molière that some mischievous former student had slipped into the library. We had the first act written all out in limericks before they caught us at it and confiscated the book."

For a moment she glowed, remembering, and Catherine caught her breath—but then the light flickered out and Miss Muchelney looked so bereft that Catherine nearly handed her the handkerchief again.

A suspicion glimmered in Catherine's mind. "Was this . . . the same friend you mentioned last night?" she asked.

Miss Muchelney's glance was sharp and startled.

Catherine kept her own face smooth from long practice.

"Yes," the girl admitted. Cautiously, as was only prudent. "We met at Cramlington. She was the dearest friend I've ever had."

"Until her marriage."

Miss Muchelney nodded. Her jaw was tense. Her eyes defiant. And her spine could have taught steel how not to bend.

Catherine didn't know why she was pushing this subject. It was not at all a proper line of inquiry. She didn't even dare name what it was. But the questions were sprouting so thick and so fast—How had it started? Ended? Had it been a mutual discovery of attraction or a deliberate seduction?—that she couldn't fend them all off in time the way she usually did.

So she picked the safest one, and used it as a shield against all the dangerous questions around it. "What was her name?"

"Priscilla." There was no mistaking it. Only love could make the name drip from Miss Muchelney's mouth in those honeyed tones. Even a love in mourning still had sparks in it.

Catherine, who would have given much *not* to hear it, couldn't deny the truth. She wanted to make some excuse and leave the room, to find her bearings again, but she couldn't in good conscience abandon her guest after upsetting her like this. Not for a second time. Every one of the women of the Kenwick ancestral shades would come howling out of the wallpaper in protest, a horde of hospitable poltergeists.

Instead Catherine stood and walked toward the windows, where the sunlight was slinking in beneath the long velvet curtains. It took her a couple good pulls to open them—the moss-green panels moved reluctantly, though the staff had kept them pristine—but soon enough they had parted to let in the tender light of a spring morning.

"The light is much better on this side of the house," Catherine said, her voice deliberately calm. "Would it disturb you if I were to bring my needlework in here for a while?"

"Not at all," Miss Muchelney said, with a blink.

Catherine, relieved, went off to fetch her silks.

Chapter Three

W hile the countess was gone, Lucy rummaged through the library's writing desk in quest of paper, pen, and ink. If she were going to try and dazzle the Polite Science Society with a sample passage, she might as well start working on it now.

She was three sentences in when Lady Moth returned with her tambour hoop, her hook, and a fall of light muslin half worked with blossoms of such an astonishingly vivid poppy red that Lucy dripped ink on half a paragraph's worth of paper before she could stop staring. She blotted the splatters with a mutter of annoyance.

Lady Moth only smiled indulgently and sat in the other armchair, the base of the hoop frame resting on her lap.

Lucy bit her lip, unable to sink back into French or physics. Priscilla had always wanted to be entertained while she worked, and Lucy was finding it hard not to break the silence with a story or a question.

The countess worked calmly, though, as though the embroidery were something to escape into, rather than escape from. The muslin was stretched between the two wooden arcs of the hoop, the hook pierced the light fabric, and the slender silk thread was pulled through and formed into long chains of close-set stitches. Through all this, Lucy watched the countess surreptitiously from the corner of her eye. The pale sunlight gave her gold hair an angel's gleam, and the muslin frothed cloudlike down from the hoop and past her knees. She was a complete confection, a richly, roundly luscious, perfectly domestic delicacy. Like the Renaissance Madonna Stephen had once copied from an Italian gallery.

Except: the Madonna's colors were blue and white, and the countess's hands were full of red.

With that sharp hook and that blinding skein of silk, Lady Moth stabbed into the white muslin over and over, like the daintiest possible murder. Another blossom took shape beneath her hands: choppy, almost square petals stacked atop one another in a blunt cone. It wasn't like any flower Lucy had ever seen before: it was like a mosaic tile, or a polished gemstone, or a dragon scale. Somehow stark and decadent at the same time.

"What kind of plant is that?" she blurted, before she could stop herself.

Lady Moth answered easily enough. "The pineapple ginger. It grows in many places in the South Seas."

"It's . . . striking."

Lady Moth's rosebud mouth was at its best when she smiled. "It is, isn't it?" She finished the last petal and started another one. "They grow right up out of the ground, on leafless stalks. Bursting into bloom. Almost like torches."

"I noticed the cushion in the parlor yesterday. You have quite an eye for tropical flowers."

The countess stopped stitching and looked up, eyes wary.

Lucy swallowed hard but forged onward. "Did you ever think about studying botany?"

The countess's shoulders tensed, as if she were resisting the urge to hunch them. "Until the last trip, all our expeditions were with Mr. Lateshaw. With so distinguished a botanist onboard, they hardly had time to humor my amateur curiosity." Lucy made a wordless noise of affront, but Lady Moth only shifted her hoop a quarter turn to get a better angle on her embroidery. "I was much more welcome as a needlewoman, to those gentlemen who had left their wives at home. Or who had no wives at all. Like Captain Lateshaw. I put a border of lilies on one of his waistcoats to cover up some mending, and he said that they were so lifelike he could feel the cool English rain even beneath the heat of the southern sun." Her hand paused briefly, the tambour hook buried in ivory and scarlet. "He was always so kind to me."

You could never mistake the sound of true grief, once you had felt it yourself. It made the mettle of the soul ring in sympathy, like one bell softly chiming whenever its neighbor was struck. Lucy could feel the echo in her whole body, softening her. "He sounds like a true friend."

"He was." Lady Moth's eyes were misty as she resumed her work.

Lucy let the subject drop, but her mind refused to put it entirely away. She dawdled at her translation, trying to unravel the tangled skein of her thoughts.

Evidence: when she'd been brought to the library, the maid had had to remove several dust covers from the furniture before leaving Lucy to read in peace. The doors had creaked when they were opened, and the sofa had squeaked beneath the countess, and the curtain rings had rattled and resisted being moved.

Conclusion: this library was a place nobody had used for a good long while. Obviously not in the years the couple were traveling, but apparently also not since George St. Day's death two years ago. Lady Moth was putting up a good front of serenity, but every now and again her eyes would flick to one side or the other, and her lips would purse, betraying her uneasiness with the surroundings.

This room must have been her husband's domain. It was hardly surprising that a widow would be unsettled by memories of her lost spouse. But her voice had warmed more when she'd spoken of Captain Lateshaw than when she'd told stories about the late Mr. St. Day.

Lucy had a few shrewd ideas about why Lady Moth might not be grieving her husband's loss too deeply. But none of them were the kind of thing you just came out and said in the open. Especially not when they involved questions of rather an intimate nature.

Growing up, Lucy had always known she liked girls more than boys. She'd been deeply relieved to find other girls who felt the same: there'd been a number of them at Cramlington, as well as girls who had no preference in that way. And some of her brother's painter friends had had semisecret affairs that could get them transported (or worse) under the full force of law.

But this felt like more than just the usual camouflage for that kind of taste. This wasn't about Lady Moth's feelings about men: this was about how Lady Moth had felt about one particular man.

This was specific: George St. Day had treated her abominably.

Lucy remembered what the countess had said about her husband: *Things were never English enough for him.* She'd been on a great voyage of scientific discovery, and they'd restricted her to mending and embroidery. You could take a robin, put it in a cage, and carry it with you around the world—but if you never opened the cage door, how much of a difference would you have made to the robin's life? All it would know was the view through the bars.

Lady Moth, Lucy decided, had been *stifled*.

It was an awful thought. Lucy couldn't imagine what she'd have done about her love of astronomy if her father had discouraged her. But he'd been her champion ever since she first demanded to be allowed to study the same things Stephen did. Albert Muchelney had eventually been grateful for his daughter's assistance as she'd grown older and he'd grown frail. Even though he'd grumbled more than once about wishing he could still do all of it himself.

She had helped make his work possible. And if she'd had to mask her scientific efforts under her father's name, at least she'd been able to do what she'd dreamed of. Even if nobody had known it was her work.

That thought rang a little hollower now than it had before.

Still, her father had at least understood. Her brother never had. But Stephen's dismissal of her work had never stung deeply until he was in a position to make her discontinue it.

Lucy had only this brief window to grapple with Oléron, and also perhaps to help another woman find her way toward science.

But how to do it? As the younger woman, Lucy would find it awkward in the extreme to assume a position of authority over the countess, and anyway, Lucy was no botanist. All her efforts had been focused on other worlds, other orbits, and the distant stars.

The same stars whose movements Oléron was explaining in this first section on the principles of gravitation. Lucy looked over the work she'd done with new eyes. The translation had offered no significant difficulties yet—the author's writing was precise and elegant, but shied away from overadornment—except that, if you had no mathematics, it was incomprehensible.

Wasn't that to be expected? The author was writing for fellow astronomers, after all. Even Lady Moth, who had spent her life in the company of learned men, did not think her abilities were equal to the text.

All of a sudden it struck Lucy that there were many more inexperienced people about than there were experts in this new field. The long-range reflector telescopes of the last forty years had seen a veritable explosion of new stars, nebulae, comets, moons, and even a new planet. Balloon ascents and royal astronomy grants had caught the public's attention, and surely whetted countless appetites for knowledge. Why shouldn't they want to read a book that helped them explore all these newly widened fields?

Her project crystallized in an instant: Lucy wasn't going to merely translate Oléron's words from French into English. She was going to make Oléron's importance apparent to everyone, astronomers and amateurs alike.

She was going to write an introduction to astronomy for Lady Moth. Not a child's schoolbook, but a celebration of the wonders of the universe and the forces that kept the stars spinning.

Lucy put a bold X through the plain translation, picked up a new sheet of paper, cast one more sidelong glance at the countess, and went to work.

It was only later, as Narayan helped her undress, that Catherine rediscovered the handkerchief she'd absently tucked in her sleeve. She returned it to Brinkworth the next morning when she went down to breakfast. "Thank you for lending it to our guest," she said. "The white work is beautifully done."

Brinkworth took the scrap of linen back as though it were made of pure gold. "Thank you, ma'am. My daughter's work." A little fond pride crept into his voice, before he caught himself and smoothed his features back to proper impassivity.

Catherine blinked. Eliza Brinkworth was the newest housemaid, just turned fifteen. A dutiful girl, with a pleasant manner—but her job had her more often cleaning fireplace grates and emptying chamber pots than doing delicate embroidery. Perhaps, though, if she were to be trained as a lady's maid . . .

"Is there something else, ma'am?" the butler inquired.

Catherine shook off her meandering thoughts, and dismissed him.

The day of the Society dinner, Miss Muchelney wore the embroidered muslin gown again. Catherine's eye traced anew the vines and flowers of the bodice, and an envious ember flared briefly in her belly.

The girl caught Catherine's keen glance and shivered.

"Do you need a shawl, Miss Muchelney?" Catherine asked, chagrined. "It is an unseasonably cool night."

"I don't have one fine enough for evening company," Miss Muchelney demurred, flushing.

"Then you shall borrow one of mine, of course." The girl tried to protest, but Catherine was adamant. She fetched a green wrap of wool lined with silk, and told herself she felt no relief at seeing the infamous Priscilla's handiwork hidden from sight.

They climbed into the carriage, Catherine spreading out her brown striped silk to avoid wrinkling before they arrived. Miss Muchelney held the wrap at her throat with one hand; the other clutched the papers of her translation of Oléron, which she had insisted upon bringing with her to the dinner.

"Better to have it and not want it, than want it and not have brought it," she'd said, a practical attitude with which Catherine couldn't argue.

"That's a fair bit of translating in just a few days—you do work quickly." Miss Muchelney flushed and bit her lip, but made no reply.

Nerves, surely. And no wonder. Catherine sat back and let the girl have a bit of quiet. Tonight's event was only a cordial gathering of the members closest to London, and not one of the twice-yearly great symposia, but it would be Miss Muchelney's first appearance before the Society.

But surely not her last. For nearly a week now Catherine had watched her guest work: steady, concentrated, focused bouts of effort. It was no longer difficult for her to imagine Miss Muchelney filling pages with exact calculations and figures—or fitting data to theories, or arguing upon observable evidence. She had watched enough men doing science that she couldn't fail to recognize it when it happened right in front of her.

Perhaps she had not seen women doing it before because she'd spent so many years away from England.

It was not precisely a comfortable thought, and it decided her: she was going to throw her full support behind Miss Muchelney as translator. After all, the Kenwick fortune was partly sponsoring the work. George had used Catherine's money to influence the results of similar Society arguments in the past, so she knew Mr. Hawley was susceptible to that line of persuasion.

Mr. Hawley's cozy brick home was dwarfed by the glasshouses glittering to either side—the one a cool, shaded space for Alpine flowers, mosses, and lichens, the other a hothouse for tropical species, where the air had so much warmth and moisture going through the door was like walking into a cube of soup. His parlor had a smaller replica of this on a low table, so that Mr. Hawley could display his best specimens for learned guests.

Their host was showing off a star-like cluster of white blooms in this miniature edifice when Catherine and Miss Muchelney arrived. "Ah, my dear," he said, his cheeks flushed red with excitement, "do let me introduce my latest discovery." But instead of the flowers, he turned to a gentleman next to him with rich brown skin. "May I present Mr. William Frampton, our newest addition to the Society? His father is a musician at court, and Mr. Frampton has already published several mathematical letters that have been well received by the membership."

The gentleman bowed.

Catherine introduced Lucy in turn, and Mr. Hawley exclaimed and clasped her hands warmly in both of his. "My dear Miss Muchelney," he said. "My deepest sympathies on your family's loss. Your father was one of our grandest lights, and Science's sky is darker for his absence."

Miss Muchelney lowered her head. "He would be touched to hear you say so—he had no better friend than you, Mr. Hawley."

The president's florid face folded into an indulgent smile.

Miss Muchelney turned to Mr. Frampton. "My father was also a musician, sir, before astronomy diverted him. He always said music and mathematics were two sides of a single tongue."

Mr. Frampton's smile was slight, but sincere. "I would

agree, but my father would turn up his nose and insist that music is an art, not a science."

Miss Muchelney laughed in recognition.

Catherine left them talking under Mr. Hawley's eager supervision and went to greet her aunt Kelmarsh, who was on the other side of the room with the chemist Mr. Chattenden and his wife.

"Catherine, my love," said the older woman, gray hair piled high and green eyes twinkling. "It's been an age."

Catherine bent to kiss the smaller woman's parchment cheek, a flash of warmth making her relax a little beneath the tension. Aunt Kelmarsh wasn't a blood relative, but she'd lived at Ruche Abbey with Catherine's mother for fully the last decade of the seventh countess's life. She'd been Aunt Attleborough then. Twice widowed, she often still dressed in black for Mr. Kelmarsh, a quiet parson with a brilliant gift for botany whom she'd married while Catherine and George were away on their Egyptian expedition.

Before long the sallow Sir Eldon Wilby arrived to join them, along with his pleasingly plump and pinkish wife. For a while all was talk, until a noise at the door had all eyes turning: a young man burst in—color high, white forehead gleaming beneath a shock of brown hair, tugging at his slightly askew cravat. "My apologies for being so late," he said with a hasty bow.

"Nonsense," Sir Eldon said, and waved the young man over.

He turned out to be Mr. Richard Wilby, Sir Eldon's

nephew. Catherine eyed him consideringly as he joined the conversation flowing around her. So this was one of Miss Muchelney's fellow candidates for the translation work? He seemed bright enough and talked a great deal—but the impression he gave was of still being slightly underbaked. He tugged at his hair and twitched at the cuffs of his coat as if it had been borrowed from someone of greater stature.

Surely Miss Muchelney had very little to fear from him as a rival.

Dinner was announced, served, and enjoyed. Conversation remained general until the courses were carried away, then Mr. Hawley sat back with a fresh glass of his favorite honey-wine and turned to the more serious subject of the evening. "Ladies and gentlemen, it is time to talk about Monsieur Oléron. Mrs. Kelmarsh, will you take notes?"

Aunt Kelmarsh smiled tightly and nodded acquiescence. She was not a Society Fellow—women had never been admitted—but she was an avid botanical illustrator and never went anywhere without a sketchbook and a pencil. She flipped past all her ferns and flowers to the next empty page, and began jotting in her elegant shorthand.

"Thank you," said Mr. Hawley. "For those of you who missed our last discussion—" nodding at Mr. Wilby "—the Society is undertaking an English edition of Gervais Oléron's *Méchanique céleste*. This book builds on Newton's great *Principia* and has collected the past fifty years' worth of advances in mathematics, gravitation, and astronomy. Which, it must be admitted, are mostly on the French side of things. It is a definite masterwork, and if our English astronomers are to catch up to our Continental counterparts, this is the absolute best place for us to begin."

"Hear hear," said Sir Eldon, raising his port. A general murmur of approval followed.

Mr. Hawley inclined his head humbly. "Now: Lady Moth has generously offered to bear half the cost of the publication, in honor of her late husband, the much-missed George St. Day. The Society membership will raise the other half of the funds. Only one question remains: Who shall we ask to undertake the translation? We shall select two names."

Sir Eldon put a hand on his nephew's slender shoulder. "Richard took a double first in mathematics and physics at Oxford. He's read Newton and replicated all the experiments in the *Principia*. He's young, I'll grant you, but that only means his mind is fresher. More flexible and full of the juices of youth than us wizened old balloons." Sir Eldon chuckled, including both himself and Mr. Hawley in this description.

The president's smile was slight. "Does he have the French for it?"

Sir Eldon huffed into his mustaches. "His French was good enough for the Tour—and anyway, the language is the easier part of the thing, is it not? Any mind that can grapple with the mathematics will surely have no trouble with mere French."

The president nodded, lips pursed. "Mr. Richard Wilby," Mr. Hawley said to Aunt Kelmarsh.

She noted it down.

Mr. Wilby's ears were red but his chin was high, as he peered around the table for any challengers.

The president rested one hand magisterially on his lapel. "I have a candidate of my own to suggest. Mr. William Frampton has been a Society Fellow for the past six months, and has already contributed several letters to our *Polite Philosophies* in that short span of time. He is a gifted autodidact who would have made a great sensation at Oxford, had his race permitted him to attend."

Mr. Frampton crooked a sardonic eyebrow at this phrasing.

Mr. Hawley continued blithely. "His grandmother was from Saint-Domingue, so he speaks French like a native, and his residence here in London makes it a simple matter to consult with him whenever an issue with the manuscript should arise." For a moment his cloud-like brow furrowed with remembered storms. "We all are, I'm sure, anxious to avoid a repetition of the kind of results Mr. Grenfuller presented us with, when we trusted him with Captain Lateshaw's papers."

The company murmured agreement. Aunt Kelmarsh looked up, her green eyes acid-bright, before returning to her notebook and jotting down Mr. Frampton's name.

Mr. Hawley took another sip of honey-wine and set the tiny cup aside. "So, shall we designate our translators in the official Society record—?"

Catherine straightened in her chair. "Excuse me."

"—or are there any objections?"

"Excuse me," Catherine said, more loudly.

Mr. Frampton cleared his throat.

Mr. Hawley beamed at him. "Mr. Frampton, my dear sir?"

"I believe Lady Moth has something she wishes to say," Mr. Frampton offered. Quite as if Mr. Hawley had not blatantly ignored Catherine a bare moment ago.

Mr. Hawley's smile stayed put. He blinked once or twice, then turned toward Catherine without a single muscle changing the placid set of his features. "My lady?"

Catherine swallowed her nervousness. She rarely addressed the Society, even in so informal a setting, preferring to make arrangements with Mr. Hawley in private and allow him to convey them to the group at large. She wished she had thought to prepare remarks in advance. Best to be direct.

"I would like to propose Miss Lucy Muchelney as a translator," she said.

A ripple of surprise ran around the table, as Lucy raised her chin and folded her hands serenely in front of her. Only Catherine, who was more than usually interested in Miss Muchelney's hands, could see how the knuckles were white with strain.

Mr. Hawley chuckled as if Catherine had said something witty. "Miss Muchelney? Translate Oléron?"

"She is of anyone the most familiar with her father's finely developed mathematics," Catherine said.

Sir Eldon wheezed a hearty laugh through the brush beneath his nose. "Letting his daughter play at astronomy is just the sort of wild hair Arthur would have gotten, don't you know."

Lucy's cheeks had twin spots of red, but her voice was

measured when she replied. "He trained me first as an assistant, but in the last year before his death I was performing all of the calculations on my own."

"While he sent us letters about Lunarians and life-forms and the rain clouds he spotted on the sun," Mr. Chattenden broke in. Mr. Chattenden was a chemist and had taken the solar letters as a personal affront, Catherine recalled.

Sir Eldon laughed and Mr. Wilby openly snickered.

Mr. Hawley only turned his kindly eyes toward Catherine. "Miss Muchelney is not a Society Fellow."

"Is Mr. Wilby?" she countered.

"Not yet," Mr. Hawley replied easily, "but no doubt his uncle will sponsor his application shortly. Miss Muchelney has not the same recourse, since Society Fellowships are forbidden to the gentler sex."

"And what if they weren't?" Catherine blurted out.

Every eye at the table swiveled toward her: some in astonishment, others in horror. Anger gave her armor. She went on. "You all know Mrs. Kelmarsh is as talented a botanist as her husband ever was. He told us often how well they worked together on many of the papers he wrote for us. Why shouldn't she have the benefit of Fellowship, as he did in his lifetime? Why shouldn't the Society have the benefit of her insight and intelligence, simply because they're *hers* rather than *his*?"

The widow's eyes were bright as stars as she looked up, as though Catherine were speaking a new language. Emboldened, Catherine continued. "If Miss Muchelney has anything like her father's gift for astronomy, surely she should be able to put it to use?"

"I think it's an excellent suggestion," said Mr. Frampton, folding his arms across his chest. There was an odd note of relief in his voice.

Mr. Hawley cut him a keen glance and sipped at his drink. "Perhaps."

Sir Eldon huffed wordlessly.

Mr. Wilby leaned forward. "But let us go about it scientifically," he said, his expression eager as a puppy on a new scent. "We must start not with assumptions, but with the fundamental questions. Several points need to be clearly determined at the outset: first, whether women are capable of astronomy; second, whether they would offer any particular benefit to astronomy; third, whether astronomy would be of any use or benefit to women; fourth, whether it would harm the needs of mankind to encourage women to put their efforts toward the sciences rather than the continuation of the species."

Mr. Chattenden nodded. "That is a proper scientific line of enquiry, Mr. Wilby."

Aunt Kelmarsh looked nauseated. Miss Muchelney reeled back as though she'd been slapped.

Catherine's body went hot with rage. The men of the Society had almost always talked over her, of course—but she'd always thought that was because she was no expert in their chosen fields of study. She hadn't known they'd been imagining she was inferior simply because she was a woman. But here was Miss Muchelney—brilliant, sensitive Lucy Muchelney—being talked about as if she had no more brain than a child, simply because she was wearing skirts instead of breeches.

Words like embers danced on her tongue and she feared the lightest breath would kindle them into flame.

Mr. Hawley stayed cool. "Fruitful as such a debate would be," he declared, "I'm afraid that it can be no solution to our present quandary. You know, my dear Lady Moth," he said, reaching a hand out and placing it on the table in front of Catherine, "the idea was for our translator to work with the men of the Society. Surely you will see the impropriety of Miss Muchelney being closeted for long stretches of time with so many single men, in what must be ardent and rather volatile circumstances?"

Catherine let her eyes narrow. It was one thing to worry about the girl living with a bachelor—but merely existing in the same room? "Are you suggesting not all Society Fellows are to be trusted to behave like gentlemen?" There was a jumbled general outcry at this. Catherine pressed her advantage. "If that is your only concern, then I would happily attend as chaperone whenever Miss Muchelney is working in consultation with the other translators. Her expertise with the mathematics is paramount, and not to be tossed aside."

Mr. Hawley shook his head, his face all apology. "My dear lady, it is out of the question." He pulled his hand away and leaned back, eyes distant, the topic clearly finished in his mind.

"You might at least take a look at her work before you dismiss it," Catherine insisted stubbornly. "She's already made a good start on the first volume."

Lucy said not a word as she pulled her handwritten pages out of her pocket and set them on the table in front of the Society president.

Mr. Hawley kept his eyes on Catherine, swept out his hand, and brushed the pages, unread, to the floor.

Aunt Kelmarsh gasped, hand over her mouth, and Mr. Frampton's eyebrows shot up.

Mr. Hawley sighed. His tone was all sweet disappointment. "My dear countess: you must know you are being unreasonable." While Catherine choked on shock and outrage, he turned to Miss Muchelney, putting a hand on her wrist and gripping it with earnest entreaty. "Please do not think I disparage your eagerness to help, my dear girl—it is only that as men of science, we must uphold certain standards if our work is to be accorded its proper value in the community. You understand, of course."

"Oh yes, Mr. Hawley," Miss Muchelney replied tightly. "I understand you perfectly."

Catherine rested both her palms onto the dinner table and stood. Chairs scraped as the others hastened to follow her to their feet. Old oak creaked as Catherine leaned forward. "Mr. Hawley, you have your standards, and I have mine. This behavior fails to meet them on every level. I officially retract my half of the funds for this publication."

Mr. Hawley's mouth went tight with fury. "You think to bully me, Lady Moth—but the Society will go ahead with a proper scientific translation, with or without your support."

Catherine ignored him and gave the rest of the company a tight nod of farewell. "Mr. Frampton, Mr. Wilby, I wish you every good fortune with your work. Miss Muchelney." She swallowed hard. "If you prefer to stay awhile longer, I can have the carriage return for you."

Miss Muchelney stood easily. Her voice was all sunshine when she replied: "No need, my lady. I shall intrude no longer on Mr. Hawley's kindness." Catherine saw, with vicious glee, one corner of the president's mouth tighten as he caught the bright, bitter undertone. Aunt Kelmarsh's lips quirked as she caught it, too, and she sent Catherine an eloquent look. Miss Muchelney made a very pretty curtsy, set her chin at a most stubborn angle, and marched out of the room.

Her discarded manuscript pages fluttered farewell as she passed.

A s soon as the carriage began to move, Miss Muchelney's invulnerability cracked. Her shoulders shook and her eyes went wild and she clutched Catherine's green wrap around her as though she were caught in the sudden blast of an arctic howler. Catherine twisted her hands together, feeling helpless. "I'm so sorry," she said. "I should have gathered up your manuscript pages . . ."

"Oh, that." Miss Muchelney half laughed, a sound like a wild thing. "That was only a clean copy. I still have the rough version and all my notes, safe and sound where they belong." She pursed her lips. "Mr. Hawley only *thought* he was trampling all my hopes and ambitions."

Relief was a river, deep and quiet. Catherine's fingers relaxed. "I'm glad," she breathed.

"You tried to warn me how it would be," Miss Muchelney replied. Her voice was watery, forewarning Catherine about the tears that soon began to spill from her eyes. The girl scrubbed at her cheeks with the heel of her palm. "I should have listened."

"I had no idea they would be like *that*," Catherine said. The upswelling anger that had sent her storming away from Mr. Hawley's dinner table still sizzled just beneath her skin. "I had expected them to grapple with you about mathematical formulas or how you interpreted your French verb tenses. They have those sorts of arguments constantly. I thought they might question your expertise, yes. I never thought they might question your existence!"

For that is what Mr. Wilby's argument had amounted to. He had wanted to debate the very fact of women's intelligence, when the intelligent woman seated across the table from him ought to have been proof in and of herself.

Miss Muchelney turned her head to stare out the window at the passing city. Light from a streetlamp passed briefly over her face, and then was gone. "They think of me as my father's satellite. And so they cannot see me as I am. Anyone who's ever looked through a telescope should know: perspectives can be distorting."

"Trust an astronomer to consider it a problem of angles." Miss Muchelney chuckled weakly, and Catherine's anxious tension eased, though her heart wouldn't stop aching. "Not everything can be explained by geometry."

"I shouldn't have surprised them," Miss Muchelney went on. Her hands fell to her lap and fidgeted with the edging of the wrap. "It is sometimes difficult for men to change course once they have set their minds to something. I should have talked them round more, led up to the idea. I thought they would be like my father—but of course they were more like my brother."

Catherine hadn't known that Albert Muchelney had a second child. "Does your brother not encourage your pursuit of astronomy?"

Miss Muchelney let out a wordless choked laugh. "He has talked about selling my telescope." Catherine gasped. Miss Muchelney's lips curved briefly at the sound. "The day I left for London, Stephen told me nobody would employ a female astronomer." She stopped herself, then burst out: "I *hate* that he's right."

"He isn't right." Catherine leaned forward and clasped her hands around Miss Muchelney's. "He's only an astronomer— and astronomers spend a great deal of time being wrong before they come to realize it."

"He's not an astronomer. He's an artist."

"Then he's doomed to be wrong his whole life."

Lucy laughed, but even in the dimness the tears sparkled as they fell from her eyes. "I'm always crying in front of you, aren't I?"

Catherine lifted one hand and brushed the tears away. "I wish you had fewer reasons for it." Lucy's eyes were star-bright. Her lips parted on a breath that was far too soft for a sigh. Catherine's whole body went tight and liquid—how easy would it be to just lean forward, and press her mouth to Lucy's, and taste that sound on her own tongue?

She wanted it so much that it frightened her. She yanked herself away and tucked her hands tightly beneath her knees.

Lucy's breath hitched, but after a moment she turned

away and stared out the window again. "I suppose I must pack my things in the morning, then. Head back to Lyme."

"Must you?" Catherine swayed in her seat—surely it was only a tight turn of the carriage that staggered her, and not the thought of parting from Lucy. Catherine cleared her throat and tried again. "Couldn't you continue the work on your own?"

Lucy's shoulders rose and fell, a shadowed shrug. "I could—but without the imprimatur of the Polite Science Society, who would publish it?"

"I would," Catherine said at once. Imagination raced ahead, mapping out the path ahead of her, obstacles and their solutions and all. Nothing struck her as insurmountable. "Yes," she said, more confidently, "I absolutely would. How soon do you think you can have the first volume translated?"

Lucy frowned, as Catherine fidgeted, impatient for an answer. "Less than six months, for certain," she said. "Perhaps as little as four."

"Excellent," Catherine said. "You continue working, and I will ask about for a good publisher for this kind of thing. I'm sure someone can recommend a few names for us." Lucy was staring, and Catherine dropped her eyes back to her hands. "You are, of course, welcome to stay with me for the duration. If—if for any reason you don't fancy going home just yet."

Lucy tilted her head, birdlike. "I confess, Lyme does not hold much appeal at present." Another streetlamp flashed over the younger woman's hesitant smile, and Catherine let out a long, silent breath in the darkness. "And I can write to Stephen—to tell him I've found work. For a while, at least."

Catherine was relieved; she was fearful; she didn't know what she felt, as they disembarked at the townhouse and made their way separately to bed. Her nerves flickered like the candles as Narayan helped her undress. Only one thought felt solid, and she clung to it like a compass heading in the fog: Lucy Muchelney was going to have a chance to do the work she had so much talent and passion for.

That was something.

"One of these buttons is loose," the maid murmured, fingering the cuff of the brown silk. "I'll resew it for you tomorrow, my lady."

"Thank you," Catherine answered, and sat a little longer after her maid departed, drumming her fingers on the polished wood and staring into the depths of the mirror.

Chapter Four

The moon took twenty-nine days to show off all her phases in the heavens. The sun allowed himself the whole of the calendar year to creep back and forth along the horizon. Rarer events, such as Halley's celebrated comet, only graced the Earth once every several decades. In such astronomical terms, two weeks was nothing. A minute. A moment. A blink, here and gone.

Catherine and Lucy passed the next two weeks orbiting one another like a double star: ever moving, never touching, never truly separating. Between breakfast and luncheon they worked companionably in the library. After luncheon Lucy returned there, while Catherine took to her writing desk in the parlor to attend to her never-ending correspondence: letters to friends (many asking about printing houses), to colleagues, to Polite Science Society connections. She and Lucy met briefly for tea, then parted again until dinner, which Catherine took care was served *en famille* after that first disastrous night. To an outside observer it looked regular as clockwork.

Catherine was not an outside observer, no more than a sailor clinging to a spar in a wreck was an outside observer of storms. She felt lightning-struck. Every conversation, every joke, every blush and averted glance sent another bolt through her. Whole territories were beginning to burn in parts of her soul that she'd always kept carefully darkened.

She threw herself into busyness, hoping that forward momentum would leave any uncomfortable revelations trailing far behind. She found the housekeeper Mrs. Shaw in the still-room, her sleeves rolled up to her elbows and her hair a cloud of white curls above a face the color of antique parchment.

"What would you think about training young Eliza Brinkworth as a lady's maid?" Catherine asked.

Mrs. Shaw set aside the twine she was using to cut a large cake of soap into smaller bars. She had already heaped up some dozen of them in a pyramid, laid crosswise on top of one another to leave room for air between them. Her lips pursed, her displeasure plain. "I wouldn't advise it, my lady."

"Why not?"

"Both Joan and Charlotte have been with us longer, and would be better fit for the promotion." Her tone was sure, but her hands were shaking a little, causing flakes of rosewater soap to flutter down from the twine like a snowstorm in miniature.

Catherine's irritation jabbed her like an errant pin. "Are either Joan or Charlotte as talented with a needle as Eliza seems to be?"

"Has she shown you that sketchbook of hers?" Mrs. Shaw blew out a long breath. "She promised me she would only waste her own time on that, my lady. I grant you it's all very pretty—the girl has a knack, and no mistake—but she needs to develop some discipline to go along with it, or she'll be no good to anyone."

"She hasn't spoken to me," Catherine said. "I happened to see some of her work, and now that Miss Muchelney will be staying with us for a while, I thought Eliza might do for her."

Mrs. Shaw chewed on her lip a little, the pink coming and going from her cheeks. "May I speak plainly, my lady?"

Catherine blinked. "Of course."

"Moving Eliza up wouldn't look right. Because she's Mr. Brinkworth's daughter, you see—the other girls might take that for the reason for the preferment, and think it's no use being diligent in their own work, since they won't see the rewards for it. In the worst case, they might come to resent Mr. Brinkworth's authority. And mine."

Now Catherine did frown. "You would have Eliza overlooked for the sake of her father's standing?"

"Not overlooked, my lady. Just . . . seasoned a little more, if you like. It'd be more proper."

All of a sudden Catherine was sick to death of propriety. "I have made my wishes clear, Mrs. Shaw."

The housekeeper nodded, but her mouth was an unhappy line. "Yes, ma'am."

Not even finishing a piece in the library later that afternoon could improve Catherine's mood after such an unsatisfying interview. She put the last stitch in the pineapple ginger tablecloth edging and just sat there, stroking a restless finger over the scarlet silk.

Lucy huffed out a breath and leaned back in her chair. "I've just finished the introduction," she said. "Would you like to read it?"

Yes and *no* were both right answers. Or both wrong answers. Or right for the wrong reasons. But Lucy was waiting, her gray eyes eager, and once again Catherine found she couldn't bear to disappoint her. "Yes," she said. "Of course."

She set her embroidery aside and accepted the pages of Lucy's steeply slanted writing. The letters scrabbled insect-like, as though in a hurry to get all the way across the blank page.

The moment we raised our eyes to the heavens is the very moment we became, if something less than angels, still something more than animal.

Alone of all living things, mankind dares to look up from the earth and dream of other worlds. Those worlds, howsoever distant, are connected to ours by a force so vast and ubiquitous that it went unthought-of for most of history. Yet now we know that the self-same force which sends a breadcrumb tumbling to the parlor floor keeps the moon tethered in her orbit. I speak, of course, of the power of gravitation, whereby the attractive force between two bodies is mutual and equivalent, whatever the difference of mass between them . . .

Catherine caught her breath and looked up. "I had no idea Oléron was so poetic."

Lucy dropped her eyes, shifting a little in her chair. "It's not Oléron, technically. I've decided to expand the text a little, to clarify the mathematics so that you don't have to already be an astronomer or mathematician to understand what Oléron is doing. The book is brilliant on its own—but it assumes, quite understandably for a scientific text, that you've read everything else up until this point. But a lot of those works aren't available in English, or they're only summarized in old issues of *Polite Philosophies*, or they're otherwise expensive or rarely printed or very difficult for the ordinary reader to find." She squirmed again, biting her lip. "The original text leaves so much out. But the things that aren't said are important. So I'm putting them back in. And adding this introduction to explain, of course."

"You think very highly of the ordinary reader," Catherine said.

Lucy's gaze clashed with hers, then away. "I wasn't imagining just anyone," she said softly. "I was writing as though I were explaining it all to you."

Catherine, flustered, dropped her eyes to the page again: *the attractive force between two bodies . . .* All at once it was a great deal of work simply to pull breath into her lungs, and force it out again. The words pulled her inexorably forward to the following passage:

> The ancients imagined the earth was the central point
> of the universe. Newton's discovery showed us that
> this is true, but it is not the complete truth. The earth
> is the center of a web of force that touches the moon,

the sun, the other planets, and perhaps even all those distant stars that burn so far away. But every other moon, sun, comet, planet, and star is itself a center, and exerts its own force upon all the rest.

Nothing in the universe stands alone.

Catherine's gaze flew back up to Lucy, who was watching with widened eyes and her shoulders tight with tension.

Something she saw reflected in Catherine's face set her to chattering: "I could change it, if you like. Do a proper translation, I mean, simply putting the French into comprehensible English. Which might be better, overall. More expected." She twisted her hands together, caught herself, and folded them self-consciously. "I mean, since you're funding the translation, if you'd prefer—"

"No," Catherine blurted, then brought her voice back down to a more ladylike volume. "No," she repeated, though she sounded stiff and awkward to her own ears. "I think it's a good idea. A kind idea." She looked back down at the pages she held. "Maybe even a beautiful idea."

Lucy's shoulders relaxed in visible relief. "It's a little unusual, I admit."

Catherine's lips quirked. "Most beautiful ideas are."

Lucy blushed scarlet and turned back to the Oléron.

Catherine leaned back on the sofa and continued reading. The poetic prose of Lucy's introduction slipped more and more into mathematical explanations, some with actual figures and formulae, but so subtly that Catherine found herself racing along, eager to see what deduction came next. Before she knew it, she was on the last page, and there was no more.

The sofa creaked beneath her as she leaned back, breathless with elation. She remembered feeling like this once before on her seventh birthday, when one of her mother's guests had opened up the grandfather clock brought home by the sixth Earl of Moth after his diplomatic tour to the Turks. The old man had pointed out all the different wheels and gears and the way the whole thing fit together, and how winding the clock affected the mechanism. Catherine had been far too young to understand anything but that it glittered and seemed somehow alive; Lucy's expanded text gave her that same sense of awe and wonder and delight, without being at all childish. It was as though someone had taken the case off the universe, and let the reader peer at the naked machinery that powered the stars.

If she could keep this up for the whole of the book, Catherine realized, people were going to be hailing Lucy Muchelney as a genius.

Falling in love with a genius was a daunting thought.

At once, Catherine brought herself to heel. Nobody had said anything about love. And anyway Lucy didn't want a lover. She was still smarting from the last one, wasn't she? No, she would want a connection that was stable, untroublesome, supportive—a champion, a patron.

Or a friend.

Catherine knew how to be a good friend to an ambitious astronomer. All she had to do was tell Lucy the truth: that Lucy was right to persevere in her work. That Catherine didn't regret taking on the whole cost of publication—no, better not to mention the financials. Naturalists hated to worry about money, after all. Catherine knew that from long experience. Better to handle all the practical details on her own, and simply let Lucy get on with the science.

"Well?" Lucy said. "What do you think?"

Catherine blinked and realized she was chewing on her lip.

Lucy's gaze flicked down to her mouth and back up again.

Catherine had to swallow hard before she was able to reply. "I love it."

Lucy's smile was like sunlight, warming one all the way through to the bone. "Do you think it will compare well with the translation Mr. Frampton and Mr. Wilby are doing?"

"No."

Lucy blinked.

Catherine let herself grin, drawing the moment out. "I think it will eclipse theirs entirely."

Lucy's delighted laugh gave Catherine so much pleasure she had to excuse herself from the room on the pretext of a missing skein of silk. It took fifteen minutes for her heart to stop racing, and a full half hour before she trusted her hands to be steady again. By then Lucy was intently focused on translating the next passage of Oléron, and Catherine, relieved, resumed her proper orbit.

The safety of routine was interrupted again the next day by an invitation from Aunt Kelmarsh:

Damn this absurdly chill spring, but the garden's lovely anyway. This English moss is so stubbornly green, even beneath the snow. Come and have tea, the pair of you.

Catherine traced amused fingers over the purple-and-green thistle that spread its prickly self out beneath the older woman's signature. Aunt Kelmarsh's letters always had blossoms pasted into them, incredibly life-like recreations made from scraps of cut and colored paper. She'd been taught to cut silhouettes as a child in the early years of the last century, but the older she got, the more she enjoyed composing the portraits of plants rather than people. Once, while on an extended trip to the Continent, she'd sent young Catherine a letter that was nothing but a series of blossoms, painstakingly glued down to the paper in a regular grid so the letter could be folded small enough to post. Catherine had taken several days to decrypt the whole, bedeviling her mother's pet botanist and several of the Ruche Abbey gardeners in the process.

It had seemed like a game at the time. It seemed less so after her marriage, with George laying first claim to all arriving correspondence—ostensibly since much of it was vital to his scientific pursuits—so that every letter Catherine received had been opened and scrutinized long before it reached her.

Soon she didn't trust him not to read her outgoing letters as well—so she would compose long descriptions of the weather wherever they were, and border them with sketches of worm-eaten rose leaves bristling with thorns, or quiet, tense bundles of forget-me-nots. Aunt Kelmarsh would respond with equally polite replies about the state of English roads, but her bright additions of lilies and willows and myrtle would offer palpable solace in answer to Catherine's wordless plea. Catherine still had them all, upstairs, tied up safely with ribbons.

After her husband's death, Catherine had written Aunt Kelmarsh two lines:

George dead. Write as you please.

Aunt Kelmarsh had replied with a single word on the first page, underlined three times and sent halfway round the world:

Good.

The second page of the letter had been absolutely covered with detailed, precise, and glorious recreated apple blossoms, which Catherine had no trouble interpreting: *Better things ahead.*

All of which was to say: Aunt Kelmarsh's letters were never trifles. She meant something by this invitation.

Catherine sent a note back to accept—with an unseasonable mistletoe sprig doodled in the corner—and the next morning she and Lucy set out.

The wind coming off the river was sharp and cold on the westbound road. It warmed only slightly when the carriage turned off the main thoroughfare and into the dell cottage Aunt Kelmarsh had inherited from her late husband. The house sat with its back against a row of stony hillocks, draped in green boughs and protected from the worst of the weather.

The older woman waved to them from the door, swathed in a gown of deep emerald wool. Cranberries in red and thorns in ochre silk twined around the gown's collar, cuffs, and hem. "I'm afraid nothing is blooming yet," Aunt Kelmarsh said, once they'd all clasped hands and kissed cheeks. "I'm starting to worry it'll never warm." She turned to Lucy with a welcoming smile. "But first let me tell you, Miss Muchelney, I regret not storming out with you after dinner the other night. Roger Hawley has always been a tedious rule-follower, and none of us are the better for it. I can't get you membership the way Sir Eldon's doing for that Wilby pup. I can, however, let you know that you aren't alone." As Lucy blinked at this frank declaration, the old woman jammed her hands into the muff at her waist. "Let me show you the garden, and then we'll have a spot of something warming in front of a good fire."

Catherine hadn't seen the cottage garden in ten years—an eternity, in gardening time. She'd been expecting something orderly, charming rows and tiers of plants the way they'd been at Ruche Abbey. But those grounds had been expansive, even without counting the glasshouses and the aviary. This tiny place was knobbly and closed-in. Anyone in search of a vista would have thrown hands up in frank despair.

Aunt Kelmarsh had seen the place for what it was, not what it could be improved into. She'd seen the gray stone and the shaded spaces, the water and the woods and the quietness. Instead of a long line to the horizon, she'd made a path to wind between stacks of flat stone, lush with moss and overhung by the trailing arms of willows. Every turn brought some new discovery: a branching arbor overhung with vines waiting for summer, a pond frost-fed by a stream, a gathering of slender gray birches that leaned genteelly together like elven maidens at a faerie court. Catherine saw foliage of a few of the plants that the late Mr. Kelmarsh had been such a student of: peas and roses and flowering raspberry. The farther they walked, the thicker the frost became, icing everything over, until they turned the final corner.

Catherine stopped dead.

"Here it is," Aunt Kelmarsh said, her tone rich with satisfaction. "My shell grotto."

Round arches of irregular stone blocks enclosed a small space, just large enough for two people to stand out of the weather. Onto these walls a careful hand had placed thousands of seashells, small and large, their colors painfully vivid against the gray of the sky and the white of the spring frost. Lucy gasped and moved forward wonderingly, her hand tracing the dizzying patterns. Here a column of overlapped mussel shells rose tall and straight as the spine of some ancient dragon; there tiny snail shells were arranged in a spiral like the eye of a storm. Some arrangements looked as pristine as a church spire, others were wild, gorgeous encrustations like the palace of some decadent undersea queen.

Catherine looked at Aunt Kelmarsh and only then noticed the worried crinkle between her brows. "It's not as large as the one we had at the abbey," the older woman said apologetically.

"I heard the new owners knocked it down," Catherine replied against the ache in her throat.

Aunt Kelmarsh's lips thinned. "I heard that, too."

"Are these . . ." Catherine stopped, breathed hard, and tried again. "Are these all from Mother's collection?"

"As many as I could save. A lot of the rare, fancy ones went to other naturalists in the auction—but I bought as many as I could. Even the boxes and boxes she hadn't gotten around to cataloging yet. I put them in my attic for years, but when I married Mr. Kelmarsh and began work on the garden, I realized what I'd been saving them for." She blinked hard to clear the mist from her eyes. "I consider it a memorial to her."

"It's beautiful," Catherine said, moving forward. Close up, she recognized several species, though when she'd seen them last they'd been displayed in rows under glass, each one carefully labeled. This was not that sort of arrangement. That had been science; this was closer to art.

But as her eye followed the lines, variations of shape and style and color shifting like gradients, one species shaded almost imperceptibly into another, Catherine realized there was a science here as well. "Mother would love it," she said softly, and was rewarded when Aunt Kelmarsh set her mouth and coughed as if to pretend it was not tears tickling the back of her throat.

Lucy paused in her spot in the center of the grotto. "You must miss her very much."

Aunt Kelmarsh went utterly still, staring at Lucy.

Lucy looked back, her face calm, her eyes soft.

Tension crackled in the air, making Catherine tense her shoulders and bite her tongue to silence questions.

Aunt Kelmarsh sent her one flicker of a glance—and straightened, lifting her chin in the air. "She was my very soul."

Lucy nodded, as if this were a perfectly expected reply, and went back to admiring the grotto.

For a heartbeat, Catherine was too stunned to move. Then memories washed over her, of all the years Aunt Kelmarsh had spent with Mother at Ruche Abbey. Picnics in the summer. Walking together every evening at twilight. Letters flowing back and forth whenever they were separated by so much as a single day. As she watched, the light flickered and shifted, the blurred lens of a young girl's notice sharpening into the more precise view of mature adulthood.

Of course it was a love affair. It had been love the whole time.

Catherine's shock broke beneath the weight of this truth, leaving behind only the embarrassed feeling that she should have seen it properly long, long before now.

Her aunt was watching her warily. As soon as Catherine was able to meet her eye, Aunt Kelmarsh said: "They don't let you have anything whole, you know. If you don't follow the pattern. You have to find your happiness in bits and pieces instead. But it can still add up to something beautiful."

"Even if it all comes to nothing," Lucy said, ducking past an arch to peer at the shell-studded dome above her, "what else are you to do? Sit around being miserable and bemoaning the ways of the world?"

Aunt Kelmarsh snorted genially. "The ways of the world aren't so permanent as they say, my dear. It was quite different in the last century. There were times and places one could be open and free about such things."

Lucy's smile was knowing. "And there aren't now?"

Aunt Kelmarsh pursed her lips, amused. "If you know where to look for them."

"Or who to ask, apparently."

Aunt Kelmarsh put on her most mysterious air, humming innocently.

Lucy laughed.

Catherine was having trouble finding her footing in the conversation. She felt as brittle and stiff as the leaves of the willow beside her, their edges sharp with ice, every little lick of wind making them shiver. She'd known marriage could exist separately from love—it had taken less than a year for her own affections for George to wither like a plant unwatered—but she had never openly acknowledged that the reverse must be true as well: love could exist—could even thrive—quite apart from the paper forms of marriage and classifications of sex. It was all at once appalling that she and George had been bitterly bound to one another in the sight of the world, while these devoted souls had had to cloak their joy and hide it behind walls and walks and secret gardens.

Aunt Kelmarsh might have been a stepmother, instead of an aunt.

It was a thought to break the heart. Catherine valued family all the more for having so little left of it. She knew an embrace was not to her aunt's taste, so instead she tucked her arm in Aunt Kelmarsh's and leaned gently into the older woman's shoulder. "Thank you for bringing us here," she said softly.

The older woman's cheeks were red with more than the wind. Her lips curved in relieved affection. "I'm glad to know you appreciate it for what it is." With one more glance at the bright oranges and golds of the shell grotto, she turned Catherine around on the path. "Now, let us get out of this cold and into Cook's best brandy punch."

"Can you serve brandy punch in April?" Catherine asked.

Aunt Kelmarsh chortled. "My dearest girl: who's going to stop us?"

Catherine and Lucy took their leave much later than they'd anticipated, bundled up in the sunset light with hot bricks at their feet and their cloaks wrapped tight around them. Lucy soon fell into a doze: Aunt Kelmarsh had indeed been generous with the brandy punch. Lucy's bonnet was slightly askew, and a tendril of her dark hair had come loose and trailed down her cheek. She stirred slightly now and again, lips murmuring things that weren't quite words. Catherine made herself comfortable in the opposite seat and finally opened up the box with the thoughts she'd been hiding away for most of her existence.

The inescapable truth: women could fall in love with other women.

Strange indeed that an idea could change your life so completely, and yet fit in so perfectly with all that came before. She felt the force of it in her very bones. It was less as if her biography were being rewritten, and more as though Catherine were suddenly able to read the other set of lines that lay crosswise on the familiar page. The way the curve of one woman's waist had made her heart race. The elation when that Italian viscountess with dark hair and sparkling eyes had laughed at Catherine's teasing. It was desire, the same as she'd felt for the attractive men she'd known, and some sly part of her must have recognized this all along because she had put a great deal of effort into keeping these thoughts and impulses from seeing the light of day.

And for what? For a proper, unhappy marriage and a proper, lonely widowhood. She'd taken a lover after George's death, simply because she could: she was stranded, temporarily exiled from England by the uncertainty of the wars, and her sudden freedom from George's constraints had sparked her into reckless rebellion. She'd drunk too much champagne, flirted outrageously with an embassy secretary, and embarked on an absolute tempest of an affair.

Then, at the one-year mark, her lover had gone down on one knee, and Catherine had been forced to break off the liaison. She had not known until he asked the question how deep ran her horror of putting herself once more under a man's legal, financial, and emotional control. Her lover had been shocked, and angry. The parting had been bitter on both sides, and Catherine had not repeated the experiment. Better to remain alone, if seeking physical comfort led to one party's raised hopes and everyone's ultimate painful disappointment.

She'd believed she could bear a widow's loneliness more peacefully than the misery of a bad marriage. But that was like choosing whether hemlock or belladonna was the better poison. In the end, they both sapped the life from you.

That same sly voice whispered to her now: if she had an

affair with a woman, she wouldn't have to dread the specter of marriage at all.

It would easily, naturally minimize the risks. A lady-love could assert no authority over Catherine's finances, or claim any rights in legal matters. Should desire wear itself out, separation could be done privately and discreetly, requiring no Act of Parliament to make it official. There was the considerable chance of scandal if they were found out, of course—but even there, being women, they were safer from the cruelty of the law than if they'd been two men similarly inclined. Friendship, people would call it in public, even as they prayed silently their own daughters had no such friends.

It was shocking how perfect a solution it was. She wondered everyone didn't think of it. Then again . . . maybe quite a few of them did, and Catherine just hadn't noticed. Look at Aunt Kelmarsh and her mother, in the days of their idylls at Ruche Abbey.

No doubt the rolling hills and quiet cottages of old England's countryside housed more than one pair of ladies who were as good as wed in the eyes of everyone but the church and the law.

Perhaps in past years the idea would have been nothing more than an idle philosophical game to play in the safety of her own thoughts. But now there was Lucy. Lucy, with her quick smiles and quicker mind—and who had made it perfectly clear how her tastes aligned with Catherine's. That was the greatest hurdle in the business already leaped over, at least . . .

The carriage hit a bump, jolting the both of them. Lucy grumbled something incoherent and blinked wildly, but soon the swaying lulled her back into slumber.

Catherine let out a breath and leaned back again, the interruption allowing her natural caution to flow back into its accustomed corners. She shook her head as if to clear the cobwebs. Look at her, imagining seductions and passions and parting quarrels, when she hadn't even set foot on the path yet. Hadn't she doubted just this morning that Lucy even wanted a lover? Oh, Miss Muchelney might blush and give compliments, and once or twice Catherine had caught her staring in *that* gratifying way—she knew Lucy wasn't entirely indifferent to Catherine's charms, such as they presently were. But that kind of restrained flirtation was one thing. A seduction was quite another. Especially if all Lucy wanted was a friendship—in the usual, not the euphemistic, sense.

Catherine was going to have to go about this carefully. One step at a time. Inviting, rather than pursuing. Always leaving Lucy the chance to retreat, or reject. It would sting, but that was nothing. Catherine valued Lucy's freedom in this as much as her own. *I want more; I understand if you don't.*

Best to start with something simple. A gift, that's what was needed. Something that would bring Lucy delight, but that wouldn't feel like a burden. Sweets or flowers or jewelry, the usual kind of courting gifts, felt unspecific and therefore unsatisfying. It should be something particular.

Catherine combed back through their shared days, and remembered all the times Lucy had turned those keen eyes onto her needlework, asking about the names and species of the flowers Catherine embroidered. And hadn't the infamous Priscilla worked the vines on Lucy's best gown?

Catherine was beginning to loathe the sight of that strip

of green embroidery. Lucy had worn the dress twice more in the weeks since the Society dinner. Her wardrobe was as limited as you'd expect from a girl raised in a quiet corner of the country. Perhaps Catherine could arrange a new gown or two . . .

No. Tempting as it was to send Lucy to her favorite dressmaker and say the Countess of Moth would see to the bill, doing so was a good way to make Lucy feel embarrassed and obligated and perhaps a very little bit like a pet.

Turning someone into a project was a terrible way to woo them.

Lucy shifted in her sleep, pulling her cloak more tightly around her shoulders. She must have a tendency toward chills. No wonder, as slender as she was. Catherine recalled loaning her a wrap the night of the Society dinner—and inspiration slipped in like a breath and exploded in her body like a lightning bolt. She took her notebook out of her reticule and began making sketches.

The next afternoon, when Lucy returned to the library, Catherine began gathering supplies. Her needle case, since the tambour hook wouldn't do for the kind of fine work she had in mind. Silk skeins in pale shades of white, green, gold, and silver. And a length of deep blue fabric, silk and wool blended, the drape of it light and soft and warmer than its cool color suggested.

Her initial hasty sketches she spread on the writing desk, making notes to herself about alterations and possibilities in the margins. Slowly she began working out a shape in pencil on a clean sheet of paper, refining the curves and adding long trailing lines and delicate swirls. When she was satisfied with it she would pierce the paper with tiny holes along each line and dust it with pounce, leaving a dotted version of the design on the fabric beneath, ready for needle and thread to fill in.

She hid it away when Brinkworth brought in the tea, until Lucy was gone again. By dinnertime, she had her pattern finalized and pierced and ready for the next day's embroidering. She took care to work as slowly and meticulously as she could, not only for the sake of those long, precise lines, but because each day that passed was one more day for Lucy to move further away from her earlier love affair.

Catherine wanted Lucy, but more than that, Catherine wanted Lucy to want her back. And Lucy wouldn't, if she were still pining for the girl she'd lost. So Catherine let the days flow by like water while she put in stitch after stitch after stitch, as though each one were mending a small rent in Lucy Muchelney's heart.

CHAPTER FIVE

With heartfelt passion, Lucy cursed the French subjunctive tense.

She cast a bitter eye over the scribblings of her latest efforts. Oléron deserved so much better, and Lucy was beginning to despair of capturing even a third of the crystalline clarity of the original. Two months of consistent translating and expanding still hadn't made the frustrating compromises easier to bear. She put down *might* for this verb's translation, frowned at it, crossed it out, wrote *might* again, and then in parentheses added *should* with a pair of helpless question marks.

Let Future Lucy make the ultimate decision during revisions to the text. Future Lucy was always so much more decisive, somehow. Maybe because she was ever-so-slightly closer to death than Present Lucy?

Lucy groaned and slumped back in her chair, rolling her shoulders to ease the soreness from leaning for hours over the desk. When she started musing about the inevitability of death and the terrifying brevity of the mortal lifespan, it meant she'd spent too long looking at things from the perspective of the universe. She needed something on a human scale to focus on until the framework shifted back.

A soft knock heralded Lady Moth's entrance to the library. Her dress today was a lush plum that brought out the gold in her hair and the pink in her cheeks. She looked positively radiant, and deep within Lucy a chord hummed as if a hand had strummed the very fibers of her soul and set them to music.

It ought to have been agonizing, living and working in close quarters alongside a woman so beautiful and yet so unattainable. But Lucy's heart, newly mended, was prepared to bask in any sensation that was not the sharp pain of loss—so unrequited fascination for her benefactress came not as a trial, but rather as a pleasurable seasoning to any day's difficult work. And if the feeling occasionally stole her breath and her wits and kept her awake into the small hours of the night, well, nobody had to know. Really, it was much safer and more convenient than any actual love affair would have been.

Perhaps this was how her future could best be managed: devoting her days to scientific work and spending her nights silently, secretly pining for a woman with golden hair and clever hands.

It wasn't until Lady Moth set the bundle of cloth down on the desk that Lucy realized: one, she had been staring, and two, there was quite a lot going on with that bundle of cloth. It was deep blue, rolled tight, and looked very fine indeed. "What is this?" Lucy asked.

Lady Moth sat in her usual spot on the sofa, but the way she leaned forward and the spark in her eyes had Lucy's pulse racing with anticipation. "A little something I've made," the countess said. She smiled, not without some anxiety. "A gift."

Lucy sat straight up in astonishment. "A gift for me?"

Lady Moth's laugh was always soft, as if it had been packed away in an attic for too long, unused. "Who else?"

Lucy shook her head, feeling silly, and reached out a hand. The fabric unrolled and revealed itself to be a generous shawl, and Lucy choked back a gasp.

She'd thought at first it was an ocean blue, but there in front of her was spread the whole night sky.

Each edge of the shawl glittered with comets, icy silver spheres made of spiking stitches, a few with long wispy tails of single strands stretching out toward the center of the fabric. Arranged in a line, they formed shapes like classical columns, or arches on some Palladian monument. Between these edges was a vast, starry expanse, tiny glass spangles scattered across the blue like diamonds on velvet. Lucy's trained eye picked out the familiar patterns at once—there was the boxy bulk of Ursa Major, and spiky Cassiopeia the jealous queen, and the broad shoulders of Orion the hunter. She looked back again in wonder at the comet border, marveling at the subtle color variation in the silk threads. Silver and white and gold and even a hint of palest green, each thread as precisely placed as a brushstroke on a portraitist's masterpiece, giving the impression that each comet was still somehow streaking across the nighttime sky on its impossible journey.

She wanted to wrap the whole thing around herself like armor—and oh, wouldn't it make the most of all her gowns in their simple lines and mourning colors? Her lavenders and grays would look restrained and mature, rather than simply undecorated.

"Do you like it?" Lady Moth asked.

Lucy looked up, English and French and the language of astronomy spinning madly together in her brain. "I am trying very hard not to cry on you again," she stammered, "but it's difficult—because this may be the single loveliest thing I have ever seen." She put one hand out again to feel the softness of the wool—and stopped, hand hovering over the spangles of what could only be the Pleiades. A whole stellarium, worked in silk. "Did you say you made this?"

Lady Moth nodded.

This whole scene had been carefully, painstakingly sewn one stitch at a time by Lady Moth's own talented hands. Lucy's breath caught, and she hoped her red cheeks could be mistaken for a grateful blush, but all she could imagine was Lady Moth's hands going everywhere the shawl would: curving over Lucy's shoulders, tucked tight in the crook of her elbow, cupping the tender skin on the back of her neck . . .

She swallowed and cast about for something harmless to say. "Thank you. This is astonishing. When on earth did you find the time?"

Lady Moth ducked her head. "It didn't take so very long. I work very fast, after so many years' practice."

Lucy dared to stroke her finger across one of the comets. It all but preened beneath her touch. "I've never seen embroidery with this kind of shading before," she said. "It reminds me of a painting."

"It's a technique my mother taught me. More painstaking

than tambour work, but the results are striking, aren't they? And very precise. My mother loved to create needlework depictions of the things her naturalists and botanists and explorers brought back from their travels."

Lucy folded up the shawl carefully to protect the delicate beadwork, and looked up to meet the countess's hopeful gaze. "That would be something worth seeing."

"I'd be delighted to show you." Then the countess smiled. A new smile, shy and hopeful. A smile like the first ray of dawn. Lucy was enchanted.

Lady Moth led the way to the front parlor, the palm leaves on the wallpaper gleaming green and dust motes dancing gold in the sunlight. As Lucy took a seat on the sofa, Lady Moth went to the shelf over her writing desk and pulled out her mother's sampler book.

The pages were made of linen and satin and silk and printed calico, some obviously cut from old gowns taken apart, others pulled from samples that had been bound into issues of ladies' periodicals like *Griffin's Menagerie*. Every page was stiff with age and stitching, much thicker than Lucy had anticipated: the seventh countess had died long before the new airy muslins came to be popular.

The embroidery itself was a wealth of color and shape: long chains of feathered stitches, bold bright florals, and pastoral scenes. Some were experiments, trying out color combinations and new stitches, or embroidering to fit a patterned fabric—but the more pages Lady Moth turned, the more botanical and scientific illustrations appeared, carefully rendered in blues, greens, reds, and rich browns. Vast ruffled conch shells, vivid tropical plants and flowers, and then in the midst of them, exotic for being so unexpected, one perfectly subtle, unmistakable garden snail shell. It was just like one Lucy had seen in the mosaics in Mrs. Kelmarsh's garden, that memorial to a love long hidden . . .

Oh.

Lucy went dizzy as the world rearranged itself around her. The weight of revelation kept her pinned to the sofa, even as Lady Moth continued turning the sampler pages and providing expert explanations.

Perspective, astronomers knew, was everything. Could Lucy have been viewing Lady Moth wrong from the start? Every sunrise blush, every time Lady Moth's eyes sparkled when Lucy asked her a question, the way she sometimes stared so intently. All those tiny moments—if you assumed Lady Moth only desired men, those hints were dim as faraway stars in daylight. But if you thought maybe Lady Moth could want another woman as a lover . . .

The countess had been right: astronomers spent a great deal of time being wrong before they recognized the truth.

And now Lady Moth had made her a shawl as a gift. With her own hands. If Lucy was right, every stitch might as well be a caress.

Forget all that nonsense about convenient distractions and unrequited pining: if the countess was really trying to seduce Lucy, Lucy was all for it.

She just needed a little more proof. Just to be sure.

Another page flipped over. This scene showed two female figures at a graveside, the taller one holding the smaller one's hand and the letters on the tombstone spelling out birth and death dates while a willow spread mournful arms above and around them. "Your father?" Lucy asked.

Lady Moth nodded. "I was seven," she said. "It was very sudden. Mother wore black for three years." She cocked her head. "Until Aunt Kelmarsh moved in, now that you mention it."

"Do you think . . ." Lucy swallowed hard. This was a terribly impolite question to ask, but the truth often mattered more than manners, no matter what the etiquette books said. "Do you think your mother was happier with your father, or with Mrs. Kelmarsh?"

Lady Moth stayed quiet so long that Lucy began to despair she'd truly offended. She was trying to compose apologies in her head—difficult when you couldn't openly acknowledge how you'd erred—when the countess spoke again. "I don't think love works like that. You might as well ask the earth whether the sun or the moon is more important." She blushed a little pinker and raised her eyes, star-bright. "You can't always judge by what came before. Sometimes, there is a revolution."

The words burst over Lucy like sunlight, or the flare from a newly discovered comet. She stared, dazzled.

Lady Moth held her chin high, though her breathing was coming fast.

Lucy's heart fluttered in response, as though someone had replaced the organ in her breast with something winged and frantic. Slowly, inch by inch, in case the countess changed her mind, Lucy raised her hand. Careful fingertips brushed along the line of Lady Moth's jaw, barely skimming the tender skin.

When she moved up to the sweet curve of the countess's cheek, the lady leaned into the caress, slightly but unmistakably.

Lucy had embarked on romances with less encouragement, in her youth. But maturity and pain had made her cautious. Therefore she asked, in a sound barely more than a whisper: "May I kiss you?"

Lady Moth held her breath, then let out a sigh that formed a single word: "Please."

Lucy leaned down, as the countess leaned forward, and the kiss exploded where they met.

Just a simple brush of one mouth against another, but it sent heat and light and stars through every inch of Lucy's frame. She pulled in a breath and tried it again, the same way, repeating the experiment. The same result: sparkling fire.

When the kiss broke, the countess laughed a little, sounding surprised, and Lucy couldn't blame her. She was beyond words herself. She wanted to sink her hands into the lady's hair and hold her in place and kiss her until the sun went dark and the moon went dim and the stars blew out like spent wax candles.

Fate wasn't so generous with her hours, however. Lucy was only able to kiss the countess until the tea tray rattled a warning in the hall.

The sound broke them apart, Lady Moth's hands going up anxiously to her burning cheeks and Lucy's going down to smooth out the folds of her skirt, rumpled up against the countess's.

Brinkworth set tea and cakes on the table in front of them, bowed, and vanished.

Lucy looked at the contrast between her gray muslin and the countess's fine plum silk, and felt herself bump down against the earth again. Lady Moth poured tea just as she did every day, though the pink in her cheeks was a spur to memory. By the time the last cake was eaten, there was nothing for it but for Lucy to return to the library and her translation.

The shawl was still there on the desk, patient and serene. Lucy wrapped it around her shoulders and basked in the warmth as, outside the window, day slipped softly into evening.

Lucy wore her new shawl in to dinner. Catherine went breathless when she saw it, watching the glass beads sparkle as the younger woman moved—though Lucy's eyes sparkled more, as they met Catherine's. The countess flushed from head to toe and was glad to be sitting down: she wasn't sure her knees would have supported her, had she been standing when that look was sent her way.

But there were maids and footmen and Brinkworth around them, so there was nothing to do but eat dinner.

It took two glasses of wine before Catherine found courage enough to say: "Would you like to see my own embroidery sampler?"

Lucy looked up from her plate, her utensil suspended in midair like a tuning fork. A new knowledge hummed between them, taut and arresting as the note of a violin.

"I keep it upstairs," Catherine clarified. "In my bedroom."

Lucy cocked her head at this, as Catherine wished the parquet would simply open and swallow her up. It was the least graceless invitation the girl had ever been offered, no doubt. But every time she looked at Lucy, as the afternoon's kisses thronged between them, well—all Catherine's practiced phrases deserted her in favor of blunt, direct, short arrangements of words that would hopefully let other kisses happen as soon as possible. Why cast about for artful phrases when there were much better things to do with one's mouth?

Then Lucy smiled, and for a moment her gaze darted down to Catherine's lips. It was all the countess could do not to put her fingers up to feel the heat that gaze had left there.

"I would be honored," said Lucy softly.

Finally the courses were finished, the plates were removed, and the two women were climbing the stairs to Catherine's bedchamber on the north side of the house.

It wasn't the largest room—George had claimed that for himself, in the center of the hall—but it had a small chaise and a perfect view of the back garden. Narayan was waiting to help Catherine out of her gown. "I think Miss Muchelney and I can do for one another tonight," Catherine said to her, struggling not to feel transparently bold and reckless.

Narayan flicked a curious glance at Lucy, then curtsied and departed for her own bed two floors up.

Catherine had no idea what to do with her hands. Wait, no, the sampler book. She pulled it from its place in the top drawer of her night table. "This is my second volume of samplers. The first I made as a girl," she explained, as Lucy took a seat on the chaise. Catherine joined her. "I started this one on the day George and I left on our first expedition."

She opened the book to the first page, and was deeply gratified when Lucy gasped in admiration.

The first page was a map, the familiar lines of the globe picked out in black on creamy linen. Longitude and latitude were made of running stitches curving around the doubled hemisphere. Catherine's finger traced the thicker line of stem stitch that traced a path across the sea, from England to New South Wales and through so many of the Pacific islands. At each port where they'd put in, Catherine had placed a tiny local flower, and four larger bougainvilleas lounged in each of the map sampler's corners.

Lucy let out a sigh. "This is the whole voyage?"

"The voyage out." Catherine turned the page. "This is the voyage back."

Lucy leaned in, pointing to one bright red figure. "The pineapple ginger!"

Catherine grinned. "Precisely where I first saw it." She turned more leaves, as the maps gave way to more experimental and practical embroidery, pages where Catherine was trying out new techniques of her own or practicing stitches she'd been taught by the people in the places she'd traveled to. Quilted silk patterns from India, bold geometrical shapes, and web-like stars and flowers made by winding a single thread around and between fixed stitches.

Then she turned the page and froze. She'd forgotten what came next. Lucy's hand held down the corner firmly, her gaze turning keen. "Who is that?"

Even after two years of freedom, Catherine's stomach tightened painfully as her eye traced the lines of her late hus-

band's face. "That's George." She'd shown him with his gaze
fixed on the heavens, his hair wildly curling, his skin shaded
with tan and the ruddy hues brought out by harsh sea winds.

The date carefully placed in the lower right corner mocked
her: she'd worked this portrait when her love was still shiny
new, like a pewter mug that hadn't yet been dropped into the
sea to rust and ruin. "We were newly married, and it was my
first time traveling aboard ship—everything was so exciting. Navigators and astronomers were taking readings at all
hours, the botanists were preparing to collect samples once
we landed, the naturalists were studying weather patterns
and bird flights and the sea creatures we managed to sight
along the way. And of course the sailors who kept the ship on
course and the sails stretched out to the heavens were always
working and watching the skies. But there wasn't anything
I could do to help—rather, there wasn't anything George
wanted me helping with, so I decided I could make a record
of sorts." She turned over the next page, with a throb of mingled affection and grief. An old man with a twinkling eye
and a boisterous set of whiskers. "This is Captain Lateshaw."

She turned page after embroidered page, showing Lucy
the full set—all the scholars and sailors, so many of whom
had been lost to illness and accident—as well as the landscapes she'd added later, once they'd reached the islands.

And then, of course, she came to the princess's portrait,
bare of breast with a defiant regal glint in her eyes. She'd
been a chieftain's daughter on an island whose map name
had been changed several times since the first European ar-
rivals landed there.

Catherine shook her head, a pang of shame flaring hot within her. "Nearly the whole island's population has been lost since then to disease. One of the sailors told me on our second voyage out. This portrait, clumsy and obscure and half a world away, may be all that remains of her."

"I don't know why you insist on calling your work clumsy. Your stitches look almost like brushstrokes; I doubt my brother or any of his friends could have done so much with even the most delicate brushes and perfectly blended tints . . ." Lucy glanced up at Catherine's troubled face and hastily reached out to turn the next page. "Oh," she said, startled. "Who is *that*?"

A black-haired, fox-faced woman in burgundy stared back out, her chin tilted haughtily and her hazel eyes knowing and warm. Her lips were a sensual symphony, the dimple beside her slight smile perfectly placed.

Catherine's mouth went dry. Lucy couldn't know how often she'd turned to this portrait in the privacy of her own room—or how it stirred her every time. "That is Contezza Maddalena Bricci," she said, blushing to hear how raspy her own voice had turned. "We met her on our voyage back from Egypt after our second expedition. She was a painter, and taught me many things about color and shading. You'll notice the embroidery gets markedly better after this point in the sampler."

"She's lovely," Lucy marveled.

"This portrait may be an improvement, but it still fails to do her justice," Catherine hastened to point out. "You ought to have heard her laugh . . ." She looked up to find Lucy's gaze on her, eyes narrowed in consideration. "What?" she asked.

Lucy's long mouth curved up knowingly. "I assumed I was the first woman you ever kissed," she drawled. "Was I?"

Catherine went full scarlet. "You were," she said tartly, "but I confess: you weren't the first I *wanted* to kiss."

"So you are drawn to dark-haired, troublesome women," Lucy said, leaning closer.

"God help me, it seems I am." There was only one way to end such a conversation—Catherine happily pulled Lucy forward until she could reach her lips.

The afternoon's tender delicacy was gone, replaced by a kiss that tasted lush as wine and scorched like fire. Catherine drank pleasure from Lucy's ready mouth, the girl's encouraging gasps firing her newly bold impulses. She hadn't been dizzy from the wine at dinner, but she was giddy now, the room spinning around her and the only solid thing the skin and heat and feel of the woman in her arms.

The kiss went on and on, but when Catherine's curious fingers slipped along the line of Lucy's bodice, the girl broke away with a gasp.

Catherine dropped her hand at once, panicked and aroused in equal measure. "Too fast?" She'd done it now: she'd lost control, tried to take too much, too soon . . .

Lucy laughed and reached out to pull her back. Catherine stiffened automatically, shame at her unruly desire turning her yearning into ash.

Lucy's keen eyes watched her closely. "It wasn't too fast for me—but perhaps it was too fast for you?"

Catherine fought to loosen the tangled knots of her feelings, then huffed in frustration. "I don't know."

Lucy took Catherine's hands, gently rubbing them between her own. "Then we stop."

Catherine blinked. Her senses were still a riot, her breath still coming fast and hot in her throat. "As easy as that?" She didn't know if she was protesting or demanding proof Lucy meant what she said.

"Of course," Lucy replied breezily, as though she hadn't just said one of the most puzzling things Catherine had ever heard. "The whole point is to feel excited about one another, isn't it? If you're more anxious than excited, then we wait. Simple."

Catherine narrowed her eyes. "Don't you want to do more than kiss me?"

Lucy laughed again, and the sultry echo of it slid like warmed honey down Catherine's spine. "Oh, if you wanted me to write out my full list of wants, it would be Christmas before I was through." She slipped a thumb over the inside of Catherine's wrist; the countess's pulse leaped to meet her fingers. "But all those ideas depend on you wanting those things done to you. Or wanting to do things to me. Because it's not about you doing, or me doing—it's what we do together." Her eyes turned faraway, fixed on some memory. "The very first girl who took me to bed taught me that. She was kind, and patient—and very, very creative, once I was ready." She chuckled, seeing the blush bloom on Catherine's cheeks. "But for the first six months, all we did was kiss."

Catherine's cheeks warmed further, and her eyes slipped down to Lucy's mouth. "I'm not sure I want to wait so long as that."

Lucy's gaze sharpened, and her lips parted as she sucked

in a breath, but she only said, "As long as you need. Now, since you have dismissed your maid, let me help you undress."

It was not how Catherine had imagined being disrobed by Lucy. She had had vague notions of hasty, desperate gripping and pulling and a general carelessness about buttons and laces and seams. George had been that way—until he stopped seeking her bed at all—and so had Darby; Catherine had assumed that's just how people behaved in the throes of lust. Didn't passion overwhelm people beyond the bounds of good sense, caution, or control?

But Lucy's hands were careful and soft as they unlaced the back of Catherine's gown, loosened her stays, and pulled all the pins from her tousled hair. It was closer to how Narayan would have undressed her—though Narayan would never have dropped a kiss on the back of Catherine's neck, or combed fingers through Catherine's tumbling hair in that luxurious way. It was—it was like every touch of Lucy's hand was a silken thread, painting a sunrise one skein of warm light at a time. At the end, Lucy wrapped Catherine's favorite velvet bed jacket around her shoulders and kissed her once more, sweetly. Catherine couldn't help melting a little. "Good night," she whispered.

Lucy chuckled. "Good night, my lady."

"Catherine," she corrected the girl.

Lucy paused. "Catherine." Her tongue lingered over the name, and her smile widened with pleasure. "Good night, Catherine." She slipped out the door, leaving the countess feeling equally comforted and abandoned and thoroughly, thoroughly perplexed.

Chapter Six

The next day, despite her own amorous turmoil, Lucy was careful to follow the usual routine. She couldn't stop remembering the pained throb in the countess's—in Catherine's voice, or the flash of fear in her eyes, when kisses had turned into more. Someone had hurt her before, and badly.

The obvious culprit was her late husband.

Lucy scowled around the library, as if a fierce enough gaze could banish George St. Day's ghost. His letters to her father had never been truly warm, but they had been cordial enough that Lucy had never thought to suspect him of being secretly, cruelly cold.

But then, Lucy had never predicted that the intrepid and witty Lady Moth would have such a fragile side, either, or that she would ever choose to kiss Lucy so eagerly. People could surprise you.

Tea came, and dinner afterward. Lucy kept conversation light, aided by a usefully distracting passage of Oléron on the subject of tides that was giving her a world of trouble. "If I construe the verb the one way it's talking about oscillation as a singular event," she explained, "but construed another way, it's an ongoing state. A constant. French uses the same verb tense for both things, but I cannot believe the mathematics line up properly if it is singular." She stabbed her fork viciously into the innocent roasted chicken on her plate. "How can we agree on universal truths, when between the English and the French, we can't even agree on what time *was* was! No wonder humans have had so many wars."

Catherine snorted at this.

Lucy huffed, and moved pieces of chicken around. "It makes one pine for the days when all scholarship was done in Latin, and everybody knew what one another meant when they wrote."

"Ah," Catherine said, "but weren't they then restricted by the rules and behavior of Latin grammar?"

"At least they were all restricted equally," Lucy said. "I wouldn't have to try and guess what Oléron might have been trying to say if the French tongue had had a progressive tense, like ours does."

"You're doing an expansion, not a strict translation. You're already departing from the original. Why can't you decide which verb is better within the bounds of that framework?"

"Because . . ." Lucy bit her lip, and huffed again, and finally burst out: "Because what if I get it wrong?"

Catherine pursed her lips, visibly amused. "I keep telling you: astronomers are supposed to be wrong."

"But what if I get it wrong, and Oléron gets the blame?" Lucy persisted. "I have a responsibility not to misrepresent the material I'm basing this on, even if I'm going above and beyond its original aims. Maybe especially then. This will be the first time the work appears in English, and English scientists are going to want to base their own experiments and theories upon what this text says. Any errors I introduce will not only be repeated in the work that comes after—they will be taken as errors of the original, and Oléron's reputation would suffer for my negligence." She poked twice more at the chicken carcass before sighing and setting her fork aside. "Maybe this was why Mr. Hawley wanted multiple translators working on this: so they could better catch these problems before they went out into the world and multiplied."

"Mr. Hawley wanted multiple translators so he could play them against one another," Catherine said with some aspersion. "That way he preserves his authority in the Polite Science Society, without having to do any of the actual work himself."

Lucy blinked, surprised. "That is a very harsh opinion of him."

Catherine's brow furrowed, as Lucy watched her curiously. "Yes, well, I have spent many years in the Society strictly as an unofficial observer. An aide, really. I had to know how the whole system functioned in order to help George make progress. Maybe I recognize Mr. Hawley's manipulations because I have had to resort to them at times myself. Maybe we aren't so different, and I should be more charitable to someone who may not be able to do the work in the manner that he would prefer." She sat back in her chair, her eyes going distant.

Lucy leaned forward eagerly, by now recognizing the signs of Catherine St. Day about to tell a story.

"He was on our first expedition, you remember. It was his first as well. He took ill after we set out from Van Dieman's Land. Very ill. Very nearly died. He was half a ghost still when we returned to England."

"But his results were spectacular. He proved several leading magnetic theories were quite wrong, and advanced the state of knowledge on botany by an immeasurable degree," Lucy interjected.

Catherine nodded, lips pressed together. "Oh yes, he was feted and celebrated and even invited to Windsor to speak with the King," she said. "And he enjoyed the fame and the flattery immensely. He founded the Polite Science Society in the full flush of his glory, and people were eager to apply for Fellowship. But whenever someone pushed him to fix a date for his next voyage, there was always some excuse. He was still trying to nurture samples of species he'd brought back, or there was some matter among Society Fellows that required his careful attention for a while. So other botanists started going out on voyages, and Mr. Hawley stayed home."

"But it's not as if his work here stopped," Lucy countered. "He's been more successful than anyone at cultivating rare species: orchids, arboreals, even carnivorous plants."

"I'm convinced it's not enough for him. When did the King ever come to see his orchids? It's the voyagers who get all the royal attention: the mapmakers and the navigators and those who chart the heavens. George had thoughts of unseating Mr. Hawley from the presidency, if he'd ever made a discovery big enough to justify the coup."

Lucy pursed her lips. "Do you suppose Mr. Hawley knew it?"

"I'm certain he did. So now he stays very involved with the state of all scientific topics, keeping his fingers in as many pies as possible. Some people do benefit from his guidance—George wouldn't have worked half so hard without Mr. Hawley there to needle him, I'm sure—but I have also seen him act to suppress those whose work doesn't strike him as sufficiently noble." She lifted her glass up, watching the ruby liquid swirl in the light. "He thinks of science as something to be cultivated, with offending offshoots cut away clean. And I do not always trust his judgment about which parts deserve pruning."

Lucy grinned. "You'd rather have science a wild weed growing in the lane, discoverable by any urchin and liable to take over any ground where it's planted?"

Catherine smiled. "Imagine what those urchins might think of, that we hothouse aristocrats can barely imagine."

Lucy sniffed archly and set her chin as haughtily as she knew how. "I'm not sure whether to be insulted because I'm supposed to be the urchin, or because I'm supposed to be the aristocrat."

Catherine's eyes flicked up, and the intensity there pulled all the air from Lucy's lungs and replaced it with fire. "Neither," the countess said softly. "You are the type of scholar who cares most about the truth. There is nothing so rare, and so much to be valued by the rest of us."

Lucy swallowed hard. "You flatter me."

"Do I?" Catherine's lips curved—it was a teasing smile, full of promise, and it lit Lucy up like a torch. "You've just told me how much you're working to keep your translation true to Oléron's writing. You are trying to add yourself to it without standing between the world and the original author. It's a very difficult prospect." She set down her wineglass. "It's also the exact right thing to do. And not one in a hundred other astronomers would think of doing it."

Lucy had no response to this. Her cheeks were burning and she couldn't seem to find a safe place to look for more than half a minute together.

It wasn't as though she'd never been complimented before—her father had always lauded her mind (if not her femininity), and her past lovers had had plenty to say about her wit (if not her beauty). But she couldn't offhand think of any other time when someone had been so adamant in praise of something she'd not even succeeded yet in achieving.

Catherine had complimented Lucy's judgment, and there was something in that that intoxicated her more than strong spirits might have done.

They went straight to Catherine's room after dinner, as though it were now understood.

Lady Moth's maid gave Lucy one brief, keen look, then smoothed out her expression and curtsied as she was dismissed for the night. "Will you please go and tell Eliza I won't be needing her any more this evening?" Lucy said, blushing.

"Yes, miss," Narayan said, and the door snicked softly shut behind her.

Lucy looked at Catherine, whose cheeks were pink but whose shoulders were tight and tense. She reached out and put a hand on Catherine's cheek, gratified beyond reason when the countess leaned into the caress with a sigh.

Lucy brushed the softest of kisses across the shorter woman's mouth. "I've thought about this all day," she said.

Catherine's blush deepened. "So have I. I am terribly embarrassed about how I behaved last night."

"You needn't be." Lucy guided Catherine over to the chaise and sat her down on one side. Her posture was poker-straight, but Lucy wasn't surprised. For herself, she leaned back affably against the cushioned curve. They would both feel better if they cleared the air a bit. "You said you've never kissed a woman before."

"Yes, but it's not as though I'm entirely new to the business," Catherine said tartly. "I was married for fifteen years." She glanced away. "Plenty of time to outgrow youthful ardor. And this is not precisely the kind of conversation one has with a . . . with a new lover."

"You forget," Lucy said mischievously. "I'm an astronomer, remember? I care much more about truth than about propriety."

Catherine blew out a breath. "So I am something in the nature of an experiment?"

Lucy bit her lip. "I might ask you the same question."

"But I am *not* an astronomer, nor any kind of naturalist," Catherine shot back. "I do not perform experiments."

"No," Lucy agreed. "You are a well-traveled lady of quality—prone to sudden whims and prey to dissipated impulses."

She laughed as Catherine sputtered objections. But the countess was looking less anxious, and the corners of her mouth were tilting up.

Lucy pressed onward. "Was George the only lover you've had?"

"No," Catherine replied. "There was another man, after George died. But he— I . . ." She shook her head, clearly struggling to find the words. "With George, there had been no pleasing him. I was thrilled to find a man who wanted pleasing, and I did everything he asked of me simply for the sake of that approval. But some of the things that pleased him . . ." She paused. "How much of your innocence can I ruin in the course of one evening?"

"I'm already reasonably ruined," Lucy said. "You can tell me."

Catherine bit her lip, then steeled her spine. "He was . . . rough."

"Ah," said Lucy, in a tone of complete understanding. "He hurt you."

"He never laid a hand on me in anger."

Lucy was quietly insistent. "He hurt you, and you didn't think you were permitted to object."

"He found particular ecstasy in giving pain, and I tolerated the pain because it was so novel to bring someone happiness instead of misery or anger. Sometimes when he hurt me more than I could bear I lashed out in return. He enjoyed that, too. The struggling, the hurt. I felt like a wild thing, most of the time—but my lover was ecstatic about it. It baffled me even as it gratified. And I thought, maybe all the better kind of passion had been drained from me, from too many years of neglect." She dropped her eyes. "He was always very kind, after."

"There are people who enjoy giving pain, and people who find suffering brings them pleasure." Lucy leaned forward, resting a hand on Catherine's wrist. "It doesn't make their pleasure any more or less real than yours—it's just a matter of taste. Like preferring mint tea over chamomile." She trailed her fingertips up Catherine's skin until the tender turn of the elbow. The other woman's breath hitched, and Lucy licked her lips. "And you're anything but passionless."

"What if I lose control again?" Catherine whispered.

"I understand if you're afraid," Lucy replied, "but I'm not." She lifted Catherine's hand and pressed the softest possible kiss to the back of it.

Catherine's breath shivered out on a sigh.

Lucy kept going—her fingers mapped the course of the veins in Catherine's pale wrist, and her palm smoothed over the downy hairs on her forearm. She followed the line of her collarbone, the fluted column of her neck, and the small curls that escaped all hairpins to cluster where her scalp met her spine. Catherine hummed with pleasure as Lucy worked those pins free, one by one, draping golden locks over both of them. When she finally—finally!—pressed her lips to Catherine's mouth, the countess was all but panting with delight, trembling and shivering and returning the kiss with something near to desperation.

Lucy allowed a flame of sensual triumph to flicker in her

breast, unspoken, as Catherine's arms twined luxuriously around her neck and pulled her close without the slightest hint of fear or hesitance.

The countess didn't take things any further, though. Lucy didn't mind. Patience was a game she was happy to play for the right rewards.

The next night, in between kisses, Lucy removed Catherine's dress and then her own, as well as the stays beneath, but left their chemises and stockings in place. The night after that, she peeled off a single one of Catherine's stockings, and the second the following evening. And so it went, night by night, one delicate piece of fabric at a time fluttering to the floor like seeds from a dandelion clock, until finally Lucy was able to press herself against Catherine, skin to skin.

Lucy shivered, though she felt anything but cold. Catherine was above her in the bed, sheets tangled around both their ankles, firelight flickering gently over miles of creamy, curving skin. "You're so beautiful," Lucy murmured, running a hand along the irresistible dip of the countess's waist.

Catherine bent down for another kiss, lingering and lush. She hadn't frozen up since that first day, but Lucy kept her hands soothing and steady anyway. She was determined not to rush this, no matter how hard her pulse was pounding.

Catherine slid a hand along Lucy's side, then cupped her breast. Lucy groaned happily into Catherine's mouth, her nipple going tight beneath the countess's palm. She was focusing so intently on not rushing that she was utterly shocked when Catherine straddled one thigh and slipped a hand to the aching spot between Lucy's legs.

Lucy cried out as every muscle in her body spasmed with pleasure.

Catherine froze, eyes going wide. "Too fast?"

"God, no," Lucy groaned, and arched up against her hand demandingly. Catherine's breathy laugh skittered hot over Lucy's skin as she took the nipple she'd teased into her mouth. Her fingers continued playing between Lucy's legs, and Lucy clutched her free hand hard in the sheets to keep from tangling it in Catherine's hair.

Lucy's other hand was still on Catherine's waist, so she felt it at once when the countess shifted. Lucy cracked open the eyes she'd convulsively shut just in time to watch Catherine bear down against Lucy's thigh, soft curls and wet heat grinding against Lucy's feverish skin. The countess moaned at the friction and sank her teeth into her lip, a picture of desperate yearning.

And just like that, so suddenly she didn't even have time to gasp for air, Lucy was coming. Her back bowed off the bed as pleasure stormed through her, sweeping everything else aside. Distantly, she heard Catherine whispering encouragement in her ear, and it only set her off a second time, climax rippling through her and making her shudder like the flames dancing in the hearth.

When she came back to herself, Catherine was lounging beside her, stroking her hip, the ample curves of her body tilted in languorous pride like some ancient statue of Venus. Lucy stretched out her arms above her head and laughed, half chagrined and half impressed. "Serves me right for trying to treat you like an untried virgin."

Catherine stroked more of Lucy, her hand wandering teasingly across her belly and over her small breasts. "I managed to figure out one or two things, in fifteen years of marriage," she said.

"Only one or two things?" Lucy teased. She rolled Catherine beneath her and settled on top of the countess's delectable body. Catherine splayed out eagerly as Lucy's hand roamed lower, but her eyes truly widened when Lucy slid down until she could set her shoulders beneath Catherine's knees. Lucy spotted a dimple in Catherine's left knee and pressed a sweet kiss to it, lightly spreading the other woman's legs wider. Golden, flushed, and perfect—she was even lovelier now than in all of Lucy's secret imaginings.

The countess leaned up on one elbow, the lightest furrow appearing between her golden brows. "Where on earth are you going?"

Anticipation shot through Lucy, comet-like. "Oh, so this isn't one of the things?" Her hands drifted up, from the lady's knees to her trembling thighs, and brushed her thumbs along the tender folds between the countess's legs. "Let me show you a trick I learned in my school days. Though I promise, you won't find it anywhere on the curriculum." She bent her head and licked once, precisely where she knew Catherine needed it most.

It was no small achievement, to make a countess curse.

Lucy laughed and licked Catherine again—then again, on and on, pressing hands down on the other woman's hips to hold her in place as the countess's cries spiraled higher and breathier. She used every trick of lips and tongue that she could think of, licking and sucking and flicking at the tender flesh. Judicious fingers, cunningly applied, caused another round of gorgeous cursing. Catherine sobbed as she came, Lucy's eager tongue catching every drop of her pleasure. With a long moan Catherine fell back, gasping for breath, while Lucy moved up to nuzzle into the dewy crook of her neck, satisfaction of more than the physical kind rippling through her. "How was that for a novelty?"

It was a while before Catherine essayed a reply. "I have visited many strange places and had many unique experiences in my travels," she breathed, her generous bosom heaving delightfully up and down, "but I never imagined anything quite like that." She flung an arm up above her head and stretched, the curves of her shifting into new and fascinating topographies. "I feel positively licentious."

Lucy grinned. "You ought to have stayed home and learned about good old-fashioned English debauchery, as I did."

Catherine chuckled as Lucy pulled the sheets over them both. "If you're offering to teach me, I expect you'll be a proper scholar and do it rigorously."

Lucy snorted, and nipped at Catherine's earlobe, enjoying the way it made the lady sigh and shiver. "I shall take careful notes, and make sure my experiments are repeatable." Lulled by warmth and the sweet feel of Catherine beneath her, Catherine's arms around her shoulders, Lucy drifted into sleep before she thought to stop herself.

A squeak and a clank had Catherine cracking open an eyelid at far too early an hour the next morning.

It was daylight, but barely. The clank had been the coal scuttle, banging gently against the hearth as Narayan's foot struck it. The squeak had been Narayan herself, arriving earlier than usual to lay out Catherine's morning gown for the day.

Catherine, presently wearing not a stitch, clutched the coverlet to her breast and stared wildly at the maid, whose eyes were wide with shock.

Lucy—equally nude, and apparently a restless sleeper— was tucked in the crook of Catherine's arm facing outward, the curve of her spine fitting into the curve of Catherine's waist, one long leg thrown free of the sheets. Her hands clutched the countess's arm to her chest, as though she were afraid Catherine would try to flee sometime during the night.

Narayan bent down and scooped up the garment she'd dropped. "Apologies, my lady," she squeaked. "Shall I . . . Shall I come back in a few minutes?" Her eyes flicked to Lucy and then away, and she tucked a lock of hair behind ears turned ruddy with embarrassment.

Catherine could feel her own blush singeing her cheeks. "Yes, thank you," she managed, feeling every mile of the chasm between the stiff prudery of her tone and the lewdness of her pose and attire. Or lack thereof.

Narayan gave a hasty curtsy and vanished, and Catherine flopped back onto the pillow with a fearful huff.

Some people had years to enjoy illicit vices and hidden

depravities before they were exposed to public censure. Apparently Catherine was doomed to be caught after just one night.

She slipped out of bed, pulled on the first dressing gown she could reach, and nudged Lucy.

The dark-haired woman mumbled something and rubbed at eyes gone crusty with sleep. "Morning already?" she asked.

"The maid will be coming soon," Catherine whispered, agonized. She stroked one hand down Lucy's arm from shoulder to elbow. "Narayan was just here. Lord knows what she imagined we'd been doing."

The other woman stretched and smiled, catlike. "Something fairly close to the truth, no doubt. Loan me a dressing gown?" she asked, as Catherine's blush deepened at the reminder of everything they'd done last night.

When Catherine returned with a wrap—her second-best dressing gown, all quilted green silk with lace trimmings—Lucy rolled out of bed and allowed Catherine to help her into the garment. She was moving quickly but with no panic, while Catherine fluttered like a sparrow who'd flown in the window and hadn't figured out how to fly back out.

Lucy bent down and kissed Catherine swiftly but soundly; Catherine felt her nerves settle down from a painful jangle to a bearable buzz. "We've done nothing to be ashamed about," Lucy said, her hands warm and solid against Catherine's shoulders. "No matter what anybody else thinks." Catherine nodded, putting on a brave face, and Lucy gave her a reassuring squeeze. "Surely this isn't the first secret you've had to trust the servants with?"

Catherine thought back to George's tirades, brief explosions surrounded by long spells of icy silence. When Catherine had avoided him, he'd abused the servants in her place—shouting at housemaids, demanding impossible things from the footmen, berating the gardeners. One of the reasons she'd gone on that last expedition was that it kept George's targets to a minimum: he never dared to lose his temper while onboard ship and under the captain's iron command.

Her relationship with Lucy might be an absolute scandal—but it wouldn't hurt anyone.

So Catherine kissed Lucy again and cinched the borrowed dressing gown tight. It left Lucy's long arms bare at the wrists, even as the thick silk's extra fabric bunched at the waist. "I'll see you for breakfast," she said.

Lucy grinned and blew a kiss farewell as she slipped merrily from the room.

Catherine couldn't blame her too much: she felt much the same herself, as though her soul was so light, the slightest push from below would send it flying toward the heavens.

Narayan returned a quarter of an hour later, her face carefully neutral, and began helping Catherine dress. Chemise, stays, and stockings went on with their usual precision, as Catherine struggled not to blush for thinking at how easily such things had come off under Lucy's bold ministrations the night before.

"I am so sorry I disturbed you this morning, my lady," the maid said, her eyes on the floor and tension pinching at their corners.

"Quite alright," Catherine said, sitting down in front of her toilette.

Narayan's quick fingers made short work of arranging Catherine's more than tousled hair into something restrained and respectable. She looked up, and her eyes caught Catherine's in the mirror. "May I be permitted to ask you an impertinent question, my lady?"

Catherine braced herself. "You may."

Narayan's mouth was flat and her features contained, as if she, too, feared the worst. "Did you know Miss Muchelney would end up . . . would end up sleeping here, last night when you dismissed me?"

Impertinent question indeed—but there was something about the set of her maid's shoulders that plucked at Catherine enough to make her bite back any reprimand. "I had a fair idea what would happen," Catherine admitted. Her blush was doubled, but her chin was high. "We fell asleep before we remembered to be discreet. I am sorry to have shocked and offended you."

"Offended!" Narayan's tone was all surprise, and as Catherine watched, sunrise rays of cautious hope melted the ice of her expression. "You were simply trying to hide the affair, then, my lady?"

"With little success, it seems," Catherine muttered. Truth was so difficult, and too much honesty stung appallingly.

"Oh no, ma'am—I mean, yes, I did—this morning—oh, my lady," Narayan said, and with some alarm Catherine watched all the blood rush from her face, "do you think I might sit down for just a little?"

"Oh my—of course!" Catherine caught the girl beneath the elbow and helped her to the bench at the foot of the bed.

The maid was trembling, and for a time all she could do was bend low against her knees and take long, shuddering breaths. Eventually she lifted her head, and her eyes were shining with relief. "Forgive me, my lady," she said, with a little laugh. "I have spent two weeks thinking you were about to give me the sack."

"What?" Catherine cried. "What on earth for? You've been wonderful. I cannot imagine doing something like that without good reason."

"But you are having Mrs. Shaw train Eliza up," Narayan replied. "And my sister—who is lady's maid for the Honorable Miss Cuthbert—said to watch out when they start bringing in people who are younger and—and lighter complexioned." She set her chin as she said this.

"Oh!" Catherine pressed a hand to her mouth as the facts came clear. "Oh, no wonder you were worried. I am so sorry. Eliza was brought on to do for Lucy—I insisted on it to Mrs. Shaw . . ."

Catherine faltered, but Narayan had regained her customary poise by now and was able to fold her hands and nod. "I understand, my lady." A flash of humor twigged the corners of her mouth. "You might ask young Mary to delay the hour when she lays your fire in the mornings. It would make it so you had to offer fewer explanations."

"Thank you," Catherine said. And paused, as a thought occurred. "May I ask a probing question of my own?"

Narayan blinked and some of the worry crept back into her expression, but she nodded.

"Do you earn more than your sister does with the Honorable Miss Cuthbert?"

"I make a little more in wages, my lady, but—if you'll pardon a little more frank speaking—Sara enjoys quite a bit more in the way of secondhand clothing. The Honorable Miss Cuthbert is very much in demand amongst the social set, and there is always something new expected for her wardrobe."

Which meant, Catherine knew, there would always be something older departing—something that a fashionable London debutante had enjoyed until either the novelty or the style had worn thin, but that would still be worth a considerable sum when gifted to an attentive lady's maid who knew all the right secondhand shops. Catherine sighed and shook her head, knowing that she must have cost Narayan some pain in comparison with her sister's position. She had never gone about much in those circles, and she never expected to. "I could speak to Mrs. Shaw about increasing your wages, to compensate for my appalling hermitish tendencies . . ."

The maid drew herself up stiffly. "You don't have to buy my silence, my lady. Discretion is a virtue in any good servant—Mr. Brinkworth often says so." Catherine could only stare into the mirror, but Narayan squared her shoulders. "The sky-blue dress today, do you think?"

Catherine thought of how Lucy had looked at her the last time she wore the sky-blue, when she thought Catherine wasn't watching, and nodded. "Perfect."

Chapter Seven

Lucy slipped into her bedchamber with barely a minute to spare before Eliza arrived to help her dress for breakfast. The girl looked startled to find Lucy already out of bed, and garbed in a dressing gown that had so clearly come from another woman's wardrobe.

"The countess loaned me this, as we were up rather late last evening," Lucy explained, and was proud at how her cheeks maintained only a hint of a blush.

"Of course, miss," Eliza said. "The color suits you, though—very springlike." She threw open the wardrobe doors, and both women went grim as they contemplated the very *un*-springlike spectrum of blacks, grays, lugubrious purples, and muted lavenders hung therein.

Lucy sighed. "I do miss proper colors. I share just enough of my brother's artistic temperament to be drawn to brighter shades than these. My mourning period has been over for months." She'd written to Stephen and he'd dutifully sent on her allowance since coming to London, but her funds weren't nearly enough for even one new frock at town prices. At least, not the kind of frock she could wear around a countess. Or above a countess. Or underneath a countess . . .

"It's not so bad as that, miss." Eliza fingered the sleeve of one lavender muslin. "Something might be done with some of these, to brighten them up," she offered. "Gold and green would pretty this one up in a trice. A little something around the hem, or a border at the bodice." She caught Lucy's surprised eye, and schooled her features back into a proper maidly serenity. "That is, if you like, miss."

Lucy glanced at the dress with Pris's embroidery, trailing vines over it like clinging tentacles. "I'm rather out of humor for florals, I'm afraid."

"Doesn't have to be florals, miss. Something like this, maybe?" Eliza's face brightened as she pulled a small book out of her pocket. It turned out to be a primer, well-thumbed and nearly falling to pieces—but every space that wasn't taken up by the printed text had been filled in with chalk and charcoal and pencil sketches. Portraits, cartoons, animals and ships and buildings . . . but also patterns: lines and circles and dots, odd wiggly organics and precise geometric areas sharp as broken glass. Eliza turned to one page near the back, where a blank space between nursery songs had been filled in with a profusion of dots, scattered at first but then more and more crowded.

It made Lucy's eyes water to look at it.

"But with colors, of course," Eliza said. As though this were the most obvious thing in the world.

Lucy cocked her head, in awe of the sheer amount of work

in that little book. "How often do you find time to draw, Eliza?"

"Depends on how often Mrs. Shaw catches me at it."

Lucy chortled.

Eliza went full scarlet. "I shouldn't have said that, miss."

"I won't tell." Lucy looked again at her wardrobe, and heaved a sigh. "And anything you can do for my gowns will be welcome. Time and Mrs. Shaw permitting, of course."

The maid ducked her head. "Of course, miss."

She must have persuaded the housekeeper, for by the next morning, Eliza had utterly transformed one of the purples with a slender border of white knots on bodice and hem, with extending columns of more knots that shaded into gray and then black toward the waist of the gown. Lucy admired the effect in the mirror and traipsed down to breakfast, happier than she had any right to feel.

Catherine looked up with joy—and a self-conscious blush, since Lucy had shared her bed again last night—but when her gaze drifted down to the embroidery her expression went shuttered.

"What's wrong?" Lucy asked at once.

"Nothing." The countess shook her head, attempting a smile. "It's a silly thought I had, unworthy of being spoken." Her eyes dropped to Lucy's bodice, then away. "Pris really was a very talented needlewoman."

"Yes, she was," Lucy confirmed, puzzled—then her wits caught up with her and the significance all but bowled her over. "Oh! This wasn't Pris's work. This was something Eliza did, after I lamented the state of my wardrobe."

Catherine set her coffee aside and peered more closely, while Lucy piled a plate full of food and brought it to table. "She is *very* good. Did you direct her to place those colors that way?"

"Not at all," Lucy said. "It was entirely her own notion. I couldn't have thought of such a thing if you gave me a thousand years and silk in every color of the rainbow." She held out one hand and turned it back and forth, admiring the way the dots danced along the length of her arm. "It's incredible how such a simple technique—just a smattering of stitches— can have such a powerful effect. It's lovely, isn't it?"

"Very." Lucy blushed to the roots at the warmth in her lover's voice. Catherine's smile hid behind her cup as she took another sip of coffee.

So Lucy felt well-armored for that afternoon's scientific lecture. And she was in need of it: this was the first Polite Science Society event she would be attending since that disastrous dinner at Mr. Hawley's home. She wasn't certain whether they would even permit her to attend—but Catherine snorted at the suggestion and was immovable. "It is a public lecture. You wanted to hear Mr. Edwards's thoughts on his chemical experiments, did you not?"

"Yes," Lucy admitted.

"Then we're going." Catherine tugged her gloves into place, looking every inch the respectable town society matron, ready to brook no nonsense and stand for no insult. Her blond curls were pin-neat, her gown was cerulean cotton and tailored to perfection, and a strand of pearls hung gleaming around her throat.

Lucy wondered if the pearls were still cool, or if they had already borrowed some of the warmth of Catherine's skin. She wanted to slide her lips over them, feeling the contrast between smooth gems and soft flesh.

She wished her own attire were even half as tempting, and again was glad Eliza Brinkworth had had time to do something with this gown. She wrapped the stellarium shawl around her shoulders and saw heat flare briefly in Catherine's eyes.

That was no small thing—but still Lucy wanted more.

She was still feeling somewhat sparrowish when they arrived at the lecture hall. They had cut it rather fine, and the room was full in anticipation of the event. There was a roughly equal mix of earnest amateur philosophers, poets in search of good metaphors, and *haut ton* in search of some way to fill the afternoon until they could besport themselves in a ballroom or a bordello. Lucy spotted Mr. Hawley, Sir Eldon, and Mr. and Mrs. Chattenden seated at the front of the room, talking and peering around with great interest.

Mr. Hawley caught Lucy's eye and sent them a chilly smile that could not have said *Stay away* more clearly if he'd shouted it. Mrs. Chattenden contented herself with a perfectly polite nod. Mr. Chattenden took no notice: he was tense about the jaw, glaring around him as if every single member of the audience had offended him personally.

Catherine leaned close to Lucy's ear. "Mr. Edwards brings in a great deal of money for the Society with these events, but he's almost always destroying some new or favorite theory of Mr. Chattenden's. The gentleman cannot escape, but he's always perfectly enraged to have to turn up."

Lucy grinned. "I oughtn't be so amused by that—but he looks just like a teapot on the verge of boiling over."

Catherine chuckled. "Once last year Mr. Edwards built a miniature volcano as a chemical demonstration. I overheard some young rogues from White's making bets on whether the volcano or the 'bloody furious git in the third row' would erupt first."

Lucy's answering laugh was loud enough to catch Aunt Kelmarsh's eye, above them in the gallery. She waved Lucy and Catherine up; they stepped carefully through the chattering crowd and ascended the stairs to reach her.

Mr. Frampton was there with her, and scrambled up as the ladies approached. "Delighted to see you again, Miss Muchelney," he said, bowing over her hand. "You're looking exceedingly well—may I hope that London life agrees with you?"

"You may, and it does," Lucy replied. "I am enjoying the translating immensely, when it does not make me want to pull my hair out at the roots."

Mr. Frampton bowed over Catherine's hand as well. His tone stayed equally warm when he said: "I hope you are not giving the countess too much cause for anxiety."

Lucy put in: "Lady Moth has been an exceedingly gracious hostess—and, dare I say, friend. In fact, we are growing rather inseparable."

Aunt Kelmarsh's grin was knowing and delighted.

Catherine's blush was pure scarlet, but before she could respond, a murmur in the crowd let them know that Mr. Edwards had stepped up to the dais and the lecture was about to begin.

Ambrose Edwards had dark hair, thoughtful eyes, and a smile that dazzled with boyish charm. He also, Lucy soon learned, had an intellect as wide-ranging and fierce as any she'd ever encountered. Metaphysics and poetry and words plucked from the Gospel were liberally mixed together as he discussed newly uncovered secrets of the universe. Lucy could see the theatrics of it, how he used an actor's poise and timing to draw in his audience, one careful sentence at a time.

But even knowing how it worked, she was herself enchanted, particularly toward the end when Mr. Edwards set aside the new, shining substance he had so patiently distilled before their eager eyes. "Much has been made of man's intellect, in the pursuit of these new philosophies," he said, his orator's voice making the rafters ring. "But there is no brilliance of thought, no leap of logic that can take place without the power of imagination. Our learning requires intuition and instinct as much as pure intelligence. We are not simply minds, trained like lamps on the world around us, producing light but taking nothing in: we are bodies, and hearts, and hopes, and dreams. We are men, and we are women. We are poetry and prose in equal measure. We are earth and clay, but we are all—no matter our shape—lit with a spark of something divine."

The applause was deafening. Lucy clapped as hard as she ever had. A few muttered objections, a few shaken heads could be seen in the crowd, but none of those could stop the chills running up and down Lucy's arms and the tears gathering in the corners of her eyes. Those sensations meant only one thing to her: they were the proof that she had been hearing pure and undiluted truth. It buoyed her spirits and made her shake as though a star had spun down out of the sky and fallen to land at her feet.

The crowd began talking again, and the spell was broken.

Lucy sighed and looked back toward the Society president. Mr. Hawley sent one more pointed glance up to the gallery before dragging Mr. Chattenden and Sir Eldon toward the dais to talk further with Mr. Edwards. Lucy was almost convinced she could hear Mr. Chattenden's teeth grinding all the way up here in the gallery. With them came Richard Wilby, who had escaped her notice at first by blending in with the young bucks of the *haut ton*. He all but ran forward to shake Mr. Edwards's hand and began speaking with great animation; almost as instantly, Mr. Edwards shook his head with a gentle frown and began arguing back.

Aunt Kelmarsh had a prior engagement, but Mr. Frampton happily accepted Catherine's invitation to join her and Lucy for tea after the lecture. It took the whole carriage ride for him and Lucy to fully comb over what Mr. Edwards had demonstrated: Mr. Frampton took issue with a few of his chemical hypotheses, while Lucy was equal parts captivated and puzzled by his thoughts about Newtonian prisms and identifying gaseous matter.

Catherine poured tea for them all indulgently as the learned talk wound down. Mr. Frampton was lost in thought, gazing into the distance, and the combination of tension and relief there piqued Lucy's concern. She thought of the way the mathematician had not been seated among the other Fellows of the Society during the lecture . . . "How are you getting on with Mr. Wilby?" she asked.

Mr. Frampton heaved a sigh as he accepted his teacup. "Not at all well, I am sorry to say. In fact, if you're asking me to be perfectly frank and scrupulously honest . . . we have parted ways."

"You have?" Catherine.

"Whatever for?" Lucy protested.

Mr. Frampton stared glumly into the eyes of the lizard on his teacup handle, which stared back as sympathetically as a porcelain creature could. "We had a serious disagreement over notation."

Catherine sent Lucy a glance that was full of *I told you so*, while Mr. Frampton continued.

"It turned out to be an irreconcilable difference, and the partnership has been dissolved. Well, perhaps it is more truthful to say that my part of the partnership has been dissolved. Since I quit." His mouth twisted bitterly, and he swallowed a mouthful of tea and anything else he might have wanted to say.

Lucy's own mouth made sympathetic shapes. She knew how he felt all too intimately. "Did Mr. Wilby want to translate everything into Newton's notation?"

Mr. Frampton shot upright on the sofa. "Yes! Even though several of the functions can *only* be worked with Leibnizian variables."

Lucy huffed out her disapproval. "But surely he realized that Oléron was choosing the tools needed for the work."

"Wilby seemed to be blinded by Newton's status as a genius and an Englishman. Said it was close to treason to let foreigners stand so prominently in a work aimed at English scholars." A weight seemed to have been lifted from his shoulders and he leaned back again, teacup in hand. "After three days of no work outside of this argument, I took the matter up with Mr. Hawley. I thought he might at least see my side of things—and I admit that he did. Or at least, so he said—he spent quite a lot of time telling me how well I'd done, and how clever I'd been to notice the issue I'd brought to his attention. It was intensely flattering."

"But . . ." Catherine prompted wryly.

"But," Mr. Frampton confirmed, "he said he couldn't risk offending Sir Eldon by snubbing his nephew. Sir Eldon has stepped up to take your part regarding the financial outlay, Lady Moth."

Lucy looked at Catherine, who only nodded, a resigned set to her mouth. "I supposed something like that might happen."

Lucy was feeling less and less calm the more she turned the problem around and considered it from all the angles. "So because his uncle is financing it, he gets his way?" she demanded. "That's awful. It's venal. It's—unscientific!"

"It's the duty of the president of the Polite Science Society to ensure that funds for the enterprise remain reliable," Mr. Frampton said, with the air of one quoting something he'd heard far too often. "Or else everyone's pursuit of knowledge would be jeopardized."

Lucy snorted. "As if there is no pursuit of knowledge that could thrive without Mr. Hawley's supervision."

Mr. Frampton's glum looks intensified. "I can't fault him entirely—he took it quite hard when you walked away from the translation, my lady."

"When my money walked away, you mean." Catherine lowered her eyes demurely and sipped her tea, then set the empty cup in the saucer and met Mr. Frampton's gaze with confidence. "Were you thinking of asking to join Lucy's work on Oléron, sir?"

Lucy gaped a little, surprised by this suddenly opportunistic interpretation.

Mr. Frampton had the grace to look chagrined. "It had occurred to me," he admitted, "but it seemed so painfully presumptuous that I rejected it almost immediately. I thought instead to ask you to restore your promised funding to the Society, so that my word on Leibniz might carry some weight." He let one gloved finger stroke down the spine of the teacup lizard, whose gaze now seemed reproachful. Mr. Frampton sighed again. "But I have changed my mind about that, too. Who knows? I am tempted to resign my Fellowship altogether. It has not been nearly so productive as I hoped at the beginning."

Lucy had heard enough, and sat bolt upright on the sofa. "Allow me to share the indignation on your behalf, Mr. Frampton. I went into the archives and read your papers—you have a great gift, and one that should be more celebrated. But I do wonder something . . ." Lucy picked up a slice of bread and butter. "Was the Oléron translation a pet project of yours, or did you take it up at Mr. Hawley's suggestion?"

"The latter," the mathematician replied. "I had jumped around quite a bit in my studies, and my most recent work had been focused on astronomy. Some of the same charts you and your father produced, in fact."

Lucy glowed a little at the acknowledgment—small though it was, it was more than she'd ever had. She bit into the bread and butter to hide her mixed pleasure and embarrassment.

The mathematician continued: "While he eventually admitted me as a member, Mr. Hawley hinted that my career would have to grow steadier if I was to make proper progress in the field."

"I am sure he had an abundance of suggestions," Catherine murmured.

Lucy swallowed and tilted her head as a thought occurred. "What would you be working on, if it were up to you entirely? If money were not an obstacle, and if nobody was steering you toward anything else."

"Honestly?" Mr. Frampton looked stunned, then thoughtful.

Lucy leaned forward for his reply, as Catherine watched patiently from the other side of the sofa.

At length his voice returned, slow and careful. "During my first year out of school, I was working with one of your charts, Miss Muchelney. Point by point, you showed how the path of one particular comet arced across the sky, left, and came back again. And it occurred to me that you could build a machine for calculating exactly the kind of functions you and your father compiled from St. Day's data," he said.

Lucy, breathless, felt discovery peeking over the horizon, as though her skin felt the warmth of a sun that had yet to rise. "You aren't talking about just writing out the solutions in a table," she said slowly.

Mr. Frampton nodded, and his smile turned boyish as he saw Lucy had caught his enthusiasm. "I mean a machine that can do all the actual calculating, and present you with an exact result every time."

Catherine let out a breath. "That sounds incredibly complicated."

"It is," the mathematician confirmed. "It is proving astonishingly difficult to construct. But I feel it can be done, and there are so many ways such a machine could be invaluable."

"But you would need financing," Catherine said. "Mathematics can be done admirably cheaply, but anything with machinery would entail manufacturing costs, testing, repairing, that sort of thing."

Mr. Frampton's hopefulness flickered at this chilly breeze of truth. "I admit my finances, though not my faculties, are insufficient for the challenge. I had thought to give up my music lessons by now—instead, I think I shall have to take on a few more students, to make ends meet. I was hoping the royalties from the Oléron translation would allow for at least a first attempt."

Catherine's face was carefully neutral as she asked, "Did Mr. Hawley tell you the Oléron was expected to bring in a great profit?"

Mr. Frampton turned a ring around and around on his right hand. "He stated that as an official Polite Science Society publication, and recommended pointedly in *Polite Philosophies*, it would be sure to sell a more than respectable number of copies. 'With my imprimatur as president,' et cetera. He waxed almost poetic about it."

"Hmm," was all Catherine said.

Lucy narrowed her eyes. She knew an unspoken thought when she heard one. "Is he wrong to want to encourage Society members to purchase the translation?"

"No," Catherine replied calmly. "But if he is only addressing the volume to the Society, and not to the general public, I wonder exactly how much profit would even be possible."

"*I* wonder how much of any profit would have gone to you, in return for putting up the original funds." Lucy sniffed, and attacked a scone with some ferocity.

Catherine dropped her eyes and said nothing—as she usually did, whenever money was mentioned. Oh, she was quick to offer support, as when she'd invited Lucy to stay and finish her translation, but since that first conversation she had never gone into detail about what such support actually meant: timelines, funds allocated, profits divided, that sort of thing. Lucy had tried to ask once or twice and been deflected so elegantly she hadn't realized until later.

Evidence: Catherine was uncomfortable talking about money.

Conclusion: none possible yet. More observation was apparently required. It was a delicate question at the best of times—more so when you had just started sharing a bed with your benefactor.

As Lucy swallowed her unease, Mr. Frampton finished his tea and set the lizard cup aside. "I'm afraid I must bid you farewell, my lady," he said. "I'm attending a second Society lecture this evening, and there are a few letters I should reread in advance of hearing their author speak." He rose from his chair and paused, head tilted thoughtfully to one side. "I must ask: Have you written to inform M. Oléron about your translation?"

Lucy shook her head. "I had thought to wait until I had more of it worth sending to him first. I admit, I've added so much material that it's possible it's no longer strictly a translation. More of a supplementary text." She smiled ruefully. "A phrasebook, rather than a dictionary."

"You should send those pages sooner, rather than later," Mr. Frampton warned. "Depend upon it, Mr. Hawley will be doing so. If he's able to claim the Society's translation has the original author's stamp of approval . . ."

Lucy managed to keep her temper until Mr. Frampton had departed, whereupon she set down her teacup with a vicious click and began pacing the length of the parlor. "How dare Mr. Hawley presume to know what's best for everyone!" she cried. "How dare he think that science should be limited by his own stunted imagination!"

Catherine's lips curved as she leaned back against the sofa. "It seems that you have caught some of Mr. Edwards's ideas about imagination being necessary to science." She stirred her second cup of tea. "Many young women in the city have found him quite sensational."

Lucy waved this aside. "Oh, yes, he's handsome enough." She stopped, catching an edge in Catherine's tone that made her uneasy. "Do you think he's wrong? Do you think that science is really so rigid as people like Mr. Hawley would have it?"

"It has certainly run roughshod over my life," Catherine

said. The quiet, factual way she said it made Lucy ache for her. "But no, my disagreement concerns something else. I appreciate Mr. Edwards's praise of the power of imagination—but I object to the fact that he still would put that power into science's service. He admires the arts, but only insofar as they can be made useful. But not all the great truths are scientific in nature." She sipped her tea, her eyes distant with thought. "There is—there must be real value in a poem or a painting, for its own sake."

Lucy sighed and sat down beside her on the sofa. "Or an embroidery pattern?" she asked, trailing her fingers over the scrolls stitched along the edge of Catherine's bodice.

The countess laughed and leaned into the caress, but the corners of her eyes stayed tight. "We were speaking of high arts, I thought."

Lucy nuzzled into the crook of Catherine's neck. She smelled of lemon and bergamot and sugar: irresistible. The countess let out a pleased sigh as Lucy feathered kisses along her jawline. "Maybe we shouldn't speak at all for a little while." And for a little while, they didn't.

CHAPTER EIGHT

The laggard spring became a tempestuous summer, ominously wet and chilly. Lucy, who hadn't trained a telescope on the sky since coming to London, found herself feeling restless and earthbound. Mrs. Kelmarsh offered a welcome distraction by inviting them to something called the Friendly Philosophical Salon. It was a reading club for ladies, who gathered in the back room of a ramshackle bookstore in Paternoster Row: some older women of Mrs. Kelmarsh's long acquaintance, some comfortably matron-aged like Catherine, a handful around Lucy's years. A small closet in one corner provided a discreet dressing place for anyone who felt more at ease wearing (or changing out of) shirtsleeves, jacket, and breeches among friends; the chairs and couches were much mended, much sat-upon, and much less flexible than any of the minds in the room. Catherine and Lucy's introductions were made swiftly and without fuss, and then the group erupted into a medical-philosophical debate about the potential physical location of the soul, clearly a cherished argument of long standing. Lucy joined in with a will and a sense of belonging she hadn't felt since the gates of Cramlington had clanged shut behind her.

She was very near the end of the Oléron, but had not yet managed to pin Catherine down about money. "Finish the manuscript, then we'll take it to Griffin's and see about their terms," the countess said.

To add to Lucy's puzzlement, Stephen's pointed letters on the subject of Lyme and returning to it suddenly switched tacks entirely. Apparently, instead, he was planning a journey to London himself.

"A few of Stephen's friends have paintings to show in this year's Summer Exhibition at the Royal Academy," Lucy explained to Catherine, "so they've all come down to town to celebrate. By which I mean argue, mostly. They're impossible, but very amusing to listen to. Stephen's invited me along for the afternoon." She squirmed, worried that she would be outnumbered and vulnerable and a ready target for more of Stephen's pressure. "I'd love you to join us."

"Are you quite sure you want me to meet your brother?" The countess dropped her eyes, taking one of those shy turns that Lucy had hoped were becoming less and less frequent with time and affection. "Are you certain it's wise?"

Catherine's hesitance was understandable, but it still pricked all the tender spots of Lucy's hopeful heart. "Stephen can be downright priggish where I am concerned, but he is far more liberal-minded to people who are not his sister," Lucy said. "And a few of his friends are quite talented. Their paintings alone will certainly be worth the trip."

So Lucy put on one of her gray gowns—livened up with a puce chevron trim in Eliza Brinkworth's clever hand—and they drove to the lofty neoclassical pile of Somerset House on the River Thames.

The sky outside was lumpen with clouds, portending more rain, but Lucy didn't pay this any mind. That was the one landscape she wasn't here to view today. Bubbling with excitement, she slipped her arm through Catherine's and led the countess up the curving flights of stairs and into the main Exhibition Room.

The space was busy with people, but the bright half-circle windows far up in the high ceiling made it feel airy despite the throng. Every inch of every wall was covered by paintings, small delicate landscape sketches shoved right up against huge portraits and elaborate history scenes with ornate frames. As the eye wandered up, row by row, the paintings tilted forward more and more, arcing as if they were a wave about to crest and crash down upon the throng of viewers in a flood of paint and canvas. Lucy watched Catherine's head tilt back in wonder, and wished she dared press a kiss to the graceful column of her throat.

But this place was public, and it would be dangerous for Lucy to forget herself.

They had barely wandered the length of one wall before Lucy caught the pitch of a familiar voice. Her brother and his coterie were massed in front of one of the largest paintings, hung right at eye level, a desirable placement that spoke of the judges' strong approval. The artists in front of the piece, however, seemed less in awe of its genius than one might have expected. Arms were being flung with abandon, and gestures made toward particular parts of the canvas.

The group was plainly midargument already, but if Lucy waited for the debate to end she'd be waiting until the next century. "Stephen!" she cried instead, pulling Catherine gently forward.

"My dear sister!" Her brother was looking well, as he always did after a spell in the country: all bright eyes and ruddy cheeks and the air of a burden lately lifted. He pressed a kiss to Lucy's cheek and bowed over Catherine's hand when she was introduced. "It is an honor and a delight to meet the woman who was such a constant correspondent of my father's—and who has lately taken my rather wayward sister under her wing." He shot Lucy a sharp glance.

Lucy's pleasure at seeing him went brittle, and she had a sudden terrible urge to stamp her foot and pitch a tantrum like she hadn't done since she was four years old.

Catherine only smiled serenely: all her earlier shyness hidden carefully away beneath her countess's poise. "Your sister is brilliant, Mr. Muchelney. The honor is mine, that I can enjoy her company until she has a chance to share her genius with other scholars and scientific minds."

Stephen blinked, surprised by Lady Moth's staunch defense.

Lucy felt pride and self-consciousness war with each other to burn in her cheeks, and wondered: If she were to burst into flame right here in the gallery, how many great artworks would perish with her?

She turned to the large painting they were arguing over,

hoping for a distraction. "Tell me why this one has gotten you all so stirred up."

Stephen spun on his heel, so eager was he to follow the change of subject. "It's Kelbourne's latest: *Lord Elgin Approaching the Parthenon.*"

Lucy gazed up at the painting, slightly longer than her arms could span: the Parthenon's ancient form took up most of the upper portion of the canvas, shining white and crumbling nobly against a background of rose and gold clouds. Below and to the right stood a solitary figure in a deep burgundy coat: one leg was planted up and forward, and two hands were clamped behind his back as he surveyed the ancient temple.

Stephen's best friend, Mr. Banerjee, leaned forward, a gleam in his eyes. "The question, Miss Muchelney, is whether the painting is a sunrise or a sunset. Is our hero arriving or departing this land of legend?"

"Surely it's the latter," said one of the artists.

"Preposterous. Look at the shade of that light. Rosy as the dawn."

"Dawn? Hah! That is obviously the rich, heavy gold you get at day's end when the light has had time to steep."

"Pardon me," Catherine interjected softly but firmly, "but it must be a sunrise."

Everyone stopped and stared, even Lucy.

"How do you know?" an artist asked, tones laden with suspicion.

Catherine gestured to the section of brightest light, to the left of the row of columns. "Because that is where the sun rises when you view the Parthenon from this angle."

Mr. Banerjee's voice was all eager excitement. "You speak as though you've been there."

Catherine smiled. "I have."

"So it is a sunrise," Mr. Banerjee said decisively, and frowned. "And what is the significance of the sunrise, do you think?"

And so the argument played on, with Catherine adding occasional notes to the painterly chorus.

Lucy hid a smile and drifted away to look at the rest of the Exhibition. She'd never thought painters could spend more time talking than painting, but they never seemed to run short of opinions.

"Oi, Miss Muchelney!"

Lucy spun round at the sound of the voice, and found herself looking at a big, broad-shouldered man with a face like a boulder and a boxer's broken nose. "Mr. Violet!" she cried happily, holding out her hands.

Peter Violet grasped her hands in his—not with a gentleman's chivalrous grace, but as one would grip someone's hand to seal a bet.

She felt the strength of it all the way down to her toes, and grinned. "It's wonderful to see you. Are you showing anything this year?"

"A couple things," he said, in the low-street London accent he'd never shed. "Are you here with Stephen?"

"Stephen and—a friend," Lucy said.

Mr. Violet leaned closer, his voice a low rumble. "Not the famous Priscilla?"

"No." Lucy bit her lip. "The Countess of Moth."

"Fancy you taking a liking to a nob." Mr. Violet's grin was a whole dirty joke on its own.

Lucy snorted before she could stop herself, and some tight-wound internal part of her relaxed. She'd been so careful and proper the whole time she'd been in London, and it had been more of a strain than she'd realized. It was nice to be with someone she didn't have to play the lady in front of. She took his elbow just so she could secretly pinch him in rebuke. It only made him grin wider. "Come, now—show me your exhibits, and then if you behave I shall introduce you."

He had had three paintings accepted by the judges this year, it seemed. Two were sunset studies of the sea, rocky coastlines and roiling skies expertly rendered with confident, minimal brushstrokes in black and blue and searing orange. Ships were sketched in like ghosts, hulls and sails muddied by distance and the tactile weight of light. Half the art world hated his pieces; the other half lauded him as a genius. "It's good you're seeing this one now," he said, "because the red in the center is going to fade by this time next year."

Lucy was appalled. It was one of his most successful paintings, in her semilearned opinion, and much of the vitality came from that bold red streak. "If it won't last, then why use it at all? Why not use a paint that will still be bright in ten years' time?"

Peter turned horrified eyes on her. "This red is the *right* red," he protested. "You've got to paint the colors right, even if they won't stay that way forever. Nothing lasts."

"Some things do," Lucy argued. "We've looked up at the same constellations since Aristotle's time, and even earlier."

Peter's smile was crooked, and a little sad. "They just change slower, is all." He led her to the third and final painting. It had been hung right on the line, in the center of the wall: pride of place.

Peter's voice was sly and satisfied as he told her the title: "*Medea Meeting Jason.*"

Lucy had a hard time finding the title figures, at first. The painting was mostly architectural—not surprising for Peter, who tried to avoid painting people insofar as he could—an airy confection of glowing domes and spires. At the city gate were two small and ghostly figures: a red-haired woman in flowing lilac, with touches of gold in her hair and around her wrists. Her lithe arms were wrapped around a bare-chested hero with a Grecian helmet and curling hair. He seemed to be half avoiding the embrace, head turned away and one arm raised to point down the wooded slope to a tree where the Golden Fleece hung in splendor, a guardian serpent twined around the trunk the same way Medea was trying to twine around Jason. A ship sailing away on the distant sea foreshadowed the coming moment when they would attempt to outrun doom and disaster.

"Lovely," Lucy breathed, because it was. "But not a very happy moment to have chosen. He looks half bored with her already."

"He doesn't want her," Peter explained. "He wants the Fleece, and seducing her is the easiest way to get it."

"The fastest, maybe," Lucy replied. "I'm not sure it was easy on him, at the end."

"When she kills their boys, you mean?" Peter said, chuckling. "That's going to be the next painting, to pair with this one. Jason on hands and knees, gold crown rolling from his head, and Medea sailing away in a chariot drawn by dragons. The corpses of her two littles slung all horrid over her arm. And in the background a ruined city, with towers aflame."

Lucy's eyes goggled at the description. "I'm not sure how the judges are going to feel about that."

Peter Violet's smile turned wry. "I don't paint for the judges. If they like it, that's terrific, we'll hang it up and sell copies and let everyone ooh and ahh all they want. But they could tell me it's not worth the trouble to spit on it, and I'd still choose to paint it—because there's nothing else I can do and still feel like myself."

"So what's this one really about, then?" Lucy asked. "Since unlike so many artists I know, you're capable of giving a straight answer."

Peter's eyes went grim as he looked over his own work, the product of so many months' time and effort. "It's about two people reaching out to take what they want, and getting burned." His eyes flickered away from hers to land on the vivid red tongue of fire lancing out of the dragon's open mouth.

Lucy recognized the tone in his voice. She'd heard it often enough in her own, in those first few weeks after Priscilla's wedding. Peter had known about her inclinations ever since Lucy had caught him and Mr. Banerjee together during one of their visits to her house: she'd told them about Priscilla to reassure them that she had no intention of using their secret against them. Pris had been furious, even though the two men were in a much more dangerous position than two women would be if anyone were to find out.

Peter looked so tough, with his fighter's face and the accent he refused to shed, but he felt things more deeply the less he showed it. Heartbreak would not sit easily on him.

She squeezed his arm. "The red will fade, you know," she said, since the dragon's flame was the same bright but ephemeral shade he'd used in the other painting. Sometimes the passage of time could be a comfort. "You said it yourself: nothing lasts."

Peter's smile was a hesitant, half-bitter thing, but it gave her some hope. "Let me show you my favorites by the other painters," he offered, and Lucy agreed with a laugh.

Catherine didn't know how much time had passed when she emerged from the tempest of artistic opinion and noticed Lucy was no longer at her side.

A quick glance around was enough to reassure her: there Lucy was, holding the arm of a, well, a rather rough-looking man, if Catherine were being honest. She could practically see his calluses from across the room.

Stephen Muchelney caught the direction of Catherine's gaze and smiled. "Ah, that's our Peter Violet," he said. "Born by the docks, not far from where we're standing, and he'll tell you all about it if you give him half a minute."

"But what is he doing here?" Catherine asked.

"He's got three pieces showing," Mr. Muchelney replied. "You can pay for schooling, and you can pay for paint, but there's no way to purchase genius, and Violet has that if any of us do. He and Lucy have always enjoyed each other."

As they watched, Peter's eyes lit up and he said something to make Lucy laugh. The familiar sound of it did queer things to the tight-knotted strings of Catherine's anxious heart. She pulled cold air into empty lungs.

Mr. Muchelney leaned in conspiratorially. "To be perfectly frank, Lady Moth, I rather hope they'll end up making a match of it. He may not be gently bred but he's kind to her, and works harder than any artist I know. And Lucy's not enough of a snob to sniff at his good qualities." Mr. Muchelney's smile was serpent-sly. "Maybe it won't be too long before my sister stops taking advantage of your hospitality."

They did look well together, Catherine couldn't argue with that: Lucy's height and slenderness balanced by Mr. Violet's craggy bulk.

The countess swallowed hard against the ashes in her mouth. "You seem to think your sister nothing but a burden, Mr. Muchelney," she said, hating the gravel at the bottom of her throat. "Let me assure you, the day she leaves me is not something I look forward to."

Beside her Mr. Banerjee twitched, his own face tight with a peculiar sort of intensity.

Stephen Muchelney tilted his head as he looked at her—a gesture so like his sister's that Catherine had to catch her breath. "What would you think, Lady Moth, about having my sister's portrait painted? Then you'd always have something of her to treasure." He grinned boyishly. "I happen to know an excellent portraitist presently in need of commissions."

He meant himself, of course. So either he had guessed that Catherine and Lucy were something other than simply friends—or it was blindingly obvious even to a total stranger how much Catherine cared.

Catherine didn't want to imagine what her face looked like just now. She could feel the strings of politeness's mask pulling tight, and the porcelain going brittle and thin. "Pardon me," she murmured, "but I think I will take a turn about the house and view some of the other paintings."

She walked away and found another frame to stand in front of, but could not tell you what colors had been used on the canvas or even what the subject was. She stared straight ahead, but her vision was turned inward, upon the wounds and ruins of her own heart.

Foolish, to have let herself dream so much! Catherine had been so comforted by the freedom of knowing Lucy couldn't ask to marry her, that she had lost sight of the simple fact that Lucy might very well think of marrying someone else. That was what Pris had done, after all. It's what so many young women did, even the ones who loved other women—look at Aunt Kelmarsh, who'd loved Catherine's mother deeply but who had nonetheless been married and widowed twice over in the course of her long and interesting life.

She'd been in such high and tender hopes, today, being presented to her lover's brother as though that might signify something about the nature of their connection. As though it meant Lucy cherished her a little. But Mr. Muchelney did not even seem to know about Lucy's preferences—was that a deliberate blindness on his part, or had Lucy taken care that he shouldn't know? Brothers had such power over their younger siblings, particularly sisters, and most particularly when that brother was head of the family.

And Stephen Muchelney wanted his sister to marry Peter Violet. Would he cut her off if she refused? Catherine could save Lucy from penury; the girl wouldn't end up starving on the streets. But what if Lucy came to resent that dependence? What if Catherine, watching Lucy turn cold and bitter, became a brittle, anxious tyrant like George had been? She felt nearly tyrannical already, some wild part inside her howling with pain and rage even now, here in the heart of the polite and civilized world.

She was so wrapped up in these fears that she almost stumbled headlong into Mr. Frampton. "Lady Moth!" he said. "Are you quite alright?"

She forced a smile for him, then felt it take true hold. He was familiar, and kind, and his concern steadied her. "Just a little overwhelmed, I think," she said. "There are so many people here!"

"There are," he agreed, peering down at her. His smile was sincere but a little tight, and there were worry lines in the corners of his dark eyes.

So she took him by the arm, and saw some of those worry lines fade. "Come, sir," she said. "Let us find the quietest corner and the humblest painting. Its creator will appreciate our attention more than any of the judges' darlings, I'm sure."

His lips curved in amusement. "That's one way of making an inexpert opinion valuable."

They turned their back on the chattering crowd and

wound through the rooms of the Exhibition in search of silence and quietude. Catherine caught sight of a small, mud-colored painting in a corner of the last gallery that looked like it would do, but halfway across the space she was forced to halt because Mr. Frampton had jerked to a stop as if his feet had put roots down into the floor.

His face was shocked, his lips parted as he sucked in a breath and held it.

Catherine followed his gaze and saw nothing but a portrait of a merchant. A Frenchman, according to the title—a weaver. He sat at a desk among the detritus of his trade: spools of thread, measuring sticks, bolts of fabric, a large loom frame hovering behind his shoulder. One of the merchant's hands was gripping a pair of calipers, and beside him, newly finished, lay a stack of cards with holes carefully punched in. A few other such cards were strung up on the machine behind him, waiting only for the handle to be turned.

The brushwork was fine and the colors well chosen, but Catherine couldn't see why this painting should have struck Mr. Frampton like a lightning bolt out of a clear blue sky. "Do you know this man?" she asked.

The mathematician shook his head, eyes never leaving the portrait. "Not at all. But he's given me a miracle."

Catherine had lived all her life among scientists. She knew the sound of revelation when she heard it. And she knew what to do next. "Do you need to write something down?" she asked, and began digging through her reticule for the pencil and notebook she always kept handy.

Mr. Frampton looked at her, some miracle still shining in

his eyes. "*Thank* you," he breathed, and began scribbling and sketching at once—in the back of the notebook, far away from her own botanical sketches and plant studies. Very thoughtful, even in the grip of inspiration. George had once scribbled calculations over a full-page sketch of Captain Lateshaw, and had never even seen the need to apologize.

Catherine suppressed a smile and left Mr. Frampton to his work. No doubt he would be occupied for some few minutes. She would come back in a quarter hour and see if the dream had relinquished him then.

She wandered a little farther on her own, still reluctant to return to the crowded main gallery. A stairway lured her outside to a small terrace that fronted the river, boats and barges trundling through its murky waters, and waves lapping up against the very foundations of the house. The sky above was still roiling with clouds, but the river made a break in the buildings, as though some great knife had sliced through so all the layers of the city could be seen. A brisk wind brought Catherine the scents of land and water, refreshing after the crush of perfumed, perspiring humanity within Somerset House.

Near the terrace edge, hem dancing in the breeze, sat a woman with an easel. A little older than Catherine, maybe, to judge from the silver that streaked a few of her dark locks where they escaped her simple cap. She was sketching the view, hand flying with confidence over the page. Catherine crept closer as soundlessly as she could, peering avidly while the woman's pencil conjured boats and waves and the sweep of the sky, quickly and with feeling. She seemed to know just which lines were important and should be made bold, and which ones should be skipped as unnecessary. She stopped, cocking her head to consider her work thus far—and a flutter of Catherine's skirt caught her eye and broke her concentration.

The countess flushed. "I beg your pardon. I didn't mean to trouble you."

"No trouble," the woman said, though her mouth pressed thin with something close to annoyance. Catherine noticed her clothing was serviceable but not expensive: broad cotton rather than silk, dyed soft green but mended here and there where only a careful eye could see. She wore no jewelry, but her eyes were hard and bright as gems. Something about the way she kept herself angled to face Catherine said *shopkeeper*.

As quickly as it had appeared, the annoyance on her face smoothed out into polite blandness. "Are you enjoying the Exhibition?" the woman inquired.

"Very much," Catherine said. "The landscape with Lord Elgin will be in my thoughts for some time, I think."

"Ah, yes." The other woman turned to the sketchbook on her easel and quickly flipped through to an earlier page. There in penciled shadow was Lord Elgin, an extraordinarily faithful reproduction of the painting Catherine had just been admiring. "This one?"

"You've captured it exactly," Catherine replied, eyebrows lifting in pleasure and surprise. "It's striking, is it not?"

The artist smiled. "Yes, all the artists are buzzing about it. Which means it should prove quite popular." She turned to her pencil box and pulled free a small card impressed with the image of a mythical beast, half lion and half eagle. "I'm with

Griffin's," she said, to Catherine's secret delight. "We offer quality mezzotint reproductions of interesting and notable portraits, paintings, and landscapes; commissions by special request. Also selected views of the city, with historical landmarks and points of interest. And of course, *Griffin's Menagerie*."

"I'm an ardent subscriber," Catherine said as she accepted the card. "Do you have any work in the Exhibition this year?"

"Me?" The woman scoffed. "I'm only an engraver, madam. A copyist. Not an artist. Not one the Academy would recognize, at any rate."

Catherine looked at the sketch on the easel, at the easy lines and effortlessly perfect proportions that spoke of a gifted eye and willing hand, carefully trained. She bristled. "But surely this is no different, in any essential way. Your sketches would not suffer by comparison with many of the landscapes I walked past just now."

"But those landscapes were done in oils," the woman countered. "Or watercolors, or charcoal. Each one done by hand, one stroke at a time." She tapped her pencil end against the paper. "These are mere copies. Since I did not create the initial portrait, none of them can properly be labeled art."

Catherine listened to this with dismay, but the engraver seemed to take it in weary stride.

The woman's mouth crooked wryly up at the corners. "Still, I'll sell more of them than most of the great artists whose work you've just strolled past. Reprints and scenic views and embroidery patterns—which don't count as art, either, of course."

Catherine imagined the gallery behind her full of embroidered panels instead of paintings. Tambour and scrollwork and satin-stitched florals, all flung up in one giant patchwork, while the public paid good money to admire them and the critics debated what the embroiderer's choices of stitch and color signified. It was an absurd thing to yearn for, and yet . . . she saw it so vividly, she could almost feel the texture of the threads beneath her fingertips.

The engraver began another question, but a clatter on the stairs behind Catherine cut the conversation short.

Lucy appeared in the doorway, breathless, cheeks flushed, framed like a very picture of alarm and dismay. "There you are!" she cried. "Stephen told me—" She stopped, as she registered the presence of the other woman. "Oh, I'm so sorry." She dropped a flustered curtsy. "Lucy Muchelney," she said. "Are you a friend of Lady Moth's?"

Oh, this was awkward. Catherine hadn't missed how the engraver's eyes had widened at the use of her title. Nevertheless, there were rules, so Catherine completed the introductions and nodded politely to the other woman, whose name turned out to be Mrs. Agatha Griffin. "We were discussing her work," Catherine said to Lucy, "but I am glad you found us." She turned back to the engraver. "Miss Muchelney is nearly finished with a very scholarly translation—we were hoping to approach you about printing a full run of copies."

"You'll be wanting to speak to Thomas—my husband, that is," Mrs. Griffin said. "He oversees the contracts. He's away at the moment, but he should be back in the shop on Thursday. If that suits you, my lady?"

Catherine replied that it did.

Mrs. Griffin thanked her again and returned to her sketching; Catherine and Lucy went back inside to collect Mr. Frampton.

There were still haloes in his eyes, but his frantic sketching seemed to have run its course. He showed them his pages as the carriage rattled down the street, elation crackling off him like one of Mr. Edwards's voltaic contraptions. "The trouble I've been having is not how to build the calculating machine," he said. "Even the ancients knew how to use assemblies of wheels and gears to calculate the movement of the moon and the stars. No, the trouble was that this machine would have to run different calculations for different sets of data. How do you tell it which one you want it to run? The French factory-owner's portrait had the answer right there." He pointed to a sketch he'd done, a detail of the painting. "Punched cards. That's how you tell the machine which levers to shift and which gears to turn at the right time." The rest of his sketches showed an assemblage of dense metal wheels, stacked tightly one on top of another.

Lucy turned sharp eyes on the later designs. "These are going to have to be very precise—how are you going to get them milled?"

Mr. Frampton laughed ruefully. "I'm not even convinced it's possible. If it is, it will surely be ruinously expensive. But for now it should be enough to work out the design in full and present it in a paper for *Polite Philosophies*."

They parted with the euphoric Mr. Frampton at his lodgings and continued home. Lucy reached out with one arm and half of the stellarium shawl and gathered Catherine close against her, as the gray afternoon shaded into a chill evening. Horses' hoof beats sounded a soft percussion in the quiet.

After a while Lucy asked: "What did you and Mrs. Griffin talk about?"

Catherine squirmed slightly. "Art. What it is. What it's not."

"You'll be as bad as Stephen next."

"Heaven forbid. What did you and Mr. Violet talk about?"

Lucy sighed. "Art. What it means."

Catherine plucked at the edges of the stellarium shawl, her eyes downcast. "How long have you known him?"

Lucy laughed. "Sometimes it feels like forever. Especially when he's in one of his moods. I enjoy when Mr. Violet's paintings are tortured and tempestuous—but not so Mr. Violet himself."

Catherine squeezed Lucy's waist as another pang went through her. "Does the art not mirror the artist's soul, then? I'm sure I read something about how a truly sublime painting requires the union of spirit and matter. Or soul and will, or I forget what." She righted herself and leaned back against the seat. "I can't pretend I'll ever create anything artistically sublime. There are no geniuses of embroidery, after all."

Lucy sat straight up. "And why shouldn't there be?"

Her indignation was perfectly adorable and made Catherine's fond heart beat faster. "Embroidery is a handicraft, my dear. Domestic and ladylike. Perfectly ordinary. Art is— grander, is it not?"

Lucy rejected this with a firm shake of her head. "Why should you not consider what you make to be art?"

Catherine held her breath as a door she'd thought long shut cracked open, just a sliver; it was equal parts frightening and exhilarating. Bravery had done well by her in recent months—but when did one cross the line from bravery into foolhardiness?

Lucy, noting her dawning interest, pressed harder. "I've seen you create so many wonders these past few months. Tablecloth borders, chemises, gowns—you work in unusual stitch patterns, exotic plants, bold colors, unexpected mixes. I never thought about any of these things until you showed me your work. For example."

She pulled off the stellarium shawl and stretched it out in front of them both.

"Look at this. It's sophisticated and striking and absolutely lovely. Anyone who sees it is dazzled—and the more they know about how it was worked, the more they take away from it. Everyone can admire the sparkle—but only another embroiderer can recognize the skill it took to create the design, and to make it a concrete reality. I told you once your stitches looked like brushstrokes—and I've spent enough time around artists to know a gifted eye when I see someone use it. Catherine," she said more softly, "this is *art*. You are an artist."

A lifetime's worth of struggle and frustration rose up around Catherine like a storm cloud. She fought back, instinctively. "The Academy would beg to differ. Barely any women were allowed space on those walls today. And not one—not one!—works in a medium so ephemeral and frivolous as fabric and thread."

Lucy pulled back, folding the shawl up crisply, in precise,

angry movements. Her tone was sharp as a stiletto. "Let me ask you something. Am I an astronomer?"

Catherine blinked at the swiftness of the subject change. "Of course you are."

"The Polite Science Society doesn't think so. They wouldn't accept me as a Fellow. Mr. Hawley all but threw me out of his dinner party."

Catherine shook her head, guessing where Lucy was going with her argument. "That's different—"

"*How?*"

"Because science is about truth!" Catherine cried. "We have ways of measuring it. Numbers and data and cold, irrefutable facts. When you present a scientific theory, well, people *have* to agree with you or else they're wrong, and if they're wrong then nothing they try to do in their own scientific projects will succeed. But art . . ." She huffed out a breath, and quickly sucked another one in. Her heart was racing and her cheeks were flaming and Lucy was beginning to look slightly alarmed, which only made Catherine more agitated. "Art is only art because people call it so. Art is an illusion: a reflection of something, meant to communicate a thought or a feeling or the sense of a scene. There's no possible way to be concretely, completely, objectively correct about it. Is the painting a sunrise or a sunset? And if it's a sunrise, what does that mean? Six people fought about it for half an hour and no solid consensus was reached. Because no consensus *could* be reached."

Lucy's hands were bunched in her shawl, spoiling the careful folds. "But they had to agree on *some* things. Essential things. You said it yourself: the Academy believes that embroidery is not art, and an oil portrait is."

Catherine folded her arms. "So?"

"So why can't you try to change those parameters?" Lucy said. "Why can't you try to persuade them that embroidery could be counted as art on its own merits?"

"Because I am tired!" Catherine cried. She could hear the burn of unshed tears in her own voice, as the words tore themselves from her throat. "I am tired of twisting myself into painful shapes for mere scraps of respect or consideration. Tired of bending this way and that in search of approval that will only ever be half granted."

The carriage turned a corner, and Catherine felt as if the whole world spun sideways around her.

She swallowed hard and tried to explain. "My mother sent men all over the globe to fetch trinkets for her, bits and pieces of the world that she tried to put together into something like the whole. They fought to bring her the best specimens, the rarest species from the farthest places. Her approval counted for something—but only briefly, and only as a result of her accumulation. As soon as her treasures were sold, her achievements—her learning, her science!—vanished with them. I tried for more: I went out into the wider world, and I tried to do work that lasted. Even if I could only help as an assistant, and not a full participant. And still I ended up as an outsider: I didn't have the skills or the education or the experience of men like George, Mr. Hawley, or Captain Lateshaw. They dismissed me out of hand, and I can't even blame them for doing it." She dashed hot tears from her eyes, furious that her body was betraying her with this frailty, clouding her sight when it felt like she had a chance to look at her own self clearly for the first time in her life. "And then today, talking with your brother and his friends, I was an outsider again."

Lucy shook her head. "You were the only one who knew that painting showed a sunrise."

Catherine scoffed. "One brief moment where I could offer something of use—but as soon as it was over they began to talk about Lord Elgin's pose instead, what it might signify about his character, referencing paintings from Exhibitions past that I hadn't had a chance to view and therefore can't offer thoughts about. And you—" She cut herself off, finally, more tears rushing to spill down her cheeks as she relived the horrible, helpless jealousy that had sent her fleeing the gallery.

Lucy gripped her shoulders, gray eyes soft and worried. "And I what?"

Catherine gulped in a breath. If she was going to ruin everything, best do it quickly. "And you knew everyone already, and Peter Violet made you laugh, and your brother said you might marry him."

"Oh, love." Lucy's hands slipped up to frame her face. Those gray eyes never wavered, though sorrow lurked in the corners as they held Catherine's gaze. "Peter Violet is miserably, hopelessly in love with Mr. Banerjee. He doesn't want to marry me; I'm reasonably certain he doesn't want to marry anyone. He has rather radical thoughts on the whole institution. He wrote a pamphlet once."

Catherine couldn't help the laugh that bubbled out of her, a helpless, watery sort of sound.

Lucy bent down and captured it with her mouth. Catherine kissed her back desperately, even as her heart wailed in her breast with an unquenchable loss. It wasn't enough—could never be enough . . .

The carriage jolted to a halt, and Catherine fumbled to put herself somewhat to rights. But being a countess was an old, old habit by now, and it helped that if she refused to acknowledge the tear tracks on her cheeks, nobody else would dare do differently.

There was but an hour until dinner; she announced her intention of resting in her room until then, and dismissed a worried Narayan.

As soon as they were alone, Catherine wrapped her arms around Lucy. "I can't bear the thought of losing you," she said, shaking.

Lucy's slender shape stood firm against Catherine's onslaught of emotion; she only twined her arms around her lover and held her close and steady. "Why would I go anywhere?" she whispered, her mouth hot against Catherine's temple. "Everything I want is right here, because *you* are here."

She turned Catherine around, her mouth brushing over the countess's nape, her hands undoing the line of buttons down the back of Catherine's dress. Silk whispered encouragement as it slid to the floor, and Catherine trembled as cool air rushed in where she stood in only stays, petticoats, and chemise. Lucy brushed gentle fingers over her shoulders, thin lines of fire following her touch. Shivering, Catherine turned and tugged at the laces of Lucy's gown, lavender and primrose opening beneath her hands to reveal the worn muslin beneath.

It cut her to the quick, that Lucy was still stuck with these old things when Catherine could easily have bought much finer fabrics for her to wear against her skin. She pressed apologetic kisses to Lucy's collarbone.

Lucy gasped and urged her on with breathless murmurs.

Too impatient to wait for further disrobing, Catherine pulled Lucy down atop her on the chaise.

Lucy hummed happily, her greater height blocking the wan summer sun and casting Catherine in shadow. Her arms bracketed the countess like columns as she hovered above her, and Catherine felt her panic ease a little to be so confined and protected. She slid a hand beneath Lucy's petticoats and up the long length of her thigh. Her other hand curved over the back of Lucy's neck, pulling her down for deep and ravenous kisses.

Lucy held nothing back, making *hurry up* noises in her throat and gasping into her lover's mouth when Catherine's fingers slid into the heat of her. She shook and trembled and Catherine gave her more and more until she shuddered and cried out, back bowing and fingers clutching at the upholstery. At last she collapsed on top of Catherine, who gloried in the slight, trembling, dewy weight of her.

Lucy blinked to clear her eyes of passion's mist. "But you . . . ?"

"Later," Catherine whispered, and pressed her lips to Lucy's temple.

CHAPTER NINE

Griffin's print shop was hard by Queen Square, not terribly far from Somerset House. Lucy followed Catherine through the doorway and found herself in a light- and color-filled space. It was like stepping into summer proper, with its hue and haze, and some part of her country heart sighed to see it. All around her hung framed views of London: the river Thames sparkling blue in sunlight, the great conservatory of Carleton House, the tall pagoda in St. James's Park, delicately tinted. Copies of famous landscapes and paintings she recognized from the Exhibition added more color, bright in the light that slanted down from windows set high in the walls above. A pair of young women flipped through loose prints in folios resting on their spines in V-shaped cradles, and glass-fronted cabinets behind the counter held copies of books in sheets, each manuscript stack tied neatly with twine to prevent individual pages from being lost before they could be carried to the buyer's favorite bindery.

Catherine strode through this treasury, direct as an

arrow. Lucy hurried after, head craning to take in as many sights as possible.

The young man behind the counter couldn't have been more than fifteen. He blinked anxiously at Catherine and hurried forward. "How may I help you, madam?"

"I am here to see Mr. Thomas Griffin, please," Catherine replied, and held out her card.

Lucy had to hide a smile as the young man's eyebrows fairly flew off his head at the letters announcing Catherine St. Day, Countess of Moth. "He's in the back, my lady," he said, with a quick, bobbing bow. "If you'll wait here for just a moment."

He was back again almost immediately—no wonder, with a countess waiting. Catherine sailed through the doorway after him. Lucy scurried to follow—and stopped, blinking at the sudden assault of noise.

In the far corner, an apprentice was pulling letters from a box of type and dropping them into place in a frame, his master's keen eye spotting misspellings almost before they could happen. Beside them, another man was printing on a single large handpress, pulling the iron handle to bring the press down with a deep thump Lucy could feel from her breastbone down into her toes. Every thump produced another identical sheet filled with blocks of text, which were then hung to dry before being collected and folded into signatures. In the other half of the room was a boy of thirteen or fourteen, bent over a reproduction of a famous painting, carefully shading forms in bright hues to add depth and vividness to the detail of the scene.

Supervising that boy was Mrs. Griffin, standing hawk-like above the young colorist. She glanced up with a piercing gaze; Lucy dared a small wave, and saw the engraver's mouth quirk in brief amusement.

Lucy and Catherine were let into a small office with windows looking out on the back street. With the door shut it was indeed much quieter than in the print shop itself. No doubt some of the sound was muffled by the stacks of manuscripts, prints, and pages piled every which way: the main desk was mostly clear, as were the two guest chairs in front of it, but the walls were lined with shelves and crates and cabinets from which paper burst chaotically like doves caught in the act of fleeing the coop.

Thomas Griffin was a man with a creamy complexion, white-blond curls, and a cherub's smile. He rose politely and bowed. "It's an honor to meet you in person, Lady Moth. What can I do for you today?"

Lucy sat. Catherine took possession of the left-hand guest chair as though it were a throne. "I will be direct, Mr. Griffin. My friend, Miss Lucy Muchelney—" Lucy nodded at being named, while Mr. Griffin's eyes cut to her "—has recently translated an important French astronomy text. We would like to make arrangements to have it printed and sold."

"Ah." The printer leaned back in his chair, fingers tapping lightly on the desk. "Griffin's has the luxury of being very choosy about what we print, my lady. We pride ourselves on producing a spectrum of work in which any lady of good character might take an interest. You know this quite well, of course—your name has graced our subscriber rolls for some time now." His angelic smile dimmed somewhat. "But it sounds like Miss Muchelney's work is quite scholarly and erudite—nothing wrong with that, of course . . . but perhaps you would be better served by one of the scientific presses here in town?"

Catherine's polite smile didn't budge, not a whit. "I will of course take all the financial risk of publication."

Mr. Griffin's eyes glinted at this. "In return for a larger cut of the profits, I assume."

"Naturally."

Mr. Griffin chuckled. "And what would I get out of this arrangement, for my smaller stake?"

"The chance to publish the first English translation of a significant scientific achievement from the Continent," Catherine replied easily. "You publish work that appeals to ladies of taste and intelligence—and this is a scientific text aimed at precisely such women." She tilted her head. "Have you been to any of Mr. Edwards's chemical demonstrations?"

"Yes, my son insisted on seeing the volcano eruption in person—quite dramatic."

"How many women would you say were in the audience?"

The printer bit his lip and looked thoughtful.

Catherine pressed on. "The motto of your *Menagerie* is 'A Lady's Treasury of the Arts and Sciences,' is it not?"

"It is—but we have never published anything scientific, outside of the short articles in the *Menagerie* itself." He pursed his lips. "I don't suppose you'd be interested in serializing . . . ?"

Catherine shook her head, even as she smiled to soften

the refusal. "You would prefer to test these unknown waters. It's a cautious impulse, and quite understandable. But if the serialization is a success, you'll want to publish the full volume next anyway—and if it isn't, you'll have used up some of the limited territory of your most valuable publication." She leaned ever so slightly forward, her voice dropping into an intense register, as though she were imparting secrets. "You don't have to choose one thing only. You can do both. Your *Menagerie*—that curated, ladylike collection of shorter pieces on history and science and the domestic arts which is already popular—and a substantive work of scholarly brilliance that just so happens to have a lady as an author."

Thomas Griffin stared for a long moment—but then, with a small laugh, said: "Lady Moth, I admit myself conquered."

He and Catherine began hammering out the finer details: number of copies printed, size of manuscript, costs of paper and platemaking and percentages of the profits. Most of the latter were to go to Lucy, at Catherine's insistence; Lucy herself could only listen breathlessly with the strange sense that the world was beginning to turn faster and faster around its axis.

She'd thought Catherine was afraid to discuss money.

She'd been wrong.

The woman who talked Thomas Griffin around was the same woman who'd funded three expeditions across the globe—and who'd arranged that famous pyramid dinner, in a foreign country where language and custom were significant barriers to cooperation. This woman had survived voyages with no small amount of peril involved in their very undertaking. And now she was here, in London, making Lucy's most cherished ambition into reality.

One worry clouded Lucy's happiness. How could Lucy possibly repay her for this?

Some detail about manuscript binding had Catherine and Mr. Griffin walking back out to the workroom. They bent over leather samples stamped with gilt and silver foil, arguing with apparent relish about cost and color.

Lucy didn't feel qualified to weigh in on this question herself, so instead she wandered across the busy print shop toward Mrs. Griffin.

The engraver had left the colorist to his work, and was now engaged with a piece of her own. A metal plate coated in wax had been inscribed with a flowing, floral design that Mrs. Griffin was now painstakingly carving away.

"That's quite pretty," Lucy said.

"Is it?" Mrs. Griffin had a wry twist to her lips. "I've copied out so many flower patterns this season for the embroidery pages of the *Menagerie*, I'm afraid I've lost my taste for them. But my last apprentice left us to go live with her aunt in Sussex, so there's nobody else to do them until I find another."

Lucy leaned down, watching the metal graver carve a series of careful arcs into the wax. One, two, three—and then a connecting swirl, something that just managed to suggest a flower without being so gauche as to depict one. It almost reminded her of the geometric sketches Eliza Brinkworth had done . . .

That was when it happened. One of the journeymen at the press in the back dropped his composing stick—the long piece of metal full of leaden letters hit the floor and rang like a thousand bells. The sudden commotion startled the colorist; his hand jerked in alarm, and a spray of droplets in deep Prussian blue arced off his brush and splattered against the soft gray sleeve of Lucy's dress.

"Sydney!" Mrs. Griffin exclaimed, then huffed out a sigh. "My sincerest apologies, Miss Muchelney."

"It's quite alright," Lucy hurried to say. "I'm sure it will wash out."

"Out of the fabric, perhaps—but I'm afraid it's caught some of the border as well."

She sent poor Sydney running for clean water and soap, but after a few daubs Lucy had to admit Mrs. Griffin had been correct: the blue had bitten deep into the light-hued silk chevrons.

At home, Catherine went to work on her never-ending correspondence. Lucy rang for Eliza and showed her the stained sleeve.

The maid's mouth flattened as she surveyed the ruin of her work. "Oh, damn."

There was a moment of exquisite silence.

Then Eliza clapped a hand to her mouth, her eyes teary with horror. "Oh, miss, I'm sorry—please don't tell Mrs. Shaw!"

"Of course not—"

"Or my father!"

Lucy stopped at that, her eyes narrowing. "I won't," she promised solemnly.

"I'll have it fixed at once, miss—let's get you a new gown . . ."

Eliza pulled a lavender frock from the wardrobe and helped Lucy change with shaking hands.

Lucy held her tongue while her mind turned over the known facts about Eliza Brinkworth. "Is Mrs. Shaw terribly hard on you?"

"Oh no, miss—that is, she *is*, but I'm so new, and I'm always making mistakes—one of the other girls might have been better, but Mrs. Shaw says my lady insisted . . . It's been a great trial to her, she said once, though I don't think she meant me to hear." She fastened the last button on the lavender frock and stepped back, hands clasped together in front of her. "There you are, miss."

With a quick curtsy, she gathered the stained gown into her arms and hurried back to the workroom.

Lucy stood very still for a moment, her mind putting one piece of evidence next to another and coming to a swift calculation. Last week one of the under housemaids had dropped a bucket after sweeping the fireplace and sent soot billowing out over the blue parlor; the week before, Brinkworth had horrified himself by discovering he'd walked around for the better part of an hour with a streak of silver polish on the sleeve of his coat. Two days ago Cook had had sharp words with a kitchen maid who'd scorched a caramel sauce and ruined the saucepan.

All accidental events, of course, and none of them truly

serious—but they were the kind of things that Lucy couldn't remember happening before. Now they all seemed to be happening at once.

And they'd begun around the same time Eliza had started training as a lady's maid for Lucy. Even though there were other older girls around who'd wanted the job. Catherine had insisted, according to Eliza.

Now Eliza was struggling, the staff were disheartened, and everyone's lives were slightly worse off. If only there were somewhere else for the girl to go . . .

Lucy turned on her heel and marched downstairs.

Catherine was halfway through a reply to a very curious beekeeper in Melliton when she heard a throat being cleared behind her. She smiled when she saw Lucy—though a Lucy who looked unusually stern and serious. "What is it, love?"

"Mrs. Griffin is in need of a new apprentice engraver," Lucy said. "I think we should ask Eliza Brinkworth if she'd like the job."

Catherine set her pen down and turned in her chair. "Is Eliza not improving? Mrs. Shaw said—"

"Eliza is doing as much as she can, while knowing that she's not doing as well as she ought," Lucy said, her voice quiet but steady. She bit lightly at her lip, then continued: "I know it's not my place—but I think she'd be happier with Mrs. Griffin than she is here with us."

"But her talent with a needle—"

But Lucy was already shaking her head. "Talent is not the

same thing as choice—and between embroidery and drawing, she evidently prefers the latter. She's a sweet girl, and a clever one. But she said Mrs. Shaw is always catching her drawing, that she sneaks time for it." The astronomer stepped forward and turned one palm out as she pled her case. "Why shouldn't she consider an apprenticeship in the art she loves best? Something that gives her more scope than what a single household can offer her."

And there it was; denial withered on Catherine's tongue. Of course Eliza would want to spend her paid hours doing bigger and better things than embroidery—why settle for a craft so domestic and ephemeral when she could be learning to produce art, or at least the kind of work the public would notice. "You're right," Catherine said to Lucy. "We'll ask her."

Once settled upon, the change took remarkably little time. Within a week, Eliza was happily putting her drawing and drafting skills to work as Mrs. Griffin's apprentice. Joan was promoted in Eliza's place, and the whole house seemed to take a deep breath of relief. Joan turned out to be a living treasury of stain-removal recipes, and was even able to get the Prussian blue off Lucy's gown. The occurrence of minor accidents dropped dramatically, and even Mrs. Shaw was *twice* caught humming cheerfully under her breath by the stillroom maid.

Catherine pulled another knot tight on the cushion she was covering with berry bunches. The mix of red and burgundy flowed under her hands like stage blood: dramatic and striking to the eye, but ultimately meaningless. Just something for an idle lady to do to pass the time.

As beautiful and useless as Catherine herself.

One afternoon not many days later, Catherine lifted the letter from the tray Brinkworth brought in and then dropped it again with a cry.

Lucy put down her teacup, concerned. "What is it?"

Catherine was scowling at the creamy envelope as if it were a serpent about to strike. "Mr. Hawley has finally written."

Tight fear released her shoulders, and Lucy shrugged. "He couldn't ignore you forever, I suppose."

"No," Catherine said, and Lucy paused. The countess's eyes were angry and troubled, her lips thin with displeasure. "He's written to you."

"Me?" Lucy turned this over from every possible angle, but couldn't decipher it. What could Mr. Hawley possibly have to say to her?

There was proverbially only one way to find out.

She slit the side of the envelope and once again found herself staring at the Polite Science Society president's precise, restrained hand.

My dear Miss Muchelney,

   I cannot express how deeply I regret the result of our last conversation. It pains me daily, as I'm sure it must pain you. Would you come to tea tomorrow afternoon, and see about how we might mend this breach in the name of Truth and Science?

            Yours most sincerely,
            Roger Hawley, President, PSS

Lucy handed the letter over to Catherine, trying not to find it adorable when the countess's brow furrowed and fury sparked in her blue eyes. "This letter does not contain an apology," she said, her consonants as crisp as corporal punishment.

"Maybe he wishes to apologize in person," Lucy suggested.

Catherine's skepticism melted into worry. "What will you do?"

Lucy picked up her cup again, staring into the dark depths as though guidance might be found there. But she was no mystic, to read the future in tea leaves. She could only drink, and hope whatever advice they had could be absorbed that way. "I suppose I'll have tea."

She set out the next afternoon. Catherine bid her farewell in the parlor, worrying at the corners of her sketchbook. Lucy kissed her and closed her eyes, breathing in the light notes of soap and citrus that bedewed Catherine's skin. She wished she could take those scents with her like incense to ward away malignant spirits. "I'll see you for dinner," she promised.

Catherine kissed her farewell with just as much apprehension.

It felt dramatic out of all proportion to the invitation, and Lucy scolded herself silently as the countess's carriage bounced across the London cobbles. *It's only tea*, she repeated. *It's only an afternoon.*

But lives had changed in shorter spans of time than that. She twisted her gloved hands together and swallowed against the high neck of her purple frock. None of Eliza's artistic embroidery today—Lucy wanted to look stern and serious, and Mr. Hawley was decidedly not the sort to appreciate the niceties of feminine dress and decoration.

The footman who answered the door certainly took a dim view of the plainness of her attire, judging by the curl of his lip. "Mr. Hawley is in the hothouse, miss," he told her, and conducted her toward the peaked framework of iron and glass. It was one of the rare clear days in which the year had been so sorely lacking; the bright sunlight caught on every pane of glass and metal edge, then slithered through the filter of tropical leaves and air gone heavy with rainbowed mist.

Lucy began sweating almost as soon as she entered, telltale droplets sliding uneasily down her neck and blooming at the small of her back.

The footman led her through the labyrinth of greenery, holding the larger fronds aside so she could pass, until they reached the southern-facing edge of the hothouse. The sun felt more concentrated here, almost tangible, a heaviness that slowed the limbs and dazzled the eye.

Mr. Hawley was standing before a shelf of pots full of his famous flytraps, their leaf blades ringed with needle-like teeth and brilliant pink within, gaping like a hundred hungry mouths.

"Miss Muchelney, sir," the footman said, and bowed before departing.

"Ah!" Mr. Hawley said. "You'll have to be patient a moment more, my dear—I am just about finished with the weekly feeding. If you'll just have a seat . . ." He waved at a wicker bench against the back wall. Lucy sat, taking the opportunity to loosen the neck of her gown a little. But the relief she hoped for didn't come; all she felt was a rush of a newer, hotter air down the flushed hollow of her throat.

She sweated in silence while Mr. Hawley took a thin knife to a pile of mealworms and sliced each one into careful, perfect sections. One by one he placed a section on each pink, glistening plant mouth, then used a slender forceps to brush the near-invisible trigger hairs until each trap snapped shut on its meal, teeth interlaced and leaves sealed tight to ensure the prey could not escape. Finally, the last plant was fed and Mr. Hawley set the forceps down and clapped his hands. "Now, tea!" he cried.

Lucy had lost her entire appetite.

Fortunately, Mr. Hawley did not intend to feed her there beside his digesting carnivorous trophies: instead he led her back to the house and his very proper parlor. Lucy sat on a stiffly upholstered sofa and tried not to stare too long at the smaller Venus flytrap in the miniature glasshouse. These had not been fed yet, judging by the ravenous way they gaped.

The footman brought them a pot and a selection of pastries, and Lucy agreed very anxiously to pour. Conversation was all practicalities until Mr. Hawley had sipped his tea and taken a bite of scone. "Now then," he said, leaning back in his plush, well-worn armchair. "I believe I owe you an apology, Miss Muchelney."

Lucy's heart leaped. She'd been right after all!

Mr. Hawley went on: "I should have made it utterly clear to everyone that I knew you were capable of the mathematics you claimed to understand." He leaned back and lifted his teacup to his lips, eyes glittering as he awaited her response.

Lucy blinked, fidgeting on the stiff sofa as the silence lengthened and lengthened again. That was it? That was his full apology? Nothing about denying her the project, or tossing her manuscript to the floor? Then the full sense of what little he had said caught up with her. "I beg your pardon— you knew?"

Mr. Hawley clucked his tongue as if she'd said something particularly foolish. "Of course I knew. Your father, for all his brilliance, had been fading for some time—his calculations slower, his conclusions more riddled with assumptions, his theories less ambitious. Even his fantasy seemed to grow thinner and less substantial in its speculations. And then you took over, ostensibly to save him the trouble of writing so he could better focus on observations—but a few of us saw right through that, naturally, because suddenly there were all these splendid, perfect mathematics right there in plain black ink." He nibbled at his scone again, while Lucy gaped and cast about for a response. "We thought he might have taken on a student, or some such. It was a good few months before I concluded that it must have been all your doing."

Lucy's fingers were so tight on the china of her teacup that she feared it would crack. But she didn't dare set the cup aside, either—she might slam it down onto the table to send shards flying viciously through the air. "You knew," she repeated. "And yet you still chose Richard Wilby as your translator?"

Mr. Hawley looked pained, and heaved a great sigh.

"Being the president of the Polite Science Society has been my great privilege for many decades—but I would be lying if I said it did not come with some unpleasantness from time to time. Sir Eldon has been a staunch supporter for so many years, both intellectually and, it must be said, financially, and he was so insistent on Mr. Wilby being included. There was nothing I could do." A flicker of distaste puckered his mouth briefly. "I'd hoped the nephew would take after his uncle, to be honest. But the gentleman is young, and prone to a young man's carelessness and—ahem, less high-minded passions. Much as I encourage Mr. Wilby in his enthusiasm, the truth is I could not see a way in which he would be able to work with a gentlewoman such as yourself without offering you an insult of one kind or another."

Only the faintest smudge of red on Mr. Hawley's face hinted at the less-than-proper nature of what he'd worried Mr. Wilby would attempt.

"I see," Lucy muttered. Her heart had twisted up within her, frail and flammable as a scrap of paper. One spark would turn it entirely to ash. "You shut me out for my own protection."

"Precisely." Mr. Hawley nodded and smiled, as if Lucy had surprised him by doing something clever. The edges of her paper heart crinkled further. "I had thought Mr. Frampton might provide a guiding hand on the project—but alas, Mr. Frampton rather disappointed me in that regard."

"Yes, he told me he'd given up the endeavor." Lucy kept her voice tranquil and raised her teacup to hide her teeth when Mr. Hawley's eyes narrowed.

"This must have been at Mr. Edwards's lecture," said the Society president. "I noticed you in the gallery with Lady Moth and Mrs. Kelmarsh. It was so gratifying to see our little tiff hadn't soured your taste for science entirely."

Lucy swallowed hot tea to drown a thousand hotter and more biting responses. Instead she put all the sugar she had into her tone and asked: "How is Mr. Wilby getting on alone?"

Mr. Hawley leaned forward, a smile gracing his lips though his eyes told a more anxious story. "That is precisely why I asked you here today, my dear. For you see . . ." He lowered his voice conspiratorially. "Mr. Wilby's translation is not going at all well."

"Oh," Lucy said. "Oh dear. Oh, that must be terrible." She filled her mouth with buttered bread before her lips could betray her by smiling, or her voice could break into a shamefully satisfied cackle.

"It is certainly not ideal," Mr. Hawley said. "I'm afraid as the time passes I am growing rather desperate to find ways of salvaging the book. Mr. Frampton outright refused to be lured back—something about some machine he's designing, which he imagines will be important, though I cannot for the life of me see how—and there really is nobody else doing the kind of work a manuscript like Oléron's requires." He licked his lips. "Nobody, that is, except yourself."

Lucy leaned carefully back, untangling herself from the web of someone else's hopes and demands. "You need me."

Mr. Hawley gently corrected her. "I would say, Miss Muchelney, that *science* needs you." He set his cup down and stretched his hands out entreatingly. "You have a great talent, my dear. You could do wonderful work. All you need is a little tending from an expert hand."

Lucy recalled how precisely Mr. Hawley had used the forceps on the flytraps, so carefully and tenderly feeding them bits and pieces of other living things. All for science, of course. "You think I need a mentor."

He smiled approvingly. "Just so."

"Someone who encourages me, supports me, advises me when I feel lost, and aids me when I struggle."

"Yes, yes, and yes." He rubbed his hands together.

"I have one." Lucy let her lips spread in a smile of such poisonous sweetness that by rights Mr. Hawley should have perished on the spot. "Lady Moth has been an invaluable mentor since the very instant I sought out her help on my arrival in town."

Mr. Hawley's returning smile was brittle as dried leaves. "Lady Moth has always been a loyal patroness of the Society, and I know her husband valued her abilities enormously." He leaned back on the sofa, fingers pressing against one another pyramid-like, his gaze radiating earnest concern. "But there are times I've been moved to wonder whether George St. Day might have flown higher if he'd been allowed to give his ambitions full scope. Not many people are aware of this, but . . . I trust you can be discreet with what I am inclined to reveal to you." His voice lowered still further, as if he were laying out state secrets of great international import. "His wife's inheritance was a family trust and remained within her control, you see. The previous countess had arranged it before she died, and there was no getting around whatever legal framework that aged lady had so cunningly set up. So rather than being able to direct his household funds as he saw fit, into expeditions and experiments and such, poor George was compelled to persuade and cajole when he ought to have been able simply to command."

Lucy could see it so clearly. A younger Catherine, reeling with grief, virtually alone but far from penniless; she'd have been ready prey for someone as self-interested and ruthless as George St. Day had been. No wonder he had treated her so abominably—he had expected to get access to her fortune, and he'd been prevented. So, resentfully, he had turned cold and cruel, browbeating her until she forgot she had any power over him at all. "That must have been terrible."

Of course Mr. Hawley misunderstood. "It was a great strain on him, poor man. He once confided in me that Lady Moth, though outwardly so dainty and dutiful, was often a termagant to him in private: shrill, disdainful, and capricious."

Lucy bristled a little more with every adjective.

Mr. Hawley sighed again and shook his head. "But above all other criticism, it must be pointed out that she is not herself a naturalist. I do not believe she has the necessary connections to help you progress in your work and in the Society."

Because you shut her out, Lucy realized, the cruelty of it sharp as a knife in her breast. *You shut her out and then you tell everyone she's useless.* It was a perfect, insidious kind of poison. She wondered how many other fledgling botanists, chemists, and natural philosophers he'd given this precise speech to. Did it always feature Catherine specifically, or did he switch names occasionally for variety's sake? She should ask Mr. Frampton—he'd strongly implied that he'd had just such a conversation with Mr. Hawley. Maybe more than one. No wonder he was reconsidering his position in the Society. It was by its very nature treacherous.

Her eddying thoughts were interrupted when the president leaned forward and clasped her hands in his. "Will you do this, Miss Muchelney?" he asked. "Will you take up this challenge, for the noble cause of science? Think of your father's legacy, and the good you could do for the intellectual vitality of all England." His voice was sincere in its intensity, almost pleading, as he asked: "Will you help?"

Help, Lucy thought numbly. *He praises Mr. Frampton's mind and offers him lavish profits, but he pleads with me to help him by praising my father's work, not mine.* Her answer had never been in doubt, but this last touch put her beyond sympathy. "I'm sorry, Mr. Hawley," she said, disentangling her hands from his and folding them tightly in her lap. "It is quite impossible."

He started, and went mottled red and white with consternation. "My dear Miss Muchelney, you cannot be serious."

"Please do not think I disparage your eagerness to help, sir," Lucy replied, "but I do not see why I should abandon my own completed volume to try and salvage Mr. Wilby's failed efforts." She cocked her head. "You *were* planning on keeping Mr. Wilby's name on the book, I assume, even after I made emendations?"

The president's mouth went so flat so fast that Lucy knew she'd struck home. He held on to his composure by a thread. "It would be cruel to cut him out entirely. He may have failed, but his efforts must be acknowledged."

"Must they?" Lucy shot back. "How much of the profits would you still allot to him, after everything was done?"

"Percentages can be negotiated—"

"So his failures deserve to be rewarded, while my successful work is refused and denied and scorned until you are desperate for my help—and even then I shouldn't presume I deserve a full author's share." Mr. Hawley spluttered, but Lucy wasn't finished. Her voice was a whip crack in the cozy parlor. "Would you put up my name as a full Fellow of the Polite Science Society?"

Mr. Hawley's eyes flashed, and he visibly bit back a reply. His mouth was now a tight line, lips thinned, a light sheen of perspiration glistening on his temples. "That would be asking a great deal," he said, then winced slightly at whatever he saw in Lucy's expression. "I would absolutely be willing to consider it." It was a wild final cast, a lure flung hopelessly into the heavens.

Lucy saw this for the refusal it was. "Mr. Wilby is made a Fellow already by his uncle, even though his work clearly fails to meet scientific standards. But you deny me the same honor on account of my sex even as you say I could foster the, how did you put it? The intellectual vitality of all England." She felt her mouth twist. "If I may be perfectly blunt about it: the Society seems to care less that their Fellows are men of science, and more that their Fellows are men."

Mr. Hawley choked as Lucy rose from the uncomfortable chair. He was still choking, and still seated as she walked to the door and turned. His mouth was open quite as wide as his flytraps, and in the rush of her anger and decision, Lucy had to rein in the urge to laugh and speak the comparison aloud. "When you wish to offer me full Fellowship in the Polite Science Society, you may write to me again," Lucy said. "In the meantime, I shall remain an independent scholar."

"Independent!" Mr. Hawley cried, finding his voice at last. "You are entirely dependent upon the constancy of your patroness." He rose, his brow thunderous. "Be wary of Lady Moth, my dear. She has survived fever, foreign exploration, and her astronomer husband—she will not scruple to cast you aside if you disappoint her."

Lucy yanked on her gloves and bonnet under the eye of the scornful footman. She felt utterly sure in refusing Mr. Hawley's offer, but even so, unearned regret for what she'd said in the heat of her anger was settling in, like a bruise that turns purple long after the blow has landed. She ached all the way back home—Catherine's home, of course. Familiarity had caused her to lose sight of how old and venerable the London house was: the supercilious curls on top of the columns, the arched-eyebrow curves that topped the windows, the lofty peaked roof like an admiral's cap.

But it was also Catherine's home, with Catherine inside. If Lucy couldn't trust Mr. Hawley's promises for her future—and she was bone-sure she couldn't—then there was no reason to trust him about Catherine's fickleness, either. The countess hadn't loved her husband by the end, but she'd still traveled with him and assisted him and put herself in his service.

Of course, she'd had to, hadn't she? Short of an Act of Parliament, there was nothing she could do to escape George St. Day's hold on her. Making the best of a bad situation was not the same as loving, fulsome support.

Lucy and Catherine could have no such ties. The relief was a cold one, a lump of ice in her throat untouched by the glittering sun in its azure sky.

She'd barely gotten her bonnet strings untied before Catherine flew out of the parlor and into the foyer, her eyes wide and crinkled at the edges with concern. "What did Mr. Hawley want? I hope he apologized."

"He did." Lucy stripped off her gloves, one finger at a time, as deliberate and vicious as poniard stabs. "Poorly. And then he begged me—yes, I do think *begged* is the proper word—to help him with the Society's official translation of Oléron." Oh, there was still a flare of satisfaction at being deemed worthy, even by so unworthy an authority. Lucy's smile was all arsenic, a metallic, bitter curve of lips as she all but marched back into the parlor, glared at the tea things waiting there, and stomped instead to the small decanter of sherry kept here for rare male visitors. She slopped some into a small glass and drank it all in one go, the heat of it soothing the burn in her throat where bright rage fed on shame.

Catherine perched gingerly on the sofa, her hands fluttering slightly before settling close in her lap like startled birds. "Did he offer you a proper share of the royalties, as he did with Mr. Frampton?"

Lucy poured a second glass, to sip from, and stared into the amber depths of it. She wished Catherine hadn't asked about the financials. "He offered to be my mentor." She spun the glass, watching the light dance on the liquid. "He told me I could go far, with the right sort of supervision. He mentioned my father, and that it had been clear I'd taken over the equations long ago. He laid all of English science before me and told me it was mine to cultivate and cherish."

Catherine's rosebud mouth twisted. "So he *didn't* offer you money."

"He also declined to permit me Fellowship in the Society. Even though he was asking me to step in and save them from what honestly sounds like a disaster in the making." She took another gulp of sherry and turned back to Catherine. "I told him no. Flat-out, and irretrievably. I said some accurate things for which I will not likely be forgiven. He won't be writing me again, I should think."

Catherine nodded, but some wariness held her still and stiff. "He should have offered you proper payment, if he wanted you to drop your translation and take over someone else's," she said. "That way it would have been a real choice, and you could have picked which arrangement suited you more. A bird in the hand—" She snapped her mouth shut and looked away, flinching as though she expected to be struck.

A ray of sympathy broke through the storm clouds of Lucy's mood. She plunked the sherry down on the side table and slid onto the couch. Her hands slipped into Catherine's, untangling tight fingers and warming them between her own.

"He could have offered to put the whole world in the palm of my hand, and I'd still have chosen you over him. Sweetheart, it's not about the money."

Catherine made a sound of disbelief.

Lucy shook her head, chuckling. "Yes, alright, but it's not *just* about the money. When you offered to sponsor my translation, what did you ask for in return?"

"I . . ." Catherine shook her head. "What are you talking about? I blurted it out in a moment of anger when the Society mistreated you."

"Yes—but you didn't take it back when your anger cooled. And you let me take charge of the translation as if I were an expert."

Catherine's fine brows slashed down into a piqued frown, and her hands gripped Lucy's with some ferocity. "You *are* an expert. Why would I have you work on a project if I didn't trust the work you would produce?"

"But sweetheart," Lucy said softly, "that's just what Mr. Hawley did this afternoon. And what he's done to many others, no doubt, in the course of his presidency. He demanded I undertake only the work he permits me, when and how he deems proper. But you . . ." She bent forward, brushing reverent lips against Catherine's temple. She felt the countess's soft gasp feather along the side of her neck, and smiled. "You simply made room for me to do the work *I* chose to do. You gave me a space for it and time for it and you offered support whenever I struggled. All because you believed I could do it, and do it well."

"Yes," Catherine huffed, "but it wasn't *just* about the work, either. Not after a while."

Lucy blinked and looked down.

Catherine's mouth was turned down but her eyes shone up at Lucy with helpless, hopeful affection.

Lucy slid wondering fingers along the countess's jaw, as though any movement too quick or eager would shatter the moment like glass. "Oh?" Lucy whispered. "What else was it about?"

Catherine took a deep breath and let it out again in a rush. "I am trying to tell you I love you," she said, adorably grumpy, "and you are making it impossible."

Lucy fought the urge to laugh in pure elation. "So tell me."

Catherine bit her lip, then lifted her chin. "You first."

Lucy did laugh then. Was still laughing when her mouth met Catherine's, the kiss tasting of sherry and sunlight and words still yet to be spoken.

"I love you," Lucy whispered, breaking the kiss. Her smile curved against Catherine's cheek. "Your turn."

The countess bit her lip, sighed, and drew herself up. "I love you, Lucy Muchelney."

"There," said Lucy. "That wasn't so impossible, was it?"

Catherine pulled back, her frown shading into something more serious. "The first time I told someone I loved them, I thought it was the end of all my troubles. I was young, and romantic, and very naïve. I am older now—"

"Oh, so very old," Lucy teased, and snorted. "I doubt there's a full ten years between us."

"Time weighs on you more once you're married." Catherine had meant it as a joke, but it fell rather flat.

Lucy's smile dimmed.

Catherine cleared her throat. "What I meant to say is: I've learned some since then. Loving someone shouldn't be the end of anything. It should be a beginning."

"What are we beginning?" Lucy began unpinning Catherine's hair, letting the rich gold locks trail through her fingers. "Not a marriage, this time."

"Something better," Catherine said. "Something that belongs only to us." She pulled Lucy down on top of her, golden hair haloing around her, so achingly beautiful that Lucy could almost—but not quite—believe her.

CHAPTER TEN

Reviewing the proofs of one's own book to check for typographical and mathematical errors turned out to be the most excruciating process Lucy could have imagined. Had she really written all these hundreds of thousands of words? It seemed impossible—surely some other hand had penned this striking phrase on page forty-seven. Some prankster had *definitely* written the hideous third paragraph on page one hundred sixty-two. And checking every variable and constant in every equation made her feel as if her poor eyes might never uncross again.

She did the best she could to be thorough, and resisted the urge to despair.

Eventually, however, Catherine compelled her to send the book back, even though Lucy was certain it was still rotten with clumsy substitutions and inelegant phrases. It was printed and put up for sale, half in sheets and half in plain covers, with fifty copies specially bound in a handsome octavo volume by Agatha Griffin herself. On these last the title was embossed in silver on rich blue leather: *The Lady's Guide to Celestial Mechanics*, with the author listed as L. Muchelney.

Lucy had agonized over this initial, before ultimately deciding that she would use her full name when she published her own unique work, and initials when she wanted the focus to be on the work she was translating. The women (well, mostly women) of the Friendly Philosophical Salon had graciously offered to read and discuss the book for their next meeting, so on the appointed day Catherine led a very anxious, pale-cheeked Lucy to Paternoster Row and into the back room with the worn-out sofas.

A pair of Salon members were there already, and looked up with sharp eyes at Catherine's warm greeting. "So there you are! The author who sent us to every bookshop in London."

"Or very nearly," her companion added, tucking a watch into a waistcoat pocket.

"What?" Lucy blurted, then bit her lip and looked to Catherine with worried eyes.

Lady Moth held her poise. "You had trouble finding a copy? Griffin's assured us they would send them to their usual list of booksellers."

"My favorite shop had run out," explained the first.

"So had the next three shops," her friend chimed in. "We finally found the last copy in a place on the very northern edge of town."

"We had to *share* it," the lady said with a shudder, and scowled at her friend. "You erased my notes!"

"You penciled notes in the margins of a brand-new book!"

"Where better to put my thoughts and responses? I might lose them if they weren't written right next to the passages that inspired them!"

They continued the argument while Catherine turned to Lucy with sly wonder in her eyes. "If every shop in the Row has sold out . . ." she said.

"I can't imagine," Lucy breathed.

But a few other Salon members attested to the same trouble, and a later hasty visit to Griffin's confirmed it: the initial run had very nearly all been sold, and orders for more were quickly being accumulated. A second print run was hastily undertaken from the plates of the first, and as the week passed the book began to earn notice in scientific circles. People were soon discussing Oléron's algorithms—and Lucy's expansive explanations—in letters, in lecture halls, in coffee shops, and in college courtyards. Mr. Edwards even wrote to offer his personal praise and congratulations.

But more than that, the blue-and-silver cover caught the attention of the fashionable set who found thrills in Mr. Edwards's demonstrations, so that a copy of the book became a much-sought-after accessory among the *haut ton*. Mr. Hawley, in a palpably crotchety tone, penned a review for *Polite Philosophies* that found some matters of theory upon which to quibble—but his attempt to silence Lucy backfired, as people caught the whiff of controversy and hurried to buy a copy for the pleasure of having an opinion on it. Because the book had been printed at Catherine's expense, she had taken care that the percentages of the profits had been very heavily weighted in Lucy's favor (less the blue leather-bound versions, which had been Mrs. Griffin's risk).

When Lucy saw the first accounting of how much profit she could expect from her work, she went faint and had to sit on the sofa with her head between her knees until her spotty vision steadied again.

She set some of the money aside for Stephen to deposit with the family funds, announced her intention of getting a few new dresses made, and asked Catherine if she could recommend a good modiste.

"If I may . . ." Catherine was tapping her pencil on her sketchbook, nervously, and as Lucy blinked at her, a blush rose to her cheeks. Lucy loved how the countess could be so bold in bed and so cautious when clothed. Catherine's hesitance was charming as she asked: "Would you let me embroider one of those new gowns? As a gift to you?"

Lucy was rendered speechless.

Catherine assumed this meant Lucy needed convincing, and began turning the pages of her sketchbook over to demonstrate choices. Embroidery and garment designs flew past like a flock of birds winging south for winter.

Catherine stopped on a page with the silhouette of an evening gown. Lucy's eyes widened. Long, precise silver arcs were layered over one another in dizzying arrays along the hem and at the shoulder; at some points they joined together, at others they curved apart. It looked like an armillary sphere—like music—like angels' wings.

Lucy could hardly breathe for the beauty of it.

Catherine ducked her head. "I was remembering the passage where Oléron talked about studying Saturn, and how the shape around it had to be many rings set inside one another rather than one solid piece."

"You would make this for me?" Lucy whispered.

"Of course." Catherine's answering smile was sun-bright. "I would make anything for you."

Lucy turned over the next few pages and stopped on a close-up design of a single sleeve: black fabric stark beneath the purple blooms and berries of the belladonna, entwined with a looping vine of myrtle in a sinister shade of green. It was more free-form than her other designs, without the careful symmetry and repetition: the plants almost appeared to be growing up from the wrists, stretching long, hungry tendrils toward the shoulder, either devouring or protecting the woman wearing the gown. It looked wild, and sad, and fiercely defiant—the kind of clothing a witch might wear, if she happened to be a wealthy and fashionable witch.

Catherine's mouth tilted in that particular sorrowful way she had. "That is for Aunt Kelmarsh," she said. "She rather misses the elaborate floral embroideries of her younger days."

Lucy traced the vines with one careful finger. "Myrtle?"

"For love," Catherine said.

"And belladonna?"

"Italian for *lovely lady*—but it also stands for silence."

"Because it's poisonous."

Catherine bit her lip. "Because a love silenced is something like death."

A chill ran through Lucy, but not a wholly unpleasant one. She looked down again at the gorgeous, terrifying design. It would never be a popular one with the fashionable set—it wasn't delicate or dainty or gentle enough—but it struck the eye and altered the mind, as any good painting would. "Do you have more things like this?"

"One or two. But I have never actually worked any of them. They are a bit . . . intense for everyday wear, I think. These others, however . . ."

She paged past two other glorious, blood-chilling frocks—one sea green and one ghostly gray—and revealed a sketch of an evening gown in a perfect shade of cerulean blue. White penciled-in lace gave a cloud-like fade to hem and cuffs, and the skirt had a white net overlay spangled with golden stars.

"Since you've made astronomy fashionable, I have been trying to create designs inspired by the heavens."

More sketches followed: a comet dress to match Lucy's shawl, a lighter, ladylike version of the ginger pineapple pattern, shell-like swirls in coral and peach, and a striking border design made of concentric circles and straight lines that looked Grecian to Lucy's eye, but that Catherine claimed was based on a thought she had about telescope lenses.

The word *artist* buzzed like a bee over Lucy's lips, but after the last conversation they'd had about art and artistry, she didn't want to poke at what was surely still a tender spot. "You're brilliant," she said instead. It was easy to be emphatic when you believed every word you were saying. "I would be honored to wear anything you make."

The next day they made the trek to the notorious Madame Tabot's shop. Under that lady's stern and steely eye, Lucy was fitted for four new frocks: one morning gown, a walking dress, and two evening gowns in the finest silk madame had to offer. The cuts were bold, and the fabrics deep-dyed with vivid color. Lucy was ecstatic over the thought of wearing the brightest hues she could find, though for the morning gown she did select an ivory muslin, to be embroidered with a swarm of golden bees.

For the first evening gown, thinking of Saturn's rings and Catherine's hands, she settled on a deep, rich blue that Madame Tabot's shop assistant thought was far too old and dark for her maidenly years. "Non, mam'selle, the gentlemen will want you in something daintier, as light as your figure—perhaps a robin's egg?"

"The gentlemen can go hang," Lucy said, as the assistant gasped and dropped her packet of pins. Lucy's determination was set, however. "I am not a songbird. I am an astronomer."

Madame Tabot barked a laugh from her throne-like seat in the center of the shop. "Ah, a girl after my own heart. The point of fashion is not for the gentlemen: they call it trivial because they cannot bear the thought of women having a whole silent language between themselves. Bring out that newest bolt from Crewe, if you would, Frances."

Frances recovered her pins and an expression heavy with skepticism, but did as her mistress bid. From a back corner of the shop she conjured a bolt of gold silk taffeta, shiny and lustrous as if it had been woven from pure sunshine. Madame Tabot creaked out of her throne and bobbed across the room to drape it over Lucy's shoulder, peering critically into the mirror.

The effect of the color was astonishing; it made Lucy's skin gleam like pearl and her hair shine like mahogany. The old seamstress's hands moved briskly, tucking the fabric just so around Lucy's torso and holding the shape in place until it pleased her. She nodded at Frances, who immediately began sketching the angle of the drape and the number of folds. "We keep the lines simple and strong, a bit of tulle on the bodice to soften it, a few folds along the sleeve and at the back."

Lucy dared to reach up a hand and stroke the metallic fabric, stiff and sturdy beneath the sparkle: it might look like a gown, but she knew already it would feel like a suit of armor. Perfect for walking into a soiree and slaying society dragons.

Lucy's eyes met Catherine's in the mirror. "Will it do?" she asked, suddenly anxious.

Catherine's smile was small and awed, and the heat in her gaze had Lucy's heart pounding. "'O for a muse of fire . . .'" she said softly.

Lucy's memory supplied the next part of the quote: . . . *that would ascend / the brightest heaven of invention.* Stephen had been obsessed with that play for the space of one summer, the one before he first went away to school. He'd been reading it with the tutor their father had hired, hoping to give his son an advantage in mathematics. Albert Muchelney had also engaged a governess to teach Lucy watercolors, mostly to keep her out of trouble.

This plan had failed utterly.

By the end of the first week, Lucy and Stephen were showing each other what they'd been taught; by the second, they were sneaking each other into their lessons. Of course the governess had noticed, and reported the conspiracy to Mr. Muchelney. But he had only laughed, and increased both teachers' pay, and insisted they teach both children.

Every evening after that, Lucy and Stephen would tromp through the wood to the top of the nearest hill, Stephen reciting all the best bits from *Henry V* on the way. Once at the top, he would take advantage of the summer light to fill canvas after canvas with lurid battle scenes, heroic portraits of dying knights, and blazing shipwrecks. Lucy would fill her own pages with geometrical proofs, triangles and arcs and rhombuses carefully deciphered and measured.

It had been the best summer of Lucy's young life—and it ended abruptly in the fall when Stephen started school. A sister went from being a best friend to being an embarrassment, a target of scorn for her mathematical bent, best ignored in favor of friends who cared more for art, war, and the high points of English history.

It was Lucy's first experience with heartbreak, and she had been a long while recovering from it.

The modiste pulled the gold taffeta away, and Lucy blinked at the ordinary hues of the world. Her reflection diminished in the mirror, mousy and timid.

Madame Tabot clucked in sympathy. "We shall begin work at once, Miss Muchelney. You should not have to be trapped in mourning garments for one second longer than you must." Her mouth pursed thoughtfully, and an avid glint came into her eye. "I have such a weakness for color myself, which I do not get to indulge enough in these insipid times."

They arranged for the dresses' delivery as Lucy donned her long country coat and Catherine buttoned up her smart spencer. The wind was chill but the sun was out, so they decided to walk the arcade for a ways before heading home. It seemed half of fashionable London had the same idea: everywhere couples were striding in elegant twos and fours, with the occasional lone walker or rider breasting the throng. Hackney cabs and coaches rumbled past on the cobbles, adding to the racket and the inescapable odors of horses and humans. Everything was busy and bright: haberdashers and jewelers and toy stores, sweet shops next to coffeehouses, booksellers and clockmakers and perfumeries. More modest wares like ribbons, pies, and pastries were piled on carts tucked into alleyways and on corners, gathering people into little knots on the sidewalk. Lucy had to hold Catherine quite close to keep the crowd from separating them.

It was when she pulled the countess a little leftward to go around a flower seller that she saw it. There in the window of a print shop, placed right in the heart of the display, was a copy of a painting. The engraving had been carefully hand-tinted, and it was the contrast that first caught Lucy's eye, yellow on blue.

Then she saw the subject, and her heart stopped dead in her breast.

It was her own portrait, as though she'd stopped to stare into a mirror someone had left there waiting for her. But where her mirror always showed her the truth of her looks—the long length of her nose, the narrowness of her jaw—this image had rounded her off into someone or something more unrecognizably beautiful.

This other Lucy was seated at a telescope, but she wasn't looking through it. She was looking past it, staring with naked eye up at a collection of stars. Winter and summer constellations mixed together with no regard for chart or science or season. Her languid, ladylike hand held a pen above a sheet full of numbers, and a lantern—a lantern! yellow and bright as a bonfire—cast a strong clear light over the scene and ruined any astronomer's chance at proper night vision. The ghostly figure of Albert Muchelney hovered at Lucy's shoulder—his features, she noticed, had not been beautified; the likeness was precise—his long arm pointed up at the sky, as the painted Lucy's gaze followed his guidance. Her clothing was romantically loose and drapey—where was her cloak, or even a good warm shawl? The cloth gleamed like finest silk in the lantern light, but who would wear silk while working outdoors at night? Especially pale blue and white, easily the least practical color of them all.

The title of the painting was printed below: *Miss Muchelney's Stars, or: The New Ourania*. In the corner, faithfully reproduced by the engraver, was a signature Lucy recognized with a sick floating sensation, as though the solid earth had been yanked out from underneath her.

"Oh, Stephen," she whispered, "how could you?"

Catherine's hand tightened on Lucy's arm.

She looked down to find the countess's eyes wide and her mouth a flat line. "Did he tell you he was going to do this?"

Lucy shook her head. Through the window, she saw a shop clerk pull a copy of the engraving from the top of the stack piled behind the display. Despite herself, Lucy flinched. The clerk's head snapped up at the motion, and when he saw the two women standing there, his eyes went wide as recognition dawned.

Lucy's vision went gray at the edges. *So this is what fainting feels like,* she thought, swaying on her feet and leaning heavily on Catherine.

Who, bless her, leaned back into Lucy's weight instantly, as steady and supportive as a rock in an ebbing tide. "Come," she said. "We're going home at once."

She got Lucy into the coach and thence home—Lucy would later have no memory of the journey—it felt as though she only woke up when she was in the parlor, with the stellarium shawl tucked around her shoulders, and a glass of Catherine's best port in her hand. The glass was half empty, so she must have drunk at least a little of it, but she barely tasted it on lips gone dry with dread and hurt.

Catherine was at her desk, writing what she'd told Lucy was a very sharply worded note to Stephen, but Lucy knew already that her brother would defend his actions all the more as soon as someone criticized him. The damage had already been done.

Stephen had sold the world a false image of Lucy, and he had done it for money and fame.

And so the wider world learned that L. Muchelney was a woman, and an unmarried one at that. The admiring letters Griffin's sent along to her began to take a different tone. Some previous correspondents wrote to temper their earlier enthusiasm, citing their shock at being deceived about the author's identity. They felt cheated, they said. New letters arrived from people whose flattery was much more carnal and appalling. *Polite Philosophies* ran an oily essay by Mr. Wilby that suggested Lucy might also have been the mind behind some of her father's more outré scientific speculations; the whole affair of the sun cities was brought up and laughed over anew.

There was even a rude cartoon in *Punch*, which Lucy would not have seen except that someone who claimed to be acting out of friendly concern had carefully cut it out of the magazine and posted it to her. The caricature showed Lucy as she appeared in Stephen's painting, albeit with significantly more bosom and sheerer draperies, gazing up swooningly toward an equally buxom female shape composed of stars. The stars in the most scandalous places were a particularly lurid touch.

The Nude Ourania, read the caption.

Lucy was so stunned she couldn't even move. She just sat there, the paper rustling in her trembling hand, until Catherine noticed what was happening.

The countess took one look at the cartoon, bit back a curse, snatched it out of Lucy's hand, and threw it into the fire. "How dare they," she growled, with as much rage as Lucy had ever seen from her. "How *dare* they." She went red, then white, then back again, muttering epithets and cursing every cartoon-scribbler in London.

"It's nothing," Lucy said. She pressed her hands between her knees, watching the burning paper as it curled and burned to ash. Despite the flames, she felt cold, and shaky, as though there were an unmeltable piece of ice in the center of her belly. Chills ran up and down her spine, and she hunched her shoulders against the cold. It always happened this way; nothing to do but hold on and wait for it to pass. "You should have seen the doodles Flora Gretton used to draw at school." She clenched her teeth to keep them from chattering. "Nobody could produce filth like Flora. This is practically a ladies' watercolor by comparison."

Catherine stopped pacing and looked at Lucy with dawning alarm. Her brows slashed down and her lips turned mulish. "From now on, I am opening any mail you receive from persons unknown. You have borne quite enough insults already. It shall not continue."

Lucy shook her head, even as the ice softened a little beneath the blaze of Catherine's anger on her behalf. "They'll just keep sending them until something new distracts them."

"Then we'll go away for a while. High time we both had a holiday." The countess stalked over to her writing desk and began pulling out sheets for a letter. "I have enough friends in the country, surely one of them could entertain us for a few weeks until this tempest blows over—"

"Couldn't it just be you and I?" Lucy asked. "No house parties, no hosts to be polite to." She chewed on her lip and thought for a moment. "What if . . ." It was such a big question she had to stop and take a deep breath before she asked it. "What if you came home with me?"

Catherine stilled. "Home?" she asked carefully.

"To Lyme." Catherine's face had gone blank, and rising anxiety had Lucy's tongue tripping faster than usual to get her ideas out. "Stephen's going to be busy in London for a while, riding the publicity he's garnered—"

"Stolen."

"—alright, yes, but it means he'll probably stay here in the city for at least a month, maybe two. And the house is very small but very quiet, and the garden is lovely in the summer and it would be just the two of us, we could take walks and have picnics and I could teach you how to do telescope sweeps—"

Catherine's stillness broke. She walked across the room and cupped Lucy's face with delicate hands. "It's a brilliant idea," she said fervently. "I am in love with a brilliant woman." She kissed Lucy soundly, as Lucy felt the compliment set her cheeks burning beneath Catherine's tender fingers.

CHAPTER ELEVEN

The sky was gray, the drizzle was icy, and Catherine was happier than she could ever remember being.

They had been in Lyme—or rather, a little west of Lyme—for three days, Lucy and Catherine attended by Narayan. The journey itself had been a relief, even though it required long hours on the road with only rickety inn beds to rest in at night. Catherine used her money and her title shamelessly to commandeer the best rooms and private parlors, attempting to give Lucy a more pleasant journey back than she'd had on her trip out. They arrived at Lyme in perfect cheer; Narayan had begun unpacking their trunks while Catherine and Lucy had aired Lucy's old bedroom for them both to share.

Lucy went so quiet during this work that Catherine was moved to ask if she was feeling well after the journey. "No, I'm perfectly fine," Lucy replied, "it's only . . . The last guest I had in this room was Pris."

"Ah," said Catherine, as if this were an adequate response.

Lucy tugged harder on the sheet with downcast eyes,

and Catherine wondered with a shameful pang if there were memories associated with this room—and this bed—that would sour the adventure further.

She fluffed the down pillows extra hard out of sheer pique.

But that evening, full of good country fare and wine and, finally, beautifully warm, Lucy had taken Catherine's hand and led her to the bed, heavy-curtained and pushed up against the wall to make a cozy den just large enough for two, provided they stayed pressed close against one another.

There, in the velvet darkness, far away from the endless sounds and scrutiny of the city, Catherine had lost track of the number of times Lucy's hands and mouth had made her lose track of herself.

The next morning she woke to a breakfast of toast and cheese, and the weather was clear enough to go for a bracing walk through the woods to the village market. Even when the rain returned two days later, it could not dim Catherine's mood.

And now she stood on a dismal beach, with raindrops landing on her hair and sliding down the back of her neck, cheerfully picking up rocks.

Lucy told her the locals called them snake-stones, or verteberries, but Catherine had known enough shell collectors in her youth to recognize ammonites when she saw them. But seeing one or two in a curio case was one thing—seeing a whole shoreline of them was another.

If they'd each been priceless gems, she couldn't have been more enchanted.

"Some years ago," Lucy explained from beneath her umbrella, "a young woman down the coast found a full skeleton of an ancient, terrible creature—something between a fish and a lizard. It's displayed in London now, for scholars to gawk at and attempt to guess its true age."

"We should go look ourselves, when we go back," Catherine said, and felt her happiness dim at the thought of returning. She loved London—but she'd been raised in the country and spent years away from the city.

She had needed this holiday as much as Lucy had, she realized. Perhaps even more: When had she last taken a journey simply for the pleasure of it? It appalled her that she couldn't remember.

"I would like that," Lucy said, her country coat fluttering sail-like in the relentless sea wind. She spun the umbrella handle so raindrops flew off the cloth in a sparkling arc around her.

One splashed against Catherine's cheek; she laughed and didn't bother brushing it away, since there was such a company of them.

Lucy shook her head, exasperation and amusement warring in her expression. "You'll catch your death if you aren't careful," she said, and stepped closer. The umbrella was both shelter and a symphony beneath the drumming rain, as Lucy's gloved fingers flicked the droplet away from Catherine's happiness-pinkened cheek. The smaller raindrops Lucy kissed away, cool moisture vanishing beneath warm lips and sweet breath.

Behind them, the endless sea roared approval.

Later, they wound their way back up the cliff path, Lucy leading, Catherine's pocket full of stones—some to keep, some to add to Aunt Kelmarsh's grotto. They had just reached the top when Lucy, in the lead, stopped and went, "Oh," very softly.

Another couple—a gentleman and a lady—had been about to descend. The gentleman was tall and lanky, with worried creases at the sun-browned corners of his eyes. The lady was young and slim and fair, all blond hair and blue eyes and a green wool coat embroidered with lilies-of-the-valley. She had one hand tucked in the crook of the gentleman's arm, and the other clutched a scarf tight around her throat.

The gentleman grinned and bowed most cordially. "Miss Muchelney!" he cried. "So it's true, you are back from London."

"Only briefly," Lucy said. She drew Catherine up beneath the umbrella, as a chill wind howled up from the crashing waves far below. "Lady Moth, may I present the Honorable Harry Winlock and his wife, Priscilla?"

The couple bowed, as Catherine felt her heart go as cold and stony as any ammonite.

"The Countess of Moth," Lucy went on, completing the introduction, "my benefactress and friend."

Catherine bowed politely, not missing how Mrs. Winlock's eyes flicked to where Catherine's and Lucy's arms were linked.

The infamous Pris stepped forward, pulling her hand from her husband's arm to extend it to Catherine. "So pleased to meet you. Are you the same Countess of Moth who used to write to Lucy's father?"

"The very same," Catherine murmured, accepting the handshake, two gloved hands gripping tight on the edge of a sheer cliff.

No warmth came through the fabric—perhaps the other woman was just as awkward about this meeting as Catherine was, for despite her polite expression, the corners of her eyes and mouth were tight with tension.

"Your letters were always so diverting," the new Mrs. Winlock said. "I used to try and sketch the places you described, while Lucy was going over your columns of figures. How strange to meet you at last, and so close to home."

"We have a view of the coast from the parlor, and were wondering who would brave the shore in such weather as this," Mr. Winlock added, beaming. "But we hardly expected such an intrepid traveler as yourself, Lady Moth! May we have the pleasure of asking you to take tea with us?" He unhooked the umbrella from his other arm and unfurled it, earnestness and expectation written plainly in every line of his face.

Catherine glanced at Lucy, who was looking strained beneath the polite mask. "Another time, Mr. Winlock, thank you," Catherine replied. "I'm afraid we were just heading home."

"Ah," he said, and for one moment a ghost of anxiety passed over him like the spray from a cresting wave. But then his expression smoothed out, and he tucked his wife back into the safety of his encompassing arm. "Then I shall repeat the invitation at a more convenient time," he said.

Everyone bowed and curtsied again, as was proper, and

then the two umbrellas parted ways to bob each couple back to shelter.

Catherine walked in silence, watching Lucy nervously. There was a wan tinge to the younger woman's complexion and a flatness to her mouth that made the stone in Catherine's breast weigh heavier still. There was nothing she could think of to say that felt safe, so Catherine held her tongue and her lover's arm and put one foot in front of the other.

Halfway through the wood, Lucy's silence broke. "I've always liked Harry Winlock."

A non sequitur like that was a delicate thing: pull too hard, and the thread would break. Catherine kept her face open and her voice calm. "Oh?"

She'd done exactly right: Lucy's voice gained strength as she continued. "He and Stephen used to play together, before they went off to school—but afterward, they ran in different circles. Stephen's friends were striving for genius, even then: they always wanted to be clever, or brilliant, or lauded in some way. And Harry wasn't—isn't—clever. Which isn't unusual, young boys are never half as clever as they think they are, after all—but Harry never minded. He didn't have to be the best, or the first, or the loudest. He just . . . he just *liked* everyone, despite how they treated him, and despite their own flaws. I never noticed it until I came back from Cramlington, and started helping my father with his astronomical observations. I would fall asleep in church, and all the other young people would mock me, but Harry simply asked how late I'd stayed up, and if I'd seen any comets, and how many stars I'd counted."

She paused to duck the umbrella beneath a branch that hung particularly low over the path.

"And then Pris came to visit—partly, she said, because her family was always pressuring her to marry, and I was sort of an escape." Her mouth pursed up as if she'd bitten into something sharp. "Apparently I wasn't escape enough. She met Harry, and of course he fell in love with her. Even then, I couldn't be mad at him—how could I? I'd fallen just as quickly, when I met her. But I never expected her to accept when he proposed. I left for London the day after they were married."

So quickly! Catherine thought back to Lucy's wild manner, which she'd chalked up to scientific ambition. It looked very different now in the light of this revelation. "We don't have to see them socially, if you don't like to," Catherine offered quietly. "One of the great privileges of being a countess is that people expect snobbery, so you could tell them I refuse such low connections and we could continue as we have done."

Lucy slanted her a look. "But you *aren't* snobbish, love."

"Nobody in Lyme knows that."

"But I don't want them to think it, even for a second. You deserve better."

They walked the rest of the way in silence, while Catherine alternately yearned to move on to less painful subjects and cursed herself for a coward. Narayan and Sadie had tea ready when they arrived, hot and steaming, and they gladly shed their wet things and curled up before the fire in the parlor.

Catherine had brought her ammonites in and was turning them over and over, tracing the delicate spirals of ancient life.

Lucy tilted her head. "How old do you suppose they are?"

"Older than mankind," Catherine replied. "Though by how much, I do not have learning enough to speculate. Aunt Kelmarsh might have a better idea."

"She will love these for her memorial grotto, I am sure."

"Very fitting," Catherine sighed. Pris's face wouldn't leave off haunting her. "A memento of something wondrous and beautiful, which can never die."

She must have sounded as mournful as she felt, because Lucy's hands wrapped around hers, around the stones. "This creature *has* died," she said. "It lived once, long ago. But all that remains is the impression—fixed, not animate. Its time has long passed."

Catherine could not pretend they were still talking about the ammonites, which were growing warm against her palms. Borrowing heat from their joined hands. "You loved her so much, for so long," Catherine said, as helpless tears sprang to her eyes and roughened her voice.

Lucy's lips twitched. "So long, but not so well. We fell in love as schoolgirls and hoped nothing would ever change— not me, not her, not the world. We tried to fix everything just as it was, thinking that we could preserve our happiness the way this fossil preserved the shape of ancient life. She came for long visits, but we never thought about sharing a home, either here or anywhere else. Her parents were insisting that she marry, and she couldn't put them off forever, and I was so wrapped up in helping my father with his scientific work, but not daring to claim any of it as my own . . . It seemed like the only place we could really love each other was in this frozen space between the past and the present. There was nothing truly vital in it, nothing nourishing to the heart or the mind or the soul. When I look back, the wonder is not that we parted—it's that we managed to hold on as long as we did."

She untangled her fingers, pulled the ammonites from Catherine's hands, and set them aside on the table.

Her arms went around Catherine's shoulders, and the countess returned the embrace with a quiet sob, burying her face in Lucy's neck. Somehow, at that moment, Lucy's slight figure seemed to be the one steady axis around which the entire cosmos was spinning; Catherine held on tight, fearing to be torn away by the relentless forces of nature.

Lucy's words, spoken against Catherine's temple, chimed softly against her very bones. "Loving you is entirely different. You make me feel expansive, as though my heart is big enough and strong enough to contain the whole world. As though I can become anyone I need to, or want to, without fear—I can reach higher and farther and not lose you for the striving. And oh, my love, do you know how great a gift that is?"

"We still have to be a secret," Catherine whispered.

"I know," Lucy said with a sigh. "The world is cruel that way. But just because one part of us is secret, doesn't mean our whole lives have to be lived in the shadows." Catherine could feel Lucy's lips curve in a smile, against the delicate skin beside her eye. "Aunt Kelmarsh said it used to be different, in her youth—maybe it will be different again, someday."

Her hands lazily traced the neckline of Catherine's gown, teasing and testing the swell of her breasts. Sensitive, scientific fingers followed the line of the white work embroidery Catherine had put there long ago, a series of ocean waves lapping and receding like a tide frozen in time. Lucy's eyes narrowed and pulled away slightly. "Is this design your own?"

Catherine had to bend her neck rather awkwardly to look at her own chest. "Yes," she said. "On the journey back from Egypt. I'd grown quite fascinated with the Mediterranean Sea—its lack of tides, its clear and shallow shorelines. So different from its deeper, crueller cousins: the Atlantic, Pacific, the Southern."

Lucy gripped Catherine's elbow, excitement making her gray eyes gleam like pearls. "Catherine—what if you did a pattern book?"

The countess blinked. "I beg your pardon?"

Lucy stroked the bodice edge again, making Catherine arch into the muffled touch and regret the existence of all fabric.

Lucy was undistracted. "Mrs. Griffin said they're always looking for new embroidery designs. Why shouldn't you put a collection together? Maybe something scientific, to match the *Lady's Guide?*" Her grin was somehow both shy and sly together. "She said florals were looking tired, didn't she? If the art world doesn't want you, then go where you are wanted."

But what kind of designs would I offer? Catherine thought

in despair—but as soon as the question was posed her mind leaped to supply her with answer after answer. Comets, conch shells, pineapple ginger, tides and scrolls, all sorts of botanical shapes both homely and far-flung . . .

They crowded close together and made her briefly blind and deaf to anything else.

When the vision cleared, she blinked up into Lucy's expectant face and then kissed her soundly. "You are brilliant," Catherine breathed, elation surging through her like the swell of a morning tide.

Lucy grinned, catching some of Catherine's joy. "So you'll do it?"

"I'll begin putting sample sketches together tomorrow morning," Catherine promised.

"And all it took to convince you was a kiss or two." Lucy's gaze was rich with satisfaction, almost smug, and an edge of hunger still waiting to be sated. "Imagine what I could do with a whole night. I'll bet I can have you calling yourself an artist by dawn." She flicked a hot tongue against Catherine's earlobe.

"Never." But Catherine made a throaty, wordless sound of pleasure and arched her neck for more.

They went to dinner with the Winlocks two days later. Mr. Winlock was all boyish smiles and affability, and Mrs. Winlock had apparently recovered from her surprise enough to prove a warm and gracious hostess. Dinner was simple but hearty, and afterward the foursome adjourned to the parlor for glasses of light sherry and conversation.

Catherine took care to compliment Mrs. Winlock on her needlework, which was on full display everywhere one looked: roses on the sofa cushions, ivy on the curtains, lilies-of-the-valley on the chairs, and everywhere doilies, doilies, doilies.

"One thing she never told us in her letters," Lucy chimed in, "was that she was embroidering the whole time she was traveling—she showed me a map she'd made in thread and linen, of her first expedition."

So it's my expedition now, Catherine thought with a rueful smile. *Poor George must be having a fit, wherever he is.*

"We have a map," Mr. Winlock exclaimed, eager to contribute. "Would you mind showing me the route you took, Lady Moth?"

Catherine rose from the sofa and followed him over to the writing desk in the corner—he had to remove one of the larger doilies to open the lid—and waited while he flipped to the familiar outlines of the world, sliced up and flattened out for mortal comprehension. He asked all the right questions, and Catherine lost much of her reserve in the course of satisfying his earnest curiosity. For once it did not make her feel small to see two whole years of her life laid out in so many inches of latitude and longitude.

She even felt comfortable telling him a little about the last, lonely voyage home after George's death, and he nodded with the light of understanding in his eyes. "It's much easier to leave the past behind when you can leave the place it happened in."

Laughter from across the room drew both their gazes for a moment; Lucy and Pris sharing some story about a mutual school friend. Their heads inclined toward one another, their faces alight with humor, one fair and one dark-haired.

Catherine looked quickly back at her host, but Mr. Winlock's eyes stayed fixed upon the two women. "I think that must have been one reason why Miss Muchelney left so suddenly after the wedding," he said, to Catherine's shock. "Pris felt terribly abandoned, and I did my best to comfort her, but if I'm being perfectly frank with you— and life would be so much easier if more people could be perfectly frank—it seemed like a very sensible decision on Miss Muchelney's part. And now that she has met you in person at last, well, it seems very fateful indeed." He turned to catch her glance, with a shy smile.

Catherine stared and stared, but the steadiness of his regard never faltered. "You love your wife very much, Mr. Winlock," she murmured.

"More than my very life, Lady Moth." For one moment something sad flashed in his eyes, stony and lost, but then his ebullience welled up again and his gaze grew more cheerful. "Miss Muchelney once told us you held a banquet at the Great Pyramid—is that true?"

The event was not one of Catherine's favorite memories— George had been querulous about wasting the eclipse, the weather had been mercilessly hot, and the guests unruly and demanding—but for Mr. Winlock's sake she dressed up the tale as best she could. He deserved better comfort than this, poor man, but it was all she could offer.

How strange, Lucy thought, to watch history and the future overlap. Lyme was her past: her childhood, her schoolgirl loves, her early work under her father's aegis. Catherine was her present and, Lucy devoutly hoped, her future—and yet here she was now, laughing on rocky beaches and looking anxiously at Lucy across the Winlocks' parlor. Sleeping— among other activities—in Lucy's old bed. Lucy had always been a rather lonely child, but all the old quiet places were filled now with Catherine's warmth and affectionate presence.

If she tried to count how many moments past and present were overlaid on one another in this much-compressed slice of geography, she feared she would grow dizzy and forget which moment was the real right now.

As always, when Lucy felt at sea, she sought comfort and continuity in the stars. The penultimate night of their visit was finally clear enough for Lucy to invite Catherine up to the roof for a comet-sweeping demonstration. An hour past sunset, Lucy set paper and pencil on a desk she and Narayan had hauled up from Albert Muchelney's study, and lit the lantern whose sides were thick red glass. "A threat to no-body's night vision," she said with some asperity.

"How could Stephen get such a detail wrong?" Catherine complained, the mention of Stephen's name putting her at her most haughty and countess-like. "Did he never assist you? Did he spend these nights cozy and warm and sleeping instead?" She scowled faintly and pulled her cap tighter down over her ears. The clear night had brought a chill with it, a cold steady wind blowing in off the sea and finding every place where a shawl was not wrapped tightly enough.

Lucy took a deep breath of salt- and pine-scented air before she answered. "The second time Father asked him to help, he got distracted by the shape of the moon over the trees and lit a small candle so he could sketch it. Father lifted his head to call out a doubled star and looked straight into the flame—meaning the hours he'd spent letting his eyes adjust to the darkness were wasted. He was furious."

Catherine shook her head, starlight gleaming lightly on the curls peeking out around her ears. "But we haven't been waiting for hours—our eyes won't be sensitive enough, will they?"

"Not perfectly acclimated, no. I just wanted to show you what it feels like to do this kind of work." Lucy fussed a bit with the lantern, suddenly shy. "Unless you think it's patronizing of me not to treat you as a serious astronomer . . ."

Catherine snorted. "Hardly. I'm a rank amateur. You're the famed genius now, remember?" Lucy's fears dissolved like mist in moonlight, and she was glad the dim light would hide the blush on her cheeks. She turned instead to the telescope.

Oh, how her heart had leaped when she'd climbed the spiral stairs to the roof and found that Stephen hadn't gotten around to selling it! The brass case had needed cleaning, and the mirrors would need a more thorough polish to do precise scientific observations again, but right now the seven-foot mechanism was oiled and gleaming and ready for use. The eyepiece was mounted on the higher end, a tiny parallel tube slanting back toward the observer, and the great main tube was suspended in a wooden frame by ropes that let the end be raised and lowered by very precise degrees.

The countess's shorter height meant Lucy had had to drag a stepladder up from the kitchen, and now she held Catherine's hand for balance as the smaller woman ascended the steps and fitted herself against the eyepiece. "Oh!" she exclaimed, a soft and wondrous sound. "Oh, I had no idea there would be so *many* . . ."

Above them, the sky shimmered with stars, some scattered widely in the black and others clustering more thickly in a great glowing streak arcing from horizon to horizon.

Lucy's throat closed briefly. She'd never shared this with anyone, not since her father had died. "I'm going to let go now." She gently dropped Catherine's hand and stepped back toward the notebook and chair near the lantern. "We're going to start at the tree line there, toward the south where it's clearest. I've set you up in the right spot to begin. You're going to call out what you see, and I'll take notes. When you've called out everything you can clearly see, we adjust the telescope upward using the ropes, and start over again. At the end we compare it with the chart to see if we've seen anything new."

"As simple as that?"

Lucy smiled evilly. "Precisely as simple as that."

Catherine returned to the telescope and began calling out the coordinates of stars and double stars and the fuzzy, cloudy nebulae. Lucy carefully noted their positions on the page. After ten minutes, Catherine had exhausted her spot of sky, and pulled away, blinking as her eyes adjusted to human distances again. Lucy showed her how to adjust the telescope's angle—carefully, minutely—and the process began again. And again. And again, for a full half hour, as the telescope slowly swept from horizon to zenith.

Lucy could have done the job in a third of the time, but that kind of speed came with practice and an intimate knowledge of the skies. At the end she called Catherine over and they opened up the star chart Lucy had brought up for the purpose—everything was already marked down there, aside from one single star that Catherine had seen, which was actually two small stars hovering close. "That's new!" she exclaimed.

"It would be," Lucy said, "if Mr. Clark hadn't discovered it last autumn. The paper appeared in *Polite Philosophies*, but the charts haven't been reprinted yet."

Catherine made a sound of muted fury. "Then we did all that work for nothing?"

"Not at all—you're now one of a very few people who can confirm Mr. Clark's observation as fact. A discovery isn't something you make alone, not really—it always has to be confirmed by someone else, whether you're doing an experiment or making an observation or building a new theory about how the universe works. Truth doesn't belong to any one scholar: it requires all of us."

Catherine cocked her head, considering this. "So: We move the telescope back down, and start again a few degrees to one side?"

"We could," Lucy said, "or I could show you one of my favorite sights in the night sky."

It was quick work to turn the seven-foot telescope in its stand, and only slightly longer to point it toward the glittering object she knew so well. She adjusted the telescope so the brightest orb was in the center, stepped back, and watched as Catherine mounted the stepladder and put a curious eye to the eyepiece once again.

The countess gasped and went taut as a bowstring. Lucy held her breath, but her heart was dancing in her breast. She knew what awaited Catherine's eye: a round white disc, with distinct rings arcing around it. Tiny, and perfect, and impossible to comprehend: the planet Saturn.

Catherine looked and looked, and when she raised her head and turned back to Lucy, her tears were obvious even in the soft red light of the night lantern. "It's the most beautiful thing I've ever seen," she whispered, as though they stood in a great cathedral sanctuary and not on a cottage rooftop exposed to the wind. "It's so *real*."

"And so very far away," Lucy agreed. "The only things farther are the stars themselves." She swallowed hard against her own surging sense of distance. "I grew up in this house, surrounded by woods. The ocean horizon used to be the farthest thing I could imagine. Then I looked into a telescope for the first time and there was this whole other world. Everything afterward has felt small by comparison." She slanted a look at Catherine, as tenderness rushed through her. "Well, almost everything."

Catherine cast one glance upward, to where Saturn shone like any other speck of light, its rings hidden from the unassisted eye. Then she slid bold hands into Lucy's hair, and kissed her. "Thank you," she whispered. Her lips curved, deep and lushly crimson in the lantern light. "How should we spend the rest of the night?"

Catherine felt Lucy tremble at the question. Brilliant, stubborn, delightfully lecherous Lucy, who'd taken such care with Catherine at every turn.

Well, now it was Catherine's turn, and she was done with being careful.

Maybe it was the darkness, that black expanse of sky broken only by the cold points of the stars. Or the yearning way the wind moaned in the forest that whispered around them. Maybe it was the vision of that distant planet, shining and pearl-like and perfect. So very different from the earth.

Tonight, far away from the rest of the world, where only the stars could see them, anything felt possible.

Catherine could be brave tonight. She could be bold. Not only for herself—but for Lucy, too.

She pulled the cap from her head and ran smoothing hands over her hair. Lucy watched their motion with something like envy shining in her face.

Perfect.

Catherine set the cap aside and leaned close.

"You've been giving me instructions all evening," she purred against Lucy's ear. "You're going to continue instructing me. You'll tell me where to touch, how fast, how slow, how long. When you want more." She grazed her teeth oh-so-lightly against Lucy's earlobe, wringing a breathy gasp from the astronomer's throat. "And if I like the manner of your asking, I'll do every—single—thing. Until you're too well fucked to ask for anything else."

Lucy whimpered.

Catherine's smile widened. "Is that something you'd like?"

Lucy nodded convulsively.

Catherine tapped a finger against the side of Lucy's throat. Just one finger, the tiniest rebuke, but the other woman's pulse leaped beneath her touch.

"Tell me what you want," Catherine commanded.

Lucy replied in a whisper: "You."

Catherine's lips parted in a silent, joyous laugh.

Lucy shook her head, her breath huffing out. She swallowed hard, and her chin lifted. "Kiss me."

Catherine smiled sweetly—then brushed her lips over Lucy's cheek, and away.

It was a deliberate, devilish tease of a kiss, and it made Lucy growl so low and fiercely that Catherine shivered in the cool night air.

"Kiss me *hard*," Lucy corrected herself.

Catherine obliged. She wrapped one hand around Lucy's neck and pulled the taller woman's mouth down to hers. She nipped at Lucy's lips until they opened for her, then she sank her tongue into the sweet, wet heat of Lucy's mouth and devoured her like a comet was screaming down out of the sky, and they only had time for one last kiss before the world ended.

When she felt Lucy's fingers clutch hungrily at her bodice and pluck at the buttons of her gown, Catherine ended the kiss and stepped back, out of reach.

"What next?" she demanded, though the breathiness of her own voice rather undercut the superior tone she was aiming for. Her breath whooshed in and out of her lungs, and despite the chill in the air, sweat was already trickling like a string of pearls down her spine.

Lucy's chest was heaving, too. It was not quite cool enough for her breath to fog, but even from a foot away, Catherine could feel the hot puffs of air brushing over her cheeks and collarbone. She gulped in one last breath, and waved a shaking hand at the stairwell. "Downstairs. Bed."

Catherine grasped that outflung hand and towed her lover along relentlessly. They bumped down the hallway, laughing at their own clumsiness, the sounds hidden behind furtive fingers.

Catherine pulled Lucy into the bedroom and shut the door, then pushed her up smartly against it. "Next."

Lucy's eyes were dark and hot as coals, only a single star-like spark in the pupils. She took a moment to look Catherine up and down. "Clothes."

Oh, she was far too brazen, this early in the game. Catherine pressed the heel of her hand more firmly against Lucy's shoulder, asserting a countess's authority. "Your clothes or mine?"

"Yours . . ."

"And do what with them?"

"Take them off," Lucy moaned. "Rip them, if you have to. Just hurry."

"I will do no such thing." Catherine turned on her heel, and stared haughtily back over her shoulder. "You will do one button at a time, and you will be careful about it."

Lucy laughed again, but the sound was pure need and submission, her eyes afire with yearning and her expression desperate. Her hands shook on the nape of Catherine's neck, but one by one all the buttons of the countess's gown were undone, her stays unlaced, and every last scrap of silk and linen and lace had drifted in a heap to the floor.

Catherine turned again, hands on her hips, her chin proud and high.

Lucy was still leaning against the door. Her palms pressed convulsively against the wood, fingers flexing, as her eyes roamed Catherine's glorious nakedness. The room was lit by only a single candle, one tiny sun against the darkness, bathing bared skin in undulating seas of light and shadow.

Catherine ran a hand slowly, savoringly down her own body, from shoulder to hip.

The movement pulled Lucy's gaze along like a magnet pulls a compass; Catherine felt as though she were standing at the center of the world.

She arched a single eyebrow. "Next?"

Lucy's voice was husky, low and aching. "Now my clothes. Take them off." She pushed away from the door, her hands clasping in front of her, the knuckles white. "Please."

Catherine sauntered around to stand behind Lucy. The younger woman was wearing one of her old gowns, a deep gray that had once been green—it showed on the wrong side of the cloth, when Catherine began unbuttoning and unfolding the two sides apart. Slowly she revealed the long line of Lucy's spine, the wings of her shoulder blades, the dip at the small of her back. Catherine pushed the garments to the ground and pressed herself against that shining acre of skin. The feel of Lucy's surprised gasp vibrated through blood and bone and arrowed right to Catherine's nipples, tight and aching. She shifted a little, letting herself enjoy the friction for a moment as her own hands slid forward, round Lucy's waist and higher up, until she was cupping the sweet small weight of Lucy's breasts in her two hands.

Lucy leaned back into the caress. "More," she breathed. "Please, Catherine—more, and harder."

"Good girl," Catherine murmured. "I didn't even have to prompt you that time."

She pinched Lucy's ready nipples between her fingers.

Lucy keened out, startlingly loud, and clapped a hand over her mouth in alarm.

Catherine pressed an openmouthed kiss to the nape of Lucy's neck, and pinched again. Lucy writhed in agonized pleasure.

"Careful," Catherine warned, laughter hot in her voice. "You'll have to be quieter than that."

For long minutes, under Lucy's increasingly begging direction, Catherine's hands roamed Lucy's whole sleek, supple body. The soft length of her thighs, the tender skin of her belly, the slick curls that hid her folds. Catherine's other hand pinched and plucked at her nipple every so often, uninstructed—just to keep the younger woman remembering who was in control.

But eventually, Catherine got greedy. She breathed in the hot, sweat-slicked velvet of Lucy's skin and said: "Tell me how you want me to make you come."

Lucy dipped slightly as her knees buckled—but Catherine's weight steadied her. The astronomer's fingers opened and closed helplessly around Catherine's forearm, which had banded tight across the taller woman's waist to hold her upright.

Catherine smiled against a shoulder blade, and waited.

"Put me on my knees," Lucy said, at last. Her voice was a ruin, husky and tremulous. "Stay behind me—close, just like this—but put me on my knees."

The heat that rushed through Catherine at this image sucked every atom of air from her lungs. She licked lips gone parched with lust and love and spoke from a throat dry as tinder: "Kneel, then."

Lucy dropped at once. Not helplessly: obediently, a swift, sweet fold of limbs and muscle.

It shook Catherine to her core. She stared at the curve of Lucy's bent neck, dewy in the candlelight. It tasted like salt and honey beneath her lips when she kissed it, feeling suddenly reverent. "A little wider," she bid Lucy, just to have one last command to give.

Lucy moved her knees farther apart. She was panting now, and still trembling, but there was a peacefulness to the tension that thrummed through her—as though she were perfectly content to stay poised on the edge forever, if that's what Catherine asked of her.

Catherine wasn't going to make her wait any longer.

One of Catherine's arms wrapped tight around Lucy's shoulders, holding her in place. The other hand moved down, and down—then Catherine slipped two firm fingers into Lucy's folds and began working her. She wasn't gentle about it, either: those fingers plunged in and out in a punishing rhythm. No longer teasing, Catherine was determined to possess.

Lucy shattered on the fifth stroke.

A ragged cry was torn from her throat and she bowed forward, channel clenching tight around Catherine's fingers. Catherine's heart soared and she clung to Lucy, pressing hot kisses to whatever skin she could reach, murmuring words of encouragement as the other woman's body shook and trembled in the aftermath.

Lucy relaxed, palms on the floor, chest heaving.

Catherine leaned back, smug and smiling. "Next?"

Lucy whirled around and stared. Catherine had one moment to savor the stunned, semiferal look in her eyes before her expression sharpened. Her tongue swept across her reddened lips and her eyes narrowed with carnal purpose. "Now you let me do the same to you."

Catherine's delighted laugh turned into a gasp, as Lucy pounced and rolled on top of her.

Much later, spent and sweaty and delightfully sore, Lucy fell back onto the pillow, while Catherine settled her cozy self close against her side. The countess's fingers traced Lucy's skin from freckle to freckle, making constellations out of the tiniest marks. "So you did sweeps with the telescope every night, with your father?" she asked. "Did it grow less tedious once you came to know the stars?"

"Every night, and yes, it was tedious, but it was a tedium I didn't mind too much. I like looking at stars. So I'd look at a star. Then I'd look at the next. And so on and so on, until the work was done."

Catherine's smile was everything fond. "So you became an astronomer one piece of sky at a time?"

Lucy pursed her lips, turning this over. "I don't know that there was one clear moment when I *became* an astronomer. I know I fell in love with Saturn when I was seven. I know I was calling myself an astronomer before I came home from Cramlington for the last time." She toyed with Catherine's hair, combing lazy fingers through the tousled locks.

Catherine leaned into the caress, sighing with happiness.

Lucy breathed in the scent of warm, pleasured bodies and continued: "Maybe after so many years doing an astronomer's work, it just seemed silly to avoid using the term." She lifted an eyebrow. "Why do you ask?"

Catherine chewed on her lip, something shy coming into her expression. "I've been thinking about what felt wrong about calling myself an artist," she admitted. "It was because I didn't feel that I'd earned the right to the title. I'd as soon have claimed to be Empress of Rome." She traced another constellation crown on Lucy's shoulder. "People—well, men, really—talk about art and science as though they are so noble. And they are! They're important and worthy and vital to the progress of mankind! But . . . aside from all the talk, they look quite a lot like work. Tedious, never-ending, unforgiving, excruciatingly demanding work."

Lucy chuckled. "And that's comforting to you?"

"Of course it is! I know about work. Not just physical labor—though I spent enough time on ships to know a

little about that, even though as a countess I wasn't one of
the ones being asked to actually do it—but the kind of work
that simply has to be done even though it doesn't bring you
joy or peace or any kind of satisfaction. For instance," she
said, as her voice dropped into a lower register meant for
state secrets and deathbed confessions, "I *loathe* seaming."
Lucy laughed aloud at the venom in her voice. "Loathe it,"
Catherine confirmed, the corners of her mouth twitching
up as she leaned back into the pillows. "Regular, repetitive
stitches, in a straight line, and then reinforcing it to make
sure it holds for as long as it needs to? No colors to play with,
no shapes to create, just you and two bits of cloth you want
to keep together. It's mind-numbing. But it's what makes a
dress a dress—or what keeps a table runner's weave from
unraveling—or what holds a pillow in one shape instead of
letting feathers fly loose about the parlor. So seaming must
be done. It makes all the wonderful parts possible. People
see the decoration, but they can only do that if you've put the
right invisible structures in place. And science is the same."

"All those expeditions," Lucy murmured, "and it's only
tonight that you realized science was work?"

Catherine snorted. "Of course I knew it was work—but it
was men's work, or at least my husband's work. Not *my* work,
you see. I suppose I gave them all too much credit, when they
talked about how noble it all was, how transcendent. And I
despised when they would be hypocritical about it: If it was
so noble, shouldn't it be done nobly? Not meanly, or cruelly,
or with profit as the main objective. But they were so passionate about being noble that I mistook the passion for the

nobleness. I thought they knew something I didn't—that they could tap into some vein of ecstasy or genius or intellect that I could only dimly sense."

Lucy clucked her tongue. "Because you were a woman."

"Not *just* that—but that, too. So when I wasn't being asked to fix problems I kept to my sewing: I mended clothes, I embroidered trim, and when everything else ran out I stitched portraits onto scraps of old petticoats, just to have something to do while everyone else was busy with either sailing or science. And you've talked about my stitches being like brushstrokes—but tonight it occurred to me that they're also like your telescope sweeps. I cover a great deal of ground by taking it one small bit at a time. And I get better and faster the more that I practice."

She rose on one elbow, candlelight gleaming on the slope of her shoulders and collarbone above where she'd tucked the blankets for warmth.

Her eyes were bright, and she smiled, but Lucy could see so much of the old shyness still lurking in the curve of her lips. "So I started thinking: maybe being an artist is also really about the work. It's not about standing up and trumpeting one's own genius to a throng of adoring inferiors, agog with admiration. Maybe an artist is simply one who does an artist's work, over and over. A process, not a paragon."

Lucy sat up, the better to look Catherine in the face. "So you're going to start thinking of yourself as an artist, as well as an embroiderer?"

Catherine stretched out, happy and languorous and still very, very naked. Lucy half forgot her own question. "I am going to try," Catherine said.

Lucy sighed and pretended disappointment. "Only one brief night doing science and you're taking refuge in art."

Catherine grinned and laced her fingers behind her head. "Haven't we been talking about them like they're the same thing?"

"Weren't you on the other side of the argument last time?"

"You have a point there." Catherine stared up at the bed canopy. "Good lord, what on *earth* is that?"

"Ah." Lucy rolled onto her stomach and rested on her elbows, the better not to have to view what Catherine was staring at in dawning horror. She knew its awful lineaments far too well to have to impose them upon her sight. "You've found my secret shame. Not all of us can be artists, no matter how much we may labor at our embroidery."

Catherine's gaze didn't waver. "You stitched that?"

"For my sins, I did." She slanted a gaze sideways, to where Catherine's generous bosom curved just out of sight beneath the blanket. "If you can guess what the scene is supposed to be, there's a reward."

"A reward?" Catherine did look over then, and caught Lucy's sly grin. "Ah, I see. Let me try, then."

She narrowed her expert gaze once more upon the canopy's garish blobs and figures.

"I want to say Noah and the ark, because there's a two-legged creature that must be a man, and he seems to be directing all the others four-legged things—but there's something with eight legs, and although there must have been spiders on the ark, it's far too big in scale to be a spider." Her brow crinkled up. "And his horse seems to be in the process of exploding quite violently."

"Close," Lucy sputtered, laughing helplessly. "The man is Orion the hunter. The spider is actually a scorpion, for Scorpio. Leo is the lion, and the horse is not exploding, it simply has wings, because it is not a horse but Pegasus. Other animals are—or were supposed to be—a big and little bear, a dragon, and a bull . . ."

She hunched her shoulders up, knowing Catherine had spotted the bull by the way she sputtered out a horrified laugh.

"My governess thought I might try harder in my embroidery if I stitched constellations."

"And did you?" Catherine shook her head before Lucy could reply. "No, don't answer, I can see you did."

"Can you?" Lucy rolled over, dropping her head on the pillow next to Catherine's. "How?"

"Embroidery is a language, like any other. It just takes familiarity to interpret properly."

Catherine raised an arm, her expert fingers gesturing from one stitched constellation to another, just as she'd called out the stars in the real sky earlier in the night.

"To begin with, although your technique is rough, you've covered most of the ground with stitchwork. Easier samplers always leave plenty of space, so they can be filled quickly and framed and shown off. But here everything is crowded close together: the big and little bears even overlap. The colors are different for each animal, so you had to choose them, which takes time. You've made French knots for all the eyes—French knots for a young embroiderer are the very devil, I know from experience—and then as if all that weren't enough to tell me how hard you worked, you've kept it here, hanging from your bed, ever since." Her arm dropped back down.

She wasn't laughing now, and neither was Lucy.

Catherine's gaze traced every silken thread, almost reverently. "You cared about this piece very much, too much to risk leaving it somewhere where guests—or your brother—could find it and mock it."

Lucy's throat went dry. She'd half forgotten herself; how had Catherine guessed? But it was true—the embroidery had initially been hung by her fond father in the front parlor. But then Stephen had brought an artist friend home that winter, and they'd whiled away an entire rainy afternoon storm by critiquing every last error and flaw in her work. "They said I lacked inspiration," she murmured, "and that it is inspiration which breathes life into true art. That's the root of the word, they said, trotting out all their newly acquired Latin."

Catherine stroked a hand down Lucy's arm, soothing and safe. "So you chose science instead of art?"

"I thought I had to choose between them. I knew I loved astronomy, even then—so I thought my terrible embroidery was another sign of my scientific abilities." Lucy shook her head, a flood of rare regret briefly swamping her. "I shouldn't have argued with you before, when you said the value of art lies in how other people view it."

Catherine sat up, eyes flashing. "You know what I think? I think we should stop taking your brother's self-indulgent ranting as the ultimate authority."

Lucy shook her head, but her dismay began to shade into amusement. "He's a professional painter; I'm not sure we can discount him entirely."

Catherine's gaze turned stern, her blue eyes fixing Lucy where she lay sprawled. It was an oddly schoolteacherish look, an impression which was only strengthened when the countess demanded, "How did Isaac Newton discover the principle of gravitation?"

Lucy was not yet so far removed from her school days: her reply was swift. "He saw an apple fall to the earth."

"And was he the first person to ever have seen this? Was he a discoverer of apples falling?"

Lucy let out a breathy laugh, mirth bubbling up in her. "Of course not."

"Right, because that would be absurd. So Newton looked at a perfectly ordinary apple, doing something that apples do every autumn in every orchard in the world—and not only apples, but other fruits, too, every plum and peach and orange and mango—and he came up with one of the most brilliant discoveries about the physical world, something no other living being on earth had ever realized before." Catherine folded her arms. "Now tell me that science doesn't sometimes involve inspiration, as much as hard work and a search for truth."

Lucy considered this, staring up again at the terrible evidence of her youthful feminine failures. "That's all well and good for Mr. Newton, but all I have done so far is to bring other people's thoughts into greater clarity—first with my father, and then with Oléron. I can claim no inspiration of my own."

"None?" Catherine's eyes narrowed. "What was it you said made you decide not to do a plain translation?"

Lucy sucked in a deep breath. "You," she said, sitting up again.

She picked up the end of the blanket Catherine held, pulling on it. Catherine didn't let go, but allowed herself to be pulled closer.

Lucy looked down into her lover's flushing face. "I wanted to write something to convince you that you could pursue science, if you chose. I wanted to help set you free."

Once, Catherine might have dropped her eyes, and trembled. Now she only dropped the blanket, baring her breasts and reaching out to pull Lucy into her arms.

It was Lucy who shook as the countess's hands skated over the tenderest parts of her, warm against the cool air, flickering like candlelight over her skin. "I might have taken up science once, for you," Catherine whispered. There was a sad shadow at the corner of her mouth that Lucy desperately wanted to kiss away. "But I know better now than to try and remake myself for someone else's comfort. I'm not drawn to natural philosophy, not like you are, though it's very much a part of my world. I've chosen a different path—parallel, perhaps, but not the same as yours. I want to try thinking of myself as an artist for a while, because I think it might suit me." Her hands on Lucy's shoulders clutched tighter. "But I never would have had the thought before I met you. So you see, you did set me free after all."

"I'm glad," Lucy whispered.

Chapter Twelve

All interludes must come to an end, however, and it was at last time to return to London. They stopped one night with Aunt Kelmarsh, whose garden was doing poorly in the wet, chilly summer but who still had plenty of poisonous blossoms to offer to avenge what Stephen had done.

"It doesn't have to be fatal," she explained to Catherine as Lucy went off in peals of laughter. "A single daffodil petal mixed into a salad won't kill him, but it will make him at least as uncomfortable as he deserves."

Catherine smiled and sipped her ale—summer for Aunt Kelmarsh wasn't summer without a good broad English ale to hand, no matter what the weather—as the older woman listed a few other *highly* frightening ideas. Yes, she'd done well to imagine Aunt Kelmarsh in a witch's gown. She might see about having one made up as a gift, in time for Christmas . . .

It was lucky Catherine was thinking about her art— she even stuttered over the words in the quiet of her own mind, though it was getting easier—because they returned to London to find Lucy's new wardrobe was finished and needed only the last quick fittings to be properly tailored. Suddenly Lucy looked fashionable, not at all the young country lady who'd turned up on Catherine's doorstep all those months ago.

Society began to take more notice.

Some of those noble scions who'd approved Lucy's book had not minded to learn it was the work of a woman, and had issued invitations to tea or to certain interesting lectures around the city—so Lucy was growing a small social circle of her own in town, quite separate from the gentleman naturalists, eccentrics, and dilettantes who made up the bulk of the Society's ranks.

Not that the academics were absent, of course—Mr. Edwards had come by for dinner several times with his novelist wife, and Mr. Frampton had written to ask if Lucy had sent her translation to Oléron yet. Lucy had demurred, less than eager to expose herself to more potential scorn from male bastions of astronomy.

And then there arrived a letter from Stephen, asking if he could come to Lady Moth's and apologize to Lucy in person.

Catherine thought Lucy ought to use the blue parlor, as the most formal and frigid room in the house, but Lucy chose instead to wait for her brother in the small back garden. He would be more at ease there, she was sure—and she could escape indoors if necessary and cut the interview short.

She paced for ten full minutes before a cough from behind her made her spin round.

Oh, it made her heart ache to see that even now, when he was calling at the home of a countess, he still had paint stains on his sleeve.

Before she could even speak he raised both his hands and said: "I have been a perfect ass, and if you want to ask your countess to order the footmen to beat me senseless I wouldn't blame you a bit."

Lucy laughed, and some of the awkwardness eased. They sat down beside one another on the bench beneath a cherry tree, its arms spread wide and decked with late summer's greenery.

Stephen ran a hand through his shaggy hair. "I had no idea what people would say about that painting. I'm so very sorry, Lucy."

"Why did you paint it?" Lucy blurted out. She felt hot and cold together, simultaneously angry and longing to forgive him. It nettled her, not to feel one comprehensible way. "If it was on account of the money—"

"No," he said. "Well, sort of."

"When the book was published I sent—"

"I know you did," he burst in, then ran both hands through his hair and sighed.

Lucy folded her arms and gritted her teeth.

"Father told me to take care of you," he said. "So that's what I've been trying to do. I cast countless lures out for portraits and commissions. I tried to paint what I thought would sell. I learned and studied and struggled and smiled at nearly everyone who I thought had a chance of offering me a post teaching their rambunctious brats how to draw slightly less poorly than before."

He leaned his head up to the sky, eyes closed. Sunlight filtered through the tree branches and gilded the planes of his face.

There was more strain there than Lucy remembered.

She clenched her jaw harder against the sympathetic impulse. "I managed to do quite well on my own."

The smile he turned on her was heartbreaking. "Yes. You did. You made yourself a grand success in less than a year, partly to spite me and prove me wrong—and then you sent me a large portion of the money you'd earned, with no sign that you were heading back home anytime soon. I know Lady Moth's house must be more comfortable than what we're used to in Lyme, but . . ." His hazel eyes rested on her, too observant. "Is Lady Moth a good patroness, or . . . ?"

Lucy's throat went dry and her hands clutched tight around one another. "Lady Moth has been terribly kind. We are—friends."

Stephen's gaze didn't waver. "Friends who live in her house. Eating her food. Surrounded by her servants, who are paid with her fortune."

Lucy's temper spiked at this. "If it hurts your pride to see me living here where I have friends than sending me off to solitude in Lyme—"

"My god, Lucy, if it's London you want, we'll find you a place in town. Today," Stephen burst out. "I just want to make sure you know what you're getting into. All your work was with Father, before he died—you've never had a patron before in your life. And it can be . . ."

He trailed off, his face turning away beneath the wavering summer shadows.

Lucy took a deep breath. "It can be . . . ?"

"Hard." His features were stone, his eyes fixed on some faraway point. "You think you're paid for your work, for your ideas and inspiration. But sometimes you find you've been paid for your obedience, too. Not just in regard to the object you're creating—obedience in everything. There are people who will pay you well, very well, so long as you have not a single thought or desire—or friend—outside the ones they desire you to have."

"Lady Moth isn't like that." Lucy sucked in lungfuls of air, heady with grass and earth and the last of the summer roses. She ought to tell Stephen the truth—that she and Lady Moth were in love.

But was that better, or worse? Less simple, certainly. It wasn't the money she would miss, if Catherine cut her off someday.

Her brother's words burrowed into her ears, and wouldn't leave her. She hated how easy it would be to believe him. "You're wrong."

"I hope I am." He grasped her hand, and Lucy almost sobbed at the amount of love and fear mingled in his expression. "The worst patrons—they prey on desperation," her brother said. "Your safety lies in being able to walk away."

Lucy swallowed hard.

Her brother's hands were warm on hers, the feel of them

familiar. They were like her father's hands, she noticed suddenly—the same long, artistic fingers, the dusting of light brown hair. He gripped tighter. "You know I only want the best for you. We're all the family we have. Well," his lips quirked, "except for Aunt Annabelle."

Lucy twisted her lips and hoped it passed for a smile.

Stephen hugged her and took his leave. Lucy sat for a while beneath the protective shade of the cherry tree. A movement in the corner of her eye had her gaze flickering upward—to the curtains in Catherine's private sitting room, which were just slowing down to stillness again. As if a hand had twitched them briefly aside, then let them fall.

A week passed. Lucy had been unusually quiet, and Catherine had been more and more anxious about it. Old memories of George's long silent spells haunted her like vengeful ghosts. Lucy had invited her along to a poetry reading with Mrs. Edwards, but Catherine had chosen to remain at home and work on the gown she was still embroidering for Lucy— the rings-of-Saturn design demanded a great deal of careful stitching, and the afternoon light was the kindest on her eyes.

Brinkworth brought in the post just as satin stitch was making her feel overly stabby, so Catherine decided to give her fingers a rest (if not her sight) and weed the more hateful missives from Lucy's mail. They had slowed to a mere trickle now, but until they stopped entirely, Catherine was determined to position herself as a bulwark against the tide.

She didn't register the name Mrs. Winlock until she unfolded the letter and saw the signature at the bottom: "Ever yours, Pris."

Her heart stuttered to a stop in her chest.

She shouldn't read it. She already knew it would be painful, and she had no right. It was one thing to protect Lucy from the insults of sneering strangers; it was quite another to open her more private correspondence.

But then again: the letter was already opened.

Catherine had to know.

Hesitantly, as if the words had been written in gunpowder and gall, she went over them, line by line.

> *Dearest Lucy,*
>
> *It was so good to see you in Lyme. So much has happened since we parted! This letter, I hope, finds you well. I write to tell you that I am in the city for a few days, and to ask if you would like to meet for tea tomorrow or the next day. Lyme in winter is decidedly dull and quiet, and I would like one last outing before settling in for the cold. Last Thursday's conversation was very interesting. Let's not let another six months pass before we see one another! Or else my winter months will be even duller and more dismal again by half. Very soon my husband and I travel north to visit my family, so I beg you to hurry and accept my offer.*
>
> *Ever yours,*
> *Pris*

Catherine couldn't return to her embroidery after reading such a note—her hands trembled too violently. She set the note on her desk and wondered what on earth she was going to say to Lucy.

Every phrase that sprang to her chilled lips—*Don't meet her, What did you talk about, Was it me?*—seemed both inadequate and too revealing, too much and too little at once. There was nothing *wrong* in the note itself, nothing anyone in the polite world could possibly object to. Who would be hurt if one old friend wanted to take tea with another? Hadn't they all had a cordial time at dinner? If Harry Winlock didn't object, with all a husband's right of suspicion and priority, then what claim could Catherine make in answer to this?

The serpent's fangs bit deep, and Catherine could feel her heart's blood running out and leaving her body hollow and cold, chiming beneath the little blows like a church bell in a hailstorm.

Lucy arrived home and came straight to the parlor. "Mr. Frampton said to tell you—" she began, but stopped at the look on Catherine's face. She hurried over, sinking onto the sofa beside Catherine. "What is wrong?"

The words that hadn't come before seemed to all rush upon her now, each one sharp and stinging. "A letter came for you," were the first ones out. "I wouldn't have opened it if I'd realized." She handed over the paper, and watched Lucy turn pale as she saw who it was from.

Gray eyes pierced Catherine where she sat. "You wouldn't have opened it, but since it was opened already—you did read it?"

"I did," Catherine confessed softly. The pain of admission

was perversely welcome—it was better than numbness and nothingness. If she hurt, she was still here, still in touch with the world.

Lucy nodded once, a sharp jerk of her head.

"It was a perfectly ordinary note," Catherine said. "That's no justification, though. I'm sorry."

Lucy was still frozen, and Catherine's panic redoubled—she could understand pain, or anger, or recriminations, but this long, chilly quiet made her nearly go out of her skin with dread.

Finally, Lucy turned her eyes toward the letter.

Catherine waited, still marshaling and dismissing arguments for any and all eventualities.

She was prepared for some reaction on Lucy's part—but she was not prepared for the sudden burst of violence when Lucy cried out, crumpled the letter into a ball, and hurled it across the room toward the fireplace. It missed; Lucy leaped up from the sofa and began pacing the room, cursing in a low, furious tone.

"How dare she?" were the first words Catherine was able to decipher. "How dare she, damn her!"

It was a response entirely out of proportion to the cause. Catherine froze as realization hit her: this was not the reaction of a heart fully healed from love's wound. If Lucy was this enflamed by such a tepid letter, there was still fuel to burn.

So much for fossils. Something here still lived.

Catherine's chest creaked like a glacier under strain, her tongue stiff as an icicle behind the wall of her clenched teeth.

She managed only a blunt reply: "I could not see where she erred."

She could feel it, though, plunged like a poisoned arrow into her breast. Every instinct told her that Priscilla Winlock meant no good by this.

"Oh, she's too careful for that." Lucy whirled round, unearthly fast. Catherine could almost see the sparks flying off her—or maybe that was simply the gown, which had a border of small comets Madame Tabot had patterned off the stellarium shawl. They spun and circled at her ankles as she strode back across the room. "You were meant to be fooled. Pris's parents always read her correspondence, you see—they were strict that way. She knew anything she wrote would have to pass beneath unfriendly eyes. So she wrote in code." She uncrumpled the letter halfway and flung it down onto the sofa beside Catherine. "Her real message is there, in the first letters of every sentence."

Catherine picked up the much-abused paper as Lucy resumed pacing, stopping every now and again to stomp with extra force on some thicker part of the carpet. The answer to the riddle was there in plain sight after all: I STILL LOVE.

So. Not so polite as Catherine had thought. Mrs. Winlock was making her intentions rather plain, in fact.

"What will you do?" the countess asked, setting the letter back down. She was tempted to toss it in the fireplace, where incendiaries belonged—but it was not addressed to her, after all. She had no right.

Lucy turned again, gray eyes flashing like Athena in a

rage. She stared at Catherine, who said nothing, only twisted her hands together and waited in agony for a reply.

Time stretched.

At length, Lucy spoke. "I suppose I should see her," she said. "She's come all this way. But these riddles are too childish. There is no need for them anymore."

"I don't want her in my house," Catherine said.

Lucy's head whipped up, her gaze rapier-sharp.

Catherine flinched beneath that steel.

"The kind of conversation I intend to have with Pris is best conducted in private," Lucy said coolly.

Of course she was right. Of course there would be nothing straightforward they could say unless they were somewhere safe. Catherine nodded, trying to keep from her face the feeling of a thousand needles pricking her heart.

She shouldn't have expected otherwise, really. Priscilla would make her case in person, all winning entreaty and teary eyes. They'd been together five years; Lucy and Catherine had only had a scant few months. The conclusion was inevitable.

"Of course," Catherine replied. They should have been easy syllables, mostly made of air, but they flayed her tongue like knives. She kept talking regardless. "I have a few patterns drafted to show to Mrs. Griffin—I could take them in person, and give you two the privacy you require."

Lucy's mouth was flat, and she nodded. "Perhaps that is best." A note of real relief sounded in her voice.

Catherine didn't let herself flinch again, but only rose

gracefully from the sofa. It cost her some twinges in muscles gone stiff with the effort of holding herself together, but she thought the movement played tolerably well for her intended audience. "I feel rather as though I have caught a chill from all this wet weather. I think I am going to retire early tonight." And alone—she didn't say it, but from the bleak look on Lucy's face, she didn't need to.

Catherine turned away before she could see anything worse, and made her way upstairs to a bed that seemed far bigger and emptier than it ever had before.

She spun around restlessly from side to side until the blankets were hopelessly tangled about her legs, and she had to kick violently to free herself. But her thoughts wouldn't let her rest. Curse it, the lack of permanence had been so reassuring to her, at the start of this affair! Now here she was, writhing with jealousy and envy because she didn't have any right to ask Lucy to choose her over Priscilla Winlock. She realized, with a shock, that she had never felt uncertain of George, not once, even in the years when they were barely speaking except to say something bitter to one another. She'd known he *couldn't* leave her, and some part of her had taken a secret, shameful comfort in that.

She had depended far too much on the insolubility of her marriage license, it seemed. Not on her own merits at all.

Loving another woman—loving Lucy—didn't bring any such luxuries, and all at once she felt the lack keenly. You could never sit back and let the official pieces of paper do the work for you, oh no: you had to choose the other person over and over again, every time. What's worse, you had to trust them to choose you. It was horribly frightening—as though you started every day by reminding your heart to keep beating.

Narayan came in at dawn, her dark eyes anxious, but Catherine was already awake, a dressing gown wrapped around her as she sat by the window and stared anxiously out at the back gardens. Another rainy summer day, it seemed. As if the sun itself were weeping. Narayan's eyebrows flicked up as she took in the fact that there was only one body in the room, but she helped her mistress dress and pinned her hair up without a needless word. Catherine went down to breakfast and stopped when she saw Lucy there, in the act of filling her plate.

Lucy Muchelney looked about as well rested as Catherine felt: there were dark rings beneath her eyes and a dull cast to her skin. She paused halfway to the table, a worry line appearing on her brow as she looked Catherine over from head to toe. "Still feeling ill?" she asked, setting her plate down on the table. She didn't take a seat but hovered there, hands fixed on the back of the chair, fingers opening and closing.

"I'm afraid so," Catherine replied, "but it will pass, I'm sure."

She moved to the sideboard and began putting food on her plate: thick slices of toast with as much butter and jam as they could hold, pound cake, and more eggs than a single hen could produce in a week. After a time she realized she was only stalling, gripped the plate's edge as though it were a shield, and turned back to the breakfast table.

Lucy's mouth was full, so she said nothing as Catherine

took the seat across from her. Just as they had every day—but everything felt changed now. Barren and final.

The butter dish and pitcher of cream seemed to loom over the place settings like cemetery guards. "Have you written to Mrs. Winlock?" Catherine asked.

Lucy swallowed. "She is coming by this afternoon for tea."

Toast crunched and crumbled in Catherine's mouth. She could barely focus enough to force her throat to swallow. It scraped her raw. "So soon?"

"The more I thought about it, the more delay felt intolerable." Lucy dropped her eyes back to her plate.

"Ah." Catherine had to choke down half her pound cake to fill her throat with something other than acid. So she was going to lose Lucy already. She'd known it would happen, had seen the inevitability in Lucy's reaction to the letter, but it still ripped her open like a jagged seam.

Lucy seemed no happier about the news, which Catherine found puzzling. But then, it must be awkward to be reuniting with your beloved in your new lover's house. Especially when that new lover was also your patroness.

But Catherine had forgotten: Lucy had her own funds now, didn't she? She was an independent astronomer now, established and in full flourish. What more use did she have for Catherine, if not for loving?

This was unbearable. Catherine took a long draft of tea to clear her throat, then shoved herself to her feet. "I find I have little appetite this morning."

"Clearly," Lucy replied, staring down at the piles of food on Catherine's plate.

Catherine flushed. "I should make sure the first few designs are ready for Mrs. Griffin to look over," she said. Her hands didn't seem to know what to do with themselves—they wanted to reach out, to pull Lucy close, but the temptation must be resisted. No matter how much sadness hung in those gray eyes. Catherine had no right, no right at all.

"Will I see you for dinner?" Lucy asked softly.

"I . . ." Catherine swallowed again, stomach weighing her down as though it were filled with lead. "I am not sure."

Surely those weren't her footsteps, echoing off the walls in the silence that followed. They were far too hasty, almost running. But when she reached the parlor where her sketchbook awaited her, she was breathing hard from exertion.

She grasped her sketchbook—all of it, not only the designs she'd meant to take to the engraver. This one part of her heart she could keep safe, even as she lost everything else. She took refuge in her bedroom again until early afternoon, driving Narayan mad with running back and forth for tea and cake, taking half-eaten slices back down to the kitchen to Cook's sure annoyance. Finally it was late enough that she was able to put on a walking dress, clutch her sketchbook in one hand, and mount the steps into the carriage for the trip to Griffin's print shop.

It was quieter in the shop than it had been the first time, which made Catherine grateful; the sunlight slanted in and graced every watercolor-tinted scene with a reverent halo. Catherine felt herself relax under the soothing spell of color and line, until she spotted the familiar blue of the cover of *The Lady's Guide*, displayed in pride of place to tempt readers.

She raised her chin and walked past it, though her hands tightened around her sketchbook.

Instead of the young man from before, there was a familiar face behind the counter. Eliza Brinkworth lit up with a smile of recognition and curtsied to her former mistress. "Good afternoon, Lady Moth."

Catherine smiled back. "Good afternoon, Eliza—is Mrs. Griffin available?"

The girl's smile faltered. "I'll go and see, my lady." She popped into the back—a brief hubbub swelled as the door opened and closed—and soon Catherine was being shown into the small office again.

Mrs. Griffin looked wary and got straight to the point. "If you're here to take Eliza back, you can't have her."

"What?" Catherine blinked, as the self-involved fog of misery lifted a little. "Goodness, no, that's not why I'm here." She drummed her fingers on the cover of her sketchbook. "I take it Eliza is doing well as an apprentice, then."

"The best I've had," Mrs. Griffin replied. She leaned back, some of the tension leaving her, though her eyes never lost their keenness. "So if not for that, why *are* you here, my lady?"

Catherine's mouth went desert-dry. How had it come to this? Was she really supposed to spill all her hopes and dreams out in words, like so many petals and pearls from the lips of a cursed princess, and hope that Mrs. Griffin deigned to pick some few of them up?

She cleared her throat, stalling, and the print of a world map caught her eye, hanging high on the wall behind the engraver. A line of bright dashes showed some expedition's route—maybe even one Catherine had been on.

I have sailed half a world away, she recalled, and felt confidence rush renewed up her spine like a fountain gushing with clear, cool water.

Hadn't she survived much more harrowing things than one conversation where somebody might say no?

"I have a proposition for you, Mrs. Griffin," she began, heartened by the steadiness of her tone. Words came more easily once she'd begun. "You mentioned you were always looking for more embroidery designs . . ."

She pulled out her sketchbook. The more pages she flipped, the more Mrs. Griffin's eyes gleamed, and the brighter Eliza's cheeks flushed in excitement. "Oh, yes," the engraver murmured. She lifted shrewd eyes to Catherine's. "Of course you know how much success we've had with Miss Muchelney's book. A great many more women are now talking about astronomy—and no few of those will want to flaunt this interest in their dress, while it's fashionable. You've gone and created your own captive market, my lady."

Catherine's lips pursed. "It sounds horribly sordid when you put it that way, Mrs. Griffin."

"So you won't want any of the profits from your pattern book, then?"

Catherine snorted denial.

The engraver's smile was a silverfish, flashing bright and then just as quickly gone. "I appreciate when my artists are canny about the business aspects," Mrs. Griffin went on warmly. "I'm sure we can work out percentages that will please us both."

She turned another page and stopped. It was the design Catherine had started thinking of as the siren's gown, conceived on the beach at Lyme and refined after that first meeting with Mrs. Priscilla Winlock. It was an evening dress, a deep metallic silver overlaid with a net of ocean green. Careful gathers here and there gave it the look of waves breaking, and a froth of lighter silver lace completed the marine look. It would have been soft and delicate and perfectly ladylike—except that Catherine had also added thick slashes of chestnut and amber embroidery to encircle the high waist, like tortured driftwood or a belt made from the spars of broken ships. The kind of dress someone might wear to both allure and to frighten.

Mrs. Griffin stared at it so long that Catherine felt her cheeks flush. "Not all of the designs are scientific," she said. "Or even suitable for ladies. Honestly some of them get a bit wild. But if I don't get them down on paper they just hover in my head and take up room that the more proper designs could be filling, so . . ."

She snapped her mouth shut. Mrs. Griffin wasn't listening. Her eyes were fixed on the page, but her gaze was faraway, and there was so much yearning in it that Catherine felt embarrassed to be a witness to it.

The silence stretched further. Catherine began to fidget, and coughed to clear the dryness from her throat.

Mrs. Griffin's head snapped up and she blinked, coming back from wherever it was she'd gone. "Don't even know where I'd wear it . . ." she murmured, then her dark brown eyes sharpened on Catherine with a look that was part avarice, part something very like fear. "You have a distinct taste for the fantastical, Lady Moth."

Catherine shifted uneasily. "I try my best to keep it in check."

The engraver's eyes softened. "Maybe you shouldn't try quite so hard. I look at a great deal of clothing in my work, my lady—and many great works of art, too. I recognize genius when it shows up face-to-face."

Catherine's cheeks flamed and a thrill ran through her. She was afraid to move, afraid that she'd misheard somehow.

Mrs. Griffin flickered a look back down at the siren's gown, squared her shoulders, and resumed her usual businesslike manner. "We'll start with the scientific designs— and a few of the botanicals as well, I think." They quickly reached an agreement about payment and a date for Catherine's return with the completed set of sketches, and a handshake sealed the transaction.

Catherine gripped the other woman's hand a little harder than was strictly necessary. She could feel the tears pricking the corners of her eyes. "Thank you," she said. "For the chance."

"Oh, my lady." Mrs. Griffin's other hand came up to cover both of hers. "When you get about a half dozen of those fantastical designs, will you bring those in, too?"

Catherine blinked. "Do you really think women would want to wear them?"

"I think some women will set the world on fire for the

privilege," Mrs. Griffin said, her voice low and intense. "One or two dressmakers, to start, who can well afford to pay for something this compelling . . . Perhaps not enough to justify a full print run like the others, but certainly well worth the expense of printing a few loose pages."

Catherine promised. The bargaining thus concluded, Mrs. Griffin bid Eliza show the countess out the front, while she returned to her print shop with its rattle of metal and manpower. Eliza had more of a bounce in her step than she'd had as a maid. "Are you satisfied with your apprenticeship, Miss Brinkworth?" Catherine asked.

"Oh yes, my lady," the young woman breathed. "She says I have a neat hand, and has been teaching me to make music plates for popular songs and ballads." She flushed, ducking her head. "I'm excited to get back to pattern drafting, though—I think I can persuade her to let me do a few of my own, now that I'm getting better at the engraving part."

"I am glad to hear it."

Catherine took her leave and climbed up into her carriage with a mixture of hope and regret such as she had never experienced. Hope for the future, for her own designs and the work she was already eager to return to. Regret because she had already wasted so much time. Eliza's youth was as good as a fortune: the bulk of her years spread out before her, so much space, so many hours to spend. Catherine's youth was long past, and she wasn't sure she had anything to show for it but a handful of heartbreak.

She ought to have paid more attention to her own self before now. She ought to have allowed herself to want things.

She hadn't quite known how, until Lucy. But she'd wanted Lucy, and wanting Lucy had led to wanting everything else. Now it was all changed, and even if Lucy left—or *when* Lucy left—Catherine could no more go back to her old life than she could pull out a day's worth of embroidery stitches and leave the fabric as pristine as it was at first. The needle marks would always show.

She must get used to being a person who wanted things. No, Catherine corrected herself, taking a breath and letting the cool air fill her with the first taste of the coming harvest season, she must get used to being a person who got what they wanted. Even if it didn't always last.

Lucy would go back to Priscilla, and continue being one of the great scientific minds of her age. Catherine would watch her progress with interest, at a distance, and think fondly of the time they'd shared.

It would be acceptable, if not ideal. It would hurt, but less so as time went on.

It would not destroy her, Catherine vowed. It would not. She chanted it to herself in time with the beat of the horses' hooves the whole way home.

Chapter Thirteen

Perhaps the holiday in the small house at Lyme had compressed Lucy back into a small girl again, because that afternoon the London house felt like the largest, emptiest building in the world. Especially once Catherine had departed. Three full stories, high ceilings, wooden floors, hallways that rang sepulchral with footsteps whenever the servants went ghostly about their duties. Lucy took refuge in the library, but every time she turned a page in her book, instead of printed letters and numbers she saw only Catherine's face, pale and pinched with hurt.

Lucy should have been angry. And she was. But she ought to have been *only* angry: Catherine had read her letter, then tried to keep Lucy from seeing Pris out of jealousy. Those actions merited Lucy's anger.

But the worst part was the persistent, irrefutable fear that Lucy had done something wrong, as well, unconsciously. Why else would Catherine have been jealous now, when she hadn't seemed to be at Lyme? Had Lucy done something, said something to cause Catherine to doubt?

And did the fact that Lucy was asking this question at all mean she was already tangled in the trap Stephen had described?

Three days ago, Stephen's concerns had seemed—not wrong, precisely, but misapplied. General, rather than specific.

Now, though, it seemed a far more plausible explanation. Catherine had been a guest in Lyme, a visitor to the town and to Lucy's house there. Maybe she'd thought of meeting Pris as something separate from ordinary life—the kind of strange, solemn adventure one had when one was away from home. Like visiting the ruins of Pompeii and marveling over the remnants of that ancient tragedy.

Not the sort of thing one made a habit of.

But now that Pris was coming here, Catherine protested. To protect her territory. Her home—but also Lucy. Was it so outrageous to imagine a countess being a possessive lover? Was it unreasonable to imagine she might try to use whatever power she had to keep Lucy close to her side?

Some part of Lucy refused to believe this; another part insisted it was the only logical conclusion.

She tortured herself with increasingly elaborate theories to fit contradictory evidence, until Brinkworth came in and interrupted her. "Mrs. Priscilla Winlock to see you, Miss Muchelney."

Was it her guilty imagination, or was the butler being extra-stern today? Lucy didn't know how much Narayan had let on to the other servants what Lucy and Catherine got up to together, but she couldn't suppress a flash of anxiety that Brinkworth might think she was betraying Catherine in her own home. The thought left an oily, sick feeling in its wake, and Lucy took several gulps of air to try and temper her stomach.

"I've put her in the blue parlor, miss."

Lucy's eyes narrowed, but Brinkworth's facade never cracked. He might have been pure marble, a stoic and high-moraled Senator from the glory days of Rome. "The blue parlor?" she asked pointedly.

"Yes, miss." He bowed, and held open the door.

There was nothing to be gained by delaying. Lucy shoved herself to her feet and all but stomped down the hallway.

The blue parlor was the room nearest the front door, and rarely used. The countess preferred her own cozy sitting room at the back of the house, where the light streamed through filtered by garden leaves to gild all her heirlooms. The blue parlor faced the street, tall windows stretched high like mouths open to the sight of anyone passing by on the sidewalk just outside. The decor was neoclassical, all Grecian restraint and painful elegance: thin-legged chairs, stiff and spindly, with a slender tea table between them.

Pris was perched on one of those chairs, her muslin walking dress embroidered with sprays of white work blossoms. She looked angelic, the dress glowing in the stark light, almost blinding Lucy after the comforting dimness of the library. Her gaze flicked once to Brinkworth as she rose and stepped forward to clasp Lucy's hands. "My dear Miss Muchelney," she said, her smile just the right shade of pleased without shading into a too-revealing eagerness.

Lucy couldn't avoid the kiss Pris pressed to her cheek, but was acutely conscious of Brinkworth standing behind her. "May I offer you some refreshment, Mrs. Winlock?" The name sat like a stranger's on her tongue, as Brinkworth rang for the maid to bring tea.

Lucy and Pris made empty conversation until the tea came, and then Lucy thanked Brinkworth and dismissed him with only the barest wince.

"Always happy to serve, Miss Muchelney," the butler replied. For a moment his gaze was searching, but then he caught himself and his expression went polished again. "Let me know if there is anything else you or your guest require."

There was some message here, but Lucy's wits were too strained to unravel it. Every instant of struggle only pulled the knot tighter. "Thank you," she said, and watched thoughtfully as Brinkworth shut the parlor door behind him. Then she turned to Pris—who smiled with all the old warmth, dimples appearing in her cheeks and the heat Lucy remembered so well brightening her eyes.

Once not too long ago Lucy's heart would have leaped to see it. But Lucy then was not the same woman as Lucy now, and instead she only folded her arms and asked: "How's Harry?"

"Oh!" Pris squeaked, and squirmed on her uncomfortable chair. "I know, I have been very churlish to you—but you have forgiven me, haven't you?"

She stretched out her arms to Lucy and leaned forward, lips parting—but stopped when Lucy frowned and held up a warning hand. "What do you want, Pris?"

"You, of course." Pris cocked her head, a teasing smile playing about her rose-tinted lips. "You did get my letter?"

Lucy bristled. "I am not a pet, to come when called."

"Don't be crude." Pris sighed. "Of course you're more than that. You have every right to be angry. I hurt you very badly, I know. But I have every intention of making it up to you, if you'll only let me—"

"Why now?"

Pris blinked, brought up short by the sharpness of Lucy's tone.

Lucy took a bitter satisfaction in the puzzlement on her former lover's face. More words spilled over her tongue, a fountain-jet bursting out of the rock. "Two weeks ago you behaved like a proper new wife. Six months ago you couldn't even tell me you were marrying Harry—and now you think you can just crook your finger and I'll come running back, as though nothing at all has happened since then?" Lucy shook her head. "The ink on your marriage license is hardly dry, and you're already throwing your vows aside like—like you threw me."

"It was a mistake." Pris's mouth was set in a sad pout, but Lucy could see the color starting to rise in her cheeks. She hadn't expected resistance, and it was beginning to frustrate her. Pris never had liked being thwarted. "I thought if I finally were married, my mother and father would feel they had done their duty by me and would leave me alone. Would leave *us* alone. I have my inheritance now, so I don't have to work so hard to please them." She sniffled, but if there were tears falling from her eyes, Lucy couldn't see them. "I thought we would finally be safe."

"Safe!" Lucy cried. "You left me for a husband you barely cared about! Did you really expect me not to feel hurt by that?" She narrowed her eyes. "Especially since you didn't ask me about it in advance. You let me find out when the banns were read, in the family pew, with the whole village around me to take notice of how I reacted."

"All you had to do was keep a calm head," Pris snapped, "and we could have carried on as before—only better. But you couldn't wait for that, could you? You ran away to London straight off, like a coward." She sniffed again, out of pique this time. "A married woman has a deal more freedom than an unmarried one. People ask fewer questions, people forgive a bit more eccentricities."

"Oh, was I to be an eccentricity, then?" Lucy retorted. "How flattering. Dare I ask if you informed Harry of this arrangement when you agreed to his proposal?"

"Don't be absurd—Harry has nothing to do with us."

"Pris, he is your *husband*." Lucy took a deep breath, trying to keep her volume somewhere beneath a shout. The walls would echo here. "And he loves you."

"But I don't love him. My heart is full of someone else. How could you doubt it?" Pris reached out for Lucy again, eyes wide and limpid with unshed tears.

Lucy snatched her hand away, and leaped out of the chair for good measure. "You were wrong to come here, Pris. I thought we could talk, that we could come to understand one another, but you aren't listening to me. What we had is gone now. It died the day you stood up in church and vowed to spend your life with someone else."

Pris waved this aside with one graceful hand. "A man."

"A person—who you chose," Lucy insisted. "You took his ring, you took his name, you live in his home. You never told me what you hoped for us after the wedding, and you scoff when I ask if you've told him." Pris's cheeks were flame red now, and Lucy knew there would soon be an eruption, but she barreled onward regardless. "He made his vows in earnestness and sincerity, as you apparently did not."

Pris sprang up from the chair, head high. "If you're just going to be cruel, then you're right, I should not have come. We'll talk again when you're back home, after you've had some time to come to your senses."

This deserved more than the scornful snort Lucy gave it. "You will be waiting a long time."

Pris narrowed her eyes. "How long?"

Lucy thought of Catherine's face, and anguish chimed through her. "I cannot say."

The other woman clucked her tongue at this, blond curls bouncing with the movement. "Come now. You've made your point, and I have apologized. To drag this out for pride's sake would be childish." Pris stepped forward again, reaching out, shafts of sunlight from the street outside making the pale muslin of her dress flash like lightning.

Lucy recoiled as if struck. Anger flared up, all the stronger for having gone so long unspoken. "You think I've stayed away half a year because of pride?" The selfishness of it shocked her, and Pris's wide-eyed confusion somehow made it all the worse. As if Lucy just stopped existing if she weren't standing at Pris's side, or mooning over her, or scheming how to get her back. "I have been *busy*, Pris. I have been working. I have been making a life here—it may have looked to you like I was running away, but in fact there was something I was running toward."

"And what was that?" Priscilla was seething now, the white work flowers on her dress trembling like apple blossoms in a spring storm.

"A future," Lucy replied bluntly. "A life—and a happy one. A home where I can put my talents to use, for people who will appreciate them."

"People like your Lady Moth?"

The barb struck home; Lucy couldn't hold back a revealing wince.

Pris laughed, a harsh and horrid sound. "Oh, I noticed the way you looked at her in Lyme. You'd have a time seducing such a noble old matron as that—I doubt the idea that women can enjoy it would ever occur to her."

Lucy bit hard on her lip to keep silent.

Pris cocked her head, scenting weakness, as she always had. Her eyes weighed every one of the words she spoke. "I doubt she's ever thought about it beyond spreading her legs for her dead husband and hanging on until he starts snoring. I bet she's glad widowhood removed that chore from her list. I bet she's never pulled up her own skirts and slid her hands—"

"Stop it!" Lucy cried.

"Oh, this is rich." Pris was at the full peak of her venom now, a sight Lucy hadn't seen since their school days, and had hoped never to see again. "You expect me to believe you really prefer a woman who's just a duller, withered version of me?"

"Withered? Good lord, Pris, she's only ten years—" Lucy cut herself off, with some effort. When she spoke again her voice was very soft. "I love her. That's the plain truth of it. I love her and I won't leave her for you."

Pris's smile uncurled, a small but venomous serpent beneath a rose leaf. "Maybe you won't want to," she said. "But have you considered that maybe your Lady Moth won't want to keep *you*? You're exciting now, with your youth and your brilliance and the fuss about your little book. But what happens when your lady's tastes wander?" She smoothed down the skirts of her gown, hands skimming over the delicate knots of buds and blossoms. "You can throw my marriage in my face if you must, but I have something you and Lady Moth never will. I have *certainty*. Harry can never leave me, not even if he wanted to—which he doesn't. He is bound to me, until death, in a way you could never be."

"I might have tried, if you'd asked," Lucy said gently. "But you chose someone else for that."

"And now you're doing the same thing, just to hurt me." Pris delivered this conclusion as though it were a crowning triumph. Because of course, she must be at the center of everything important. In her own mind she was the magnet the whole world's compass turned toward.

Suddenly Lucy was sick of it. The sparring, the dramatics, the way every argument spiraled deeper and deeper with never an end in sight. Victory by these terms could only ever belong to Pris—and Lucy was tired of playing a game she could not win.

Her anger and hurt evaporated, replaced instead by a

solid, steely certainty that seemed to hone the edge of every surface in the room. *I don't have to play by these rules any longer.*

She didn't even have to finish the argument—though Pris was clearly waiting eagerly for a heated reply. Lucy turned instead and walked to the door, deeply proud of the way her hands remained steady as she pulled it open. What she saw in the hallway made her smile sincerely. She pulled the door wide and folded her hands, every inch the demure young hostess. "Good afternoon, Mrs. Winlock. I hope the rest of your stay in town is pleasant."

Pris leaped forward, a cutting remark upon those rosy lips—but the words died unheard. Brinkworth was waiting in the hallway with her bonnet and gloves at the ready, a perfectly helpful expression on his face and a dagger's glint in his eyes.

Pris thanked him readily, and he bowed with all evidence of polite obedience. Pris pulled on her gloves one finger at a time, mouth set in a mulish line.

With a flash of clarity, Lucy realized she didn't have to play out the last part of this farce, either. "I believe I'll return to the library, Brinkworth. Do have one of the footmen summon a hackney for Mrs. Winlock." She could imagine the look on Pris's face at that, but didn't stop to see it. Instead she proceeded up the stairs as gracefully as she could, leaving her jilted lover to gape silently at her retreating back.

Five minutes later, Brinkworth found her again, though she was having no more luck with her book now than before. The gust of audacity that had sent her sailing upstairs had died out. Her hands were shaking as she relived the argument, agonizing over what she ought and ought not to have said.

The butler bowed, his brows knitting together with unusual concern. "If I may be so bold, miss?"

Lucy blinked. "Yes?"

"Lady Moth often found it helpful to sip a little brandy and lemon, after a conversation like the one you have just had." He held out a tray with a tumbler: three fingers of amber liquid, the gold clouded with citrus.

Lucy knew if she cried, the butler would be appalled, so she swallowed back the lump in her throat and offered him a brilliant smile as she accepted the drink. "Thank you, Brinkworth. It's very kind of you."

The butler coughed as he straightened. "Lady Moth has been more than kind to me and my family," he said softly. "She deserves everything kind in return."

Lucy's hands tightened around the crystal. Brinkworth knew. He *knew*. But his eyes were worried, not hateful or disgusted. He'd brought her a drink to soothe her nerves. And he thought Catherine deserved kindness.

Her shoulders relaxed and she met Brinkworth's gaze as directly as she could. "I completely agree."

For one moment, the corners of his mouth twitched upward—but just as Lucy, fascinated, thought it was about to tip over into a smile, he controlled himself and bowed again. "Let me know if there's anything else you need, miss." The door shut softly behind him, and Lucy leaned back on the worn, creaky sofa to sip her drink, cough in surprise at the strength of it, and watch the dust motes float in the weak afternoon sun.

By the time she'd finished the glass, warmth and lassitude had wrapped soft threads around her limbs, and a gentle rain had begun falling outside. Droplets fluttered against the windowpanes and raced one another down the glass. Lucy slumped a little lower and let the shadows gather in the high corners of the library.

It should have felt like her library now, from spending so long working here—but it wasn't, was it? It was George's library still, almost three years after his death. Which should have made it Catherine's library, really, but it didn't feel like hers, either. It felt like a place the countess tended but didn't inhabit. Like a grave. A very large and echoey grave, with book covers arrayed on the shelves like tiny tombstones.

Lucy could probably blame that image on the brandy. She put the empty glass aside, slipped off her shoes, pulled the stellarium shawl around her shoulders, and curled up tight against the arm of the sofa.

All around her were the spines of books, bound to match in sets of black and brown and poison green. Authors' names. Men's names, all of them. Except for the one small blue octavo volume, there on the shelf with the other astronomers'. Lucy had put it there herself, under Catherine's proud eye—but oh, it looked so alone amid all the other hundreds and hundreds of books. And after all, Lucy was only a translator, stringing pretty words around someone else's thoughts.

Borrowing someone else's genius.

What were the chances the next thing she wrote would

be even half as successful? Especially if she were writing it herself, not translating another volume of Oléron's masterwork. Thanks to the first, Lucy had money enough now to live for some time if she were frugal, but those funds wouldn't last forever. Eventually she would find herself dependent on someone else's charity again: Stephen's pinch-minded prudery, or Catherine's more gracious support.

What if the bloom was off the rose by then? Lucy knew she was the first woman Catherine had dallied with, the first woman she'd fallen in love with. Maybe she would decide it wasn't to her taste. She'd been married before: she knew something of permanence. Maybe she would ultimately feel held back by passing affection for a self-conscious scholar who brought nothing else to the union.

Lady Moth deserved a brighter future than that. Brinkworth was right to feel protective of his mistress. Lucy should be just as selfless, if not more so.

By the time Catherine's steady footstep was heard in the hallway outside, Lucy had sunk herself deep into a truly hopeless mood. The countess knocked softly and peered warily around the door, squinting in the dim light.

Lucy scowled harder at the thought that she ought to have lit a lamp or asked for a fire. It was growing chill as the daylight slipped away.

Catherine came into the room and stopped. She must have come straight up from the carriage: she still held her gloves in her hand, and there were raindrops glimmering in her hair. "You're still here," the countess said.

"Where else would I be?"

Catherine didn't answer, only looked at her with eyes as wide and wary as if she were looking at a ghost.

Lucy forced herself to sit up and tried to hide her melancholy; nobody liked a lover in a low mood. "How was Griffin's?"

"It was rather marvelous, actually." Catherine perched gingerly in her usual seat. "We made an arrangement for an entire book of scientific embroidery designs."

Soon half of London could be wearing Catherine's handiwork. Lucy wouldn't have that to feel special about anymore. "That's wonderful."

"But she also saw one of the more—well, she called them *fantastical* gowns," Catherine went on. "She actually wants to print a handful of those designs separately, for individual sale." Catherine shifted, hands twisting her gloves. Her expression was equal parts delight and fear. "She said she recognized genius when she meets it face-to-face."

Lucy remembered the engraver: sharp as her tools, and clear-eyed as any artist. Attractive, too, in a stern kind of way. "She would know better than anyone. I'm sure you and she will get on famously together."

Catherine froze. "I beg your pardon?"

The more she pictured it, the more Lucy's bad mood curdled further. "It's perfect, isn't it? You have the inspiration, and she has the skill and the means to make it known far and wide. She'd be a much better match for a budding artist. Much better than some star-mad astronomer who's already outraged half the scientific community in London. It's really a move for the best: you've already gotten plenty of use out of me."

It was the worst thing Lucy had ever said, and she knew it, but she knew it too late. She watched, helpless and heartsore, as Catherine's face flamed at the implication. "It is strictly a business arrangement. If you imagine otherwise, well—I am not the one who spent the afternoon in a tête-à-tête with my former lover. My conscience has nothing to feel guilty about."

"What would you have had me do?" Lucy asked. "She wasn't going to stop until she had an answer. Pris is a downright barnacle when she's fixed her mind on something."

"You might have written her a letter."

Lucy looked away, the burn of brandy and the bite of lemon making her throat ache. "You might have demanded to read anything I sent to her."

Catherine made a small noise in the back of her throat, looking stricken. "I am so sorry about that. It will never happen again," she said calmly. Too calmly. As if she expected to be forgiven. "I was just trying to protect you."

Lucy was sick of apologies; this one stung her into movement. She flung the stellarium shawl aside and stalked the library, her angry steps taking her from the sofa to the fireplace, to the window, and back to complete the triangle. It gave some vent to her feelings, but not enough. "Pris always thought I was her satellite," she said. "I could only ever orbit around her. She never believed I would choose a path for myself."

"Ah." Catherine sighed, a long, low sound that tolled like a funeral bell. "You value your independence. It's only natural."

"I value my choices," Lucy countered. "And I value people

who respect them. Stephen never did, Pris never did—nobody, really." She stopped, and turned to face the countess. "Until you. You trusted me to find my own way, even if where I was going didn't look likely or even possible to get to." Something warm trickled in and washed away some of the hurt. "And now you're forging a new path of your own. Different from mine."

"It doesn't have to be," Catherine countered. "We could arrange something . . . something permanent."

The word *permanent* crashed through Lucy like a rock through a window, leaving only a gaping, jagged-edged hole where there once had been rainbowed glass. "What?"

"I'm not sure what to call it, but . . . The solicitors would know. We could—we could arrange for you to have an allowance, perhaps—or I could see if it was possible to make you the heir to the earldom—"

"I don't want to be beholden to you!"

The shout rang off the bookshelves in George's library.

Catherine snapped her mouth shut, her face sickly pale.

Lucy fought to regain her self-control. All she could do was hold her tongue, before she said something else she'd regret.

Catherine looked so small suddenly: shoulders curled in, hands clenched tight, everything about her attempting to take up as little space as possible while ominous shadows gathered in the corners of the library. "I only wanted to take care of you. You had so little when you came to London," the countess said. "It didn't seem safe to send you back out into the city alone. That's why I invited you to stay."

Shame was a black tide, rising up to lap at Lucy's heart. "You kept me out of charity."

"You don't need charity anymore." Catherine's gaze was down now, her fingers clasped so tight they threatened to crack like overstressed porcelain. She might have been the very picture of wifely propriety—just as cold and untouchable as Pris had accused her of being.

Lucy felt her unspoken hopes wink out, one by one, like stars being covered by a cloud, as Catherine's careful sentences went on and on. "You could easily find a home of your own. Somewhere closer to the College, perhaps—or even out in the country. Better for observations, after all."

"Catherine . . ."

At the sound of her name, the countess's eyes flicked up, just for a moment—but then she dropped her gaze again.

Lucy felt as though she'd gone from noon to midnight in the space of a heartbeat. A dark chill passed over her. "Do you not see a future for us?" Lucy asked.

Catherine's shoulders rose and fell, the smallest shrug Lucy had ever seen. So slight a gesture to strike Lucy's heart so heavily. Her expression was smooth, untroubled. Unmoved. "How can there be a future? We are on different paths—different orbits, you might say. Your star is science, and mine is—well, mine has yet to be named. Art, or something close to it. A different sort of labor entirely from yours."

"Don't we both search for truth?" Lucy whispered.

"Two different truths," Catherine murmured in reply. "Two different lives. I would never dream of asking you to deviate from that course in even the smallest particular."

Lucy heard this, and knew Catherine meant well, but her fears translated it into other words from another time, another love: *I can't marry you.* She'd felt hurt then, and abandoned. She felt all that pain again now. But worse—oh, how much worse—because she knew she lost something greater this time than she ever had before in her life.

Her father's death was the only grief to equal it. Both he and Catherine had helped her find her vocation as an astronomer; how cruel of the world to take them both away. Lucy must have been greedy, because she wanted too much: she wanted science, of course—but she wanted Catherine, too, in all her beauty and her worry and her soft, stalwart steadiness.

But Catherine didn't want to be wanted like that. Lucy could see clearly now that she was pulling away, drawing into herself, hunkering down against the oncoming storm. She'd been doing it since Pris's letter yesterday.

All Lucy could do was give Catherine what she wanted. Anything else would be selfish. Lady Moth deserved to be put first, for once in her life. Even if it broke Lucy's heart to do it.

If Catherine wanted Lucy to leave, Lucy would yield.

"I will ask Mr. Frampton if he knows of any suitable lodgings near his," Lucy said. "He and I are planning to meet this evening for Mr. Edwards's lecture."

Catherine rose. "I shall arrange for an early dinner, if you like."

Lucy shook her head. She doubted she could eat, with so much anguish churning about inside of her. "I'll find something near the College." She gathered up the stellarium shawl, folding it into a square. Neat, precise, mathematical. Tidy.

Undemanding.

Catherine still sat there, statue-stiff, as Lucy walked slowly toward her. She was selfish enough—weak enough—to want one final kiss before the end. "I may be out rather late, so I will say my good-night now."

She bent down but turned coward at the last minute. Instead of claiming the countess's mouth, Lucy's lips brushed lightly over Catherine's cheek—a kiss like a moth, a nighttime creature, trembling and sad and not destined to live long.

Catherine made no move to respond; not a sound emerged from those rosy lips pressed so tightly against one another.

The last whole pane of Lucy's heart cracked straight across as the library door clicked shut behind her.

Chapter Fourteen

Lucy arrived at the College building shamefully early—the only benefit of skipping an unwanted dinner—and decided to stop by Mr. Edwards's laboratory before the lecture began. It would be quieter place to wait than in the auditorium crowd, and there was a chance that Mrs. Edwards would be there, with her kind smile and sympathetic heart. Lucy felt in desperate need of someone to guide her through the fog until her own heart was once again up to the task.

She would navigate by someone else's star, until her own shone clear again.

She'd been to the laboratory once before, with Catherine, for a private demonstration, and had no trouble finding it now. Students, scholars, and amateurs alike crowded the halls, talking ceaselessly with a roar like a dry ocean.

It was only on the third or so turn down the corridors that Lucy began to realize something strange was happening. She caught odd sounds of snickering, and excited murmurs—but whenever she turned to look, the speakers averted their eyes and abruptly ceased talking until she'd passed.

Surely her being here alone wasn't so much of a scandal as that? She was relieved when she finally pushed open Mr. Edwards's door, and could take refuge.

The curtains on the tall windows were drawn back, and the wan autumn light flowed in and caught on the smooth curves of glassware. Elements and metals and substances of all kinds and colors were arranged precisely on the shelves— some in liquid form, some stacked or wrapped in paper, some carefully corked to preserve visitors from deadly fumes. The ghosts of past experiments seemed to haunt the air: faint, tantalizing scents of metal and fire and sulfur. Mr. Edwards himself was standing bent over the large central desk, staring intently at the papers in his hands as though they held the key to the workings of the universe. Which perhaps they did.

Lucy approached softly, hoping not to startle the other scientist out of his concentration. But when he looked up at her soft cough, his face went from intent and thoughtful to outright dismay.

Dread rang alarms on Lucy's every nerve.

"Miss Muchelney," he said. "I did not expect to see you this evening."

"I am meeting Mr. Frampton to hear your latest thoughts on electrochemistry," she replied. "Has something happened?"

His dismay grew, the pain in his dark eyes and mobile mouth abundantly plain. "Then you haven't seen it?"

Lucy shook her head, and without another moment's delay he handed over what he'd been reading.

It was the latest issue of *Polite Philosophies*, dated only two days before. The most significant letter in the President's estimation always opened the issue, and this one was no different. The headline was bold and stark in large type at the top: *On the Likelihood of Miss Muchelney's Translation.*

And then in smaller letters: *An enquiry into the possibility of an earlier draft of CELESTIAL MECHANICS by Albert Muchelney, FPSS.*

The author: Richard Wilby. With the same set of letters after his name: FPSS. Fellow of the Polite Science Society.

Lucy looked up from the hideous page. "So they have officially voted him in."

Mr. Edwards nodded.

Lucy's hand shook, rattling the paper. She set it down hastily, appalled to be so transparent in her feelings. "And he is proclaiming me an imposter."

"Yes," Mr. Edwards confirmed. "It's not true, of course." His tone brooked no doubt, but his eyes . . .

Lucy almost cried out at the pity in those dark eyes. Mr. Edwards had been a Fellow long enough to know how poisonous a well-connected enemy could be. He knew just how this essay would blight Lucy's future as a scholar. How the taint of suspicion would follow her through every theory and discovery and proof, for the rest of her life and even perhaps beyond. She wasn't a Fellow, and had no official standing to counter the accusations leveled against her in the same forums where they'd been made. The theory was now a part of official Society record, and no counterargument would be enough to banish its effects. It would be like trying to empty

a forest of snakes, one at a time: there would always be another one somewhere else, slithering silently through the
underbrush—and the venom from the first would never be
wholly expunged.

It was the ruin of everything.

Mr. Edwards said something else, but Lucy didn't hear
him. She took a step back, then another, then turned and
flung open the door.

The mix of horror and fiendish joy she saw in everyone's
faces didn't puzzle her any longer: people always flocked to
the shore when there was a shipwreck to watch.

She ran around one corner—and the world kept spinning, her senses whirling and her head feeling like it was
about to separate from her shoulders and float away high into
the leaden sky . . .

She paused and leaned against a wall, shutting her
eyes until the dizziness passed. It had been a mistake to
skip dinner—worse than she'd anticipated. Her stomach
churned, her pulse hammered in her ears, and everywhere
around her was the sound of mocking, hateful laughter . . .

A hand on her elbow: a person, touching her gently.
She cracked open her eyes to see Mr. Frampton there, his
brow thunderous even as his mouth was pinched in sorrow.
"Are you alright, Miss Muchelney?" he said softly. "Can you
stand?"

Lucy nodded, gulping the air and pressing one hand to
her stomach until the world came into focus again. "Mr. Edwards showed me the letter."

She didn't have to explain further; Mr. Frampton simply

nodded and watched her closely, his eyes occasionally flicking to one side or another. With every person who passed, his face grew more and more steely. "There's something else I have to tell you," he said. "I spoke to Mr. Hawley yesterday."

"He won't print a retraction," Lucy warned. "I've wounded his pride too often."

"I wasn't asking him for a retraction," the mathematician replied. "I went to learn his answer about a request I made last week."

Lucy shook her head, too worn out for puzzles. "What was it?"

"I asked him to invite Oléron to the Symposium."

"What?" Lucy's involuntary outburst caused a momentary dip in the volume of chatter around her; she schooled her face and tried to mask her distress.

Mr. Frampton kept his face equally stoic. "I suggested Mr. Hawley might want to put Oléron's name forward as an official Foreign Member—and then invite Oléron to lecture at this year's Symposium."

"But . . . how does this concern me?" The Symposium was the dinner held for Society Fellows every winter, just after Christmas. Often a particular topic was selected for lecture or discussion, but it usually just devolved into a passionate, overstuffed, and very wine-soaked argument. Lucy's father's health had prevented him from attending, and Lucy herself of course had never been invited.

"You will surely receive an invitation," Mr. Frampton clarified, "if Mr. Hawley thinks he can get Oléron to debate you on the finer points of celestial mathematics."

"To debate . . ." Lucy yanked away, her jaw gaping open with horror. "How could you, Mr. Frampton? That's not a debate: it's a trap."

She could see it so clearly: the hall, the rowdy audience of doubting men, the laughing scorn, the smug look on Mr. Hawley's face. She swayed, and yanked her arm away again as Mr. Frampton reached out to steady her.

Fury was an anchor in the swirling storm: she turned it on him in spite of her better instincts. "I shouldn't have to perform like a dancing bear. My work should be proof enough on its own."

"Your work," he said, "is not entirely yours."

Lucy stopped short.

Mr. Frampton continued, inexorable. "It would be one thing if you'd translated the *Méchanique céleste* for the benefit of your fellow scholars. The more we share, the faster we all advance. But it was a commercial success, far beyond any expectation." His mouth was a flat line by now, his displeasure plain. "The more popular it got, the more uneasy I became with the notion that the original author had no idea your translation existed."

"So you sent it to him," Lucy whispered.

"I did." His eyes gleamed, and he leaned in again.

This time Lucy waited, though her brow furrowed in hurt.

He spoke low so there was no chance he'd be overhead. "And M. Oléron wrote back. We've been corresponding for months, now—and on account of this, I know something Mr. Hawley does not. Something about M. Oléron." Mr. Frampton tilted his head, considering his facts like any careful scientist. "Or more accurately, I have a hypothesis. But a dazzling one—and if I am right, it will make Mr. Hawley and Mr. Wilby look more foolish than either of us could ever have dreamed."

"And what about me?" Lucy all but whispered. "How foolish will I look?"

"That depends." Mr. Frampton raised an eyebrow. "How hard is it for you to admit when you've been wrong?"

Lucy's heart was treacherous, and supplied someone else's words as an answer: "Astronomers spend most of their lives being wrong." She bit her lip and took a breath. "You were right: I ought to have written to M. Oléron myself."

"Thank you. Though if you had, I would have missed out on a marvelous correspondence." Mr. Frampton squeezed her hand one final time, and bowed. "Can I convince you to let me escort you back home, or at least to your coach? I can't imagine you feel up to electrochemistry after such a shock as this."

Lucy took another breath. "No. I don't—thank you." She took his arm, grateful for the way he never wavered, no matter how many sly and stormy looks were sent their way as they wound through the curious crowds of naturalists and amateurs.

Every step, every glance seemed to add another worry to the heap.

Lucy grimaced. "I should begin going over the rest of Oléron's work—not to mention the rest of the literature. Three months is not a great deal of time in which to master a subject."

She nodded at one brave soul who'd gone out of his way to bow to her as she passed, even though his companions looked daggers at him for doing it.

They turned another corner, and Lucy's musings offered up a question. "What precisely did you mean when you say you have a theory about Oléron?"

"It was something that came up in the third letter. I feel . . . reasonably confident my suspicions are correct."

Lucy narrowed her eyes. "But not quite confident enough to tell me what they are?"

He sighed. "If I am right, it puts Oléron in a position that is at best awkward, at worst horribly vulnerable, with respect to the Society. They've already done most of the harm they can to you—I am trying to help correct that, without opening anyone else up to similar abuse. It is a very fine line to have to walk, I admit."

Lucy attempted to decode this, then gave up with a shrug and a sigh. "You are more cryptic in person than in any of your papers, Mr. Frampton. Unusual in a mathematician."

One corner of his mouth quirked up, wry and acknowledging. "I do my best."

They reached the sidewalk outside, and Mr. Frampton helped Lucy up into the countess's carriage. "Until next week, Miss Muchelney."

He bowed solemnly and stepped back as the horses leaped under the whip, dragging Lucy forward into the future.

She sat back and let herself sway with the motion of the coach. Three months. That's all the time she had—to read everything old, everything new, and everything she'd missed the first go around. The rest of Oléron's volumes on gravitation, obviously. Astronomy, mathematics, physical science—plus chemistry and the other natural sciences, if she could manage it. There was no question now about finding new lodging: she would need every spare minute if she hoped to offer an adequate defense of her translation and expansion, against the author himself.

She would need Catherine's library.

It would gall her to have to ask—and to explain the reason why—but even at this highest pinnacle of despair, Lucy knew Catherine would agree. It was not in the countess's nature to be cruel, or to enjoy someone's suffering. Lucy would spend her days in the library, and Catherine would work separately in the parlor; they might meet for dinner, or they might not. In some ways that sounded even lonelier than finding a new lodging of her own: everywhere she looked she'd be haunted by happier memories.

Nobody deserved to have their heart broken twice in the span of a single year.

Tears sprang to the corners of her eyes, but a moment later she sat up and dashed them away again. She had no time to be maudlin. Until the Symposium, she would give herself the gift of not thinking much about anything else. She would focus on the work, and not fear for how much she was about to lose.

Catherine still couldn't sleep, even though the church bells had already tolled midnight. Her pulse pounded in her ears, her temples throbbed, and her heart beat erratically in her chest. It was a long few minutes before she realized: not all the pulsing she felt was the monstrous misery hammering against her veins.

Some of the pounding was coming from the library.

She lit a lamp, tugged on a dressing gown, and padded down the hall. As she grew closer, other, more unmistakably human sounds made themselves apparent: the squeak of the library ladder, the muffled percussion of footprints, and a low, angry muttering that had the unmistakable vehement quality of someone heartily swearing.

It had to be Lucy. Nobody else would be in the library this late. And she sounded bloody furious.

The countess froze with her hand on the doorknob as moments of years past speared her with sharp familiarity. How many times had she done precisely this? Stood here outside the looming double doors, while an irate scientist who no longer loved her raged in a mounting temper? This had been her life, when George was alive and they were not on expedition somewhere. She was just as hurt and unhappy now as she'd been before.

What she wasn't, was afraid.

It was such an astonishing, irrefutable truth that Catherine had to stand there and turn it over a time or two, marveling at it. She was not afraid. It was a minor miracle. Oh, she wasn't eager to open the door and confront Lucy again; the pain of their last conversation was still raw and tender. But the poisonous dread, the shame, the sick sense of danger she'd let silence her for years in her marriage . . . she felt none of that.

A pall that had been cast over her for years—even after

George's death, during her ill-fated first affair—had somehow, in the past few months, slipped softly into nothingness while her attention had been elsewhere.

Had Lucy done it? Or had Catherine done it herself without realizing?

Another thump from the library broke through her reverie. Catherine pushed open the door before she could talk herself out of it and stepped into the darkened room beyond.

A single lamp was turned up as high as it could go, casting a bright but flickering light and making the furniture loom and hunch like Gothic gargoyles. Lucy was high on the ladder, still dressed in the gown she'd worn out this evening. The stellarium shawl was wound around her neck with its ends thrown back across her shoulders like a general's cloak, as she plucked a volume from the shelves that held the archives of *Polite Philosophies*. The collection was a complete archive of every issue since the first year of the Society's formation: George had been thorough and had them bound specially in black and gilt. Lucy had worked her way back several decades at this point: as Catherine watched curiously, she pulled one bound book from the shelf, skimmed the first few pages, muttered at what she saw, and dropped the book to the floor. It landed with a thunk on top of a pile of other volumes, spines broken and pages splayed like scattered corpses in a heap.

Catherine didn't call out, for fear of startling Lucy right off the ladder. Instead she moved carefully forward to the table and set her own lamp next to Lucy's. Turning up the wick brightened the room just enough to be noticeable, and made Lucy blink and twist around to peer down over her shoulder.

Catherine was too curious to be tactful. "What on earth are you up to at this hour?"

Lucy came down the ladder fast enough to make Catherine's heart lurch up into her throat. The astronomer's face was fierce as she began scooping up fallen books. "I am rediscovering lost geniuses."

Catherine shook her head and began helping, moving a few more books to where Lucy was stacking them on the library table. "I don't understand."

Lucy's eyes flashed, her jaw clenched so tight Catherine imagined she could hear her teeth grinding. "I thought I was the only one." Lucy pulled out one volume and flipped to the front section—the bit where letters in reply were printed, naturalists and chemists and botanists and such writing in to offer their thoughts on the previous issue's hypotheses. "Look, right there, see? *Mrs.* Jonathan Corwen, Kent. And here." She pulled out another volume. "*Miss* Annabelle Barber, Sussex, 1789. And there's more, so many more, once you know to look for them. Hiding behind initials and their husbands' names." She tossed the book onto the table; it slipped and slid and bumped up against Catherine's lamp. "Half the comets discovered in the last century were first observed by Mr. Hawley's *sister*—did you know that?"

"I didn't," Catherine replied, and subtly moved the dry, old book away from the hot glass and flame. "And nobody told you?"

Lucy flung one arm wide to indicate the towering bookfilled shelves around them. "I thought they were all *men*!"

Anguish silvered her eyes and twisted her lips; it was all Catherine could do not to reach out to hold her for comfort.

"I believed I was the first woman to really try and advance the progress of astronomy—I fancied myself a brave pioneer, an explorer like you once were. A shining beacon to girls and women of the future. It was a great comfort, whenever people like Mr. Hawley and Mr. Wilby offered insults and dismissals. All I had to do to claim victory was to prove them wrong—and don't men of science value proof more than anything? Once people saw what I did, really saw it and acknowledged it, they'd believe other women were capable of thinking, of learning, of discovering the world in the same way that men are. But tonight I learned that there were other women before me. So very, very many of them. They were here *all along*: spotting comets, naming stars, pointing telescopes at the sky alongside their fathers and brothers and sons. And *still* the men they worked with scorned them. Scoffed at them. Gave the credit and the glory to the men who *stole* their work—or borrowed it or expanded it. Rarely cited it directly. And then those men did their best to forget where the work came from. Women's ideas are treated as though they sprung from nowhere, to be claimed by the first man who comes along. Every generation had women stand up and ask to be counted—and every generation of brilliant, insightful, educated men has raised a hand and wiped those women's names from the greater historical record."

She slapped a hand down on top of the stack of *Polite Philosophies*, the sharp sound making Catherine wince.

"I am going through the archives and finding every single one of those women. I am writing to those who still live and asking them if they've kept experimenting, still observing, still collecting specimens in their field. I am going to make sure *someone* remembers these women and their work, even if it is only myself." She broke off, chest heaving on something that was almost a sob. Her voice dropped to a whisper, as if she were confessing her greatest, most agonizing secret: "Because I am sick to death of feeling alone."

"You never have to feel alone."

Lucy's eyes snapped wide at Catherine's whispered response. She caught her breath and turned toward the countess with questions written plain on her face.

There were rare moments, Catherine knew, where even the steadiest compass could shift. Bring a magnet too close to one and it would twist around to point to the magnet instead of true north; sailors told strange stories of high and icy latitudes where compasses would spin and wobble like the legs of drunken men. For some months now Catherine had felt her own internal compass spinning helplessly as the terrain beneath her shape-shifted.

But the needle had stopped spinning now: stone-steady, iron-true, and fixed irrevocably on Lucy Muchelney. "I remember what you wrote," Catherine said. "Nothing in the universe stands alone. Everything is connected—in real, mathematical, *provable* ways—across the span of the entire cosmos. As long as we live, we influence one another. You and these women you've rediscovered . . . but also you and me. I was wrong to ask you to leave. To say there could be nothing permanent between us. We're already forever." Catherine reached out a hand and slid her lamp over to blaze beside Lucy's, tapping the metal base with a deliberate finger. "We thought we were separate satellites, but we aren't. We're stars, and though we might burn separately, we'll always be in one another's orbit."

The book Lucy was holding slipped from her hands and thunked softly to the floor. "I was only leaving because I thought it's what you wanted," she said. A single silver tear spilled over and slipped sparkling down her cheek.

"I want you," Catherine whispered, and opened her arms.

Lucy dove at her, her tall, slim body slamming into Catherine's sturdier form, while her mouth opened desperately against the countess's lips. It was a hard, harsh kiss, born of fear and flame, and it seared into ash everything that had come between them.

Catherine gave over to it entirely as she buried her fingers in Lucy's hair and kissed her and kissed her and kissed her until she could no longer taste the salt of Lucy's tears.

It was only when Lucy's nails scraped Catherine's collarbone and she gasped aloud that she realized Lucy had been swiftly, determinedly untying and unbuttoning and shoving aside as much as she could of Catherine's clothing. The countess freed her hands to shrug hurriedly out of the dressing gown as Lucy's fingers dove further into the opened neck of her nightdress, pinching her nipples and pushing the fabric down to bare one shoulder. Lucy nipped newly revealed skin while Catherine moaned and let her head fall back; the dressing gown clutched in Lucy's other hand made a useful lever for her to pull Catherine down to the thick library rug.

Everything was limbs and quickening breath and the tangle of fabric, too much to strip easily in their haste. Lucy pulled away to lean over Catherine, her bodice gaping and her hair a tangle, lamplight from the table above giving her a martyr's halo as her panting breath swirled hot against Catherine's skin. "Tell me what you need," she demanded. "Anything. All of me. It's yours for the asking."

"I want . . ." Catherine began, but couldn't even wait long enough to finish the sentence. Instead she wrapped an arm around Lucy's shoulders and pulled her down for another kiss. Catherine's other hand yanked up yards of expensive, fashionable skirts with expert embroidery that the countess felt snag and pull beneath her hasty fingers. She swore to repair it with her own needle tomorrow morning.

But tomorrow morning was an age away.

Tonight there was only the woman above and the woman below, setting one another aflame.

It had been less than a day since Lucy had kissed her farewell so solemnly. Less than three since they'd last shared a bed. But it felt as though Catherine had lived a whole, empty, lonely life in that short stretch of time. Decades waiting to press Lucy's slim hip in her palm again, unseen but solid beneath the tumble of petticoats and skirts. Centuries until she could lick the sweet spot at the base of Lucy's throat, her bodice and stays spread wide as a rose in summer and her breasts rising and falling beneath her chemise as she begged for more. And a star's lifespan until Catherine could move lower and tongue the wet, hot folds between Lucy's legs, her senses dizzied by the scents of sweat and linen and musk, until Lucy cried out and shivered with the force of her need. Catherine used everything she'd learned about curling her fingers just *so*, and pressing up firmly with the angled heel of her hand, all while she licked and sucked and tongued relentlessly until Lucy broke and came with a soft sound almost like a sob.

Catherine kept going, fingers sliding through the sweet slickness and heat, until Lucy pulled back.

Strong fingers curled around Catherine's wrist, and silver eyes afire with resolve blazed against the darkness. "Bedroom. Now," she growled, and Catherine thrilled at the urgency, her pulse beating a hot and hasty tattoo.

Never had Catherine been so grateful her bedroom was close to the library. They extinguished one of the lamps and took the other with them down the hallway, mussed and heated and panting. Lucy's grip on Catherine's wrist never slackened until the door was shut behind them, and then she began stripping herself and Catherine of clothing so methodically that it made Catherine tremble. There was a fervency she hadn't seen before, a desperation that reminded her of some of the darker moments of her past.

She sucked in a breath on a shiver as her nightdress fluttered to the floor like a ghostly maiden, dead of a broken heart.

Lucy turned to face her and tilted her head, eyes glinting in the dimness. Her voice was harsh, though she spoke low. "Afraid, my love?"

Catherine swallowed. "A little. But I like it."

Lucy hummed satisfaction in the back of her throat. Gripping Catherine's shoulders, she walked her back until the older woman came up hard against the bedpost. Strong hands slid up Catherine's arms, pulling her hands high above her head. Lucy clasped her hands in place, twining them around carven oak. "Don't move unless I say," she said, and bit Catherine's earlobe.

Catherine let out a soft wordless cry, then nodded.

Lucy murmured approval, nudged Catherine's feet slightly apart, and proceeded to drive Catherine nearly out of her skin with pleasure. Lucy's hands were everywhere, sliding and teasing, every caress a prelude to the heat and slickness of that generous, tormenting mouth. Catherine gripped the wood of the bedpost until she feared it might crack, eagerly following Lucy's every whispered command: *this way, a little more, hold still, don't you dare come yet.* Moonlight silvered the long line of Lucy's back as she sank to her knees—not submissively, as one conquered, but as a queen kneels at a coronation.

Catherine was wound so tight with it all that she nearly tumbled over the edge into climax when she felt Lucy's sigh blow hot over the aching flesh between her legs. She let out a warning noise, barely more than a throaty squeak, and heard Lucy's knowing laugh unroll like velvet in the darkness. "Just a little more, love."

She trailed one hand languidly up Catherine's plump thigh, nudged her open a little wider, and slid a single finger inside her.

Catherine's head dropped back as Lucy thrust—one finger, then two. Then, while her tongue slid hot and hard against the nub buried in softly curling hair, a third. Catherine gasped as she *stretched*—more than she'd ever taken, a fit so tight it was almost like pain—but a good pain, one that sharpened every one of her senses and slid through her bright and cold as starlight as she teetered on the brink, panting as though she perched wavering on a high peak, about to step off solid rock and into the vast, welcoming nothingness beyond.

"Now," Lucy murmured, half demand and half promise. She gripped Catherine's hip to hold her in place, gave one more wicked flick of her tongue, and thrust hard with all three fingers.

Catherine exploded into orgasm with a wild, half-desperate keening. Every muscle seized and throbbed as brilliance tore through her, a flood of light and scintillation and sweet, sparkling relief. She clenched so tight around Lucy's hand that Lucy had to stop moving—a pleased murmur vibrated from Lucy's mouth into Catherine's flesh and sent her tumbling into another endless climax.

At length, as the waves faded and the world came slipping back, Lucy eased herself free and Catherine collapsed into her arms, knees weak and thighs aching with exertion. They stayed that way as Catherine's frantic breathing slowed, Lucy's tall form a bulwark against the inward storm.

Catherine's mind was as slow to recover as her body. This had been . . . different. Darker, very close in some ways to the kind of things she'd done with, and for, Darby. But oh, how much better it was to give in to someone you loved, someone you trusted. Someone who cared what you wanted. She nuzzled into the crook of Lucy's neck and kissed the sweat-salted skin there, feeling immeasurably grateful and pleasured and happy.

Loved. That was the word she was looking for. She felt loved.

CHAPTER FIFTEEN

The full and fragile teacup slipped from the countess's hand and crashed to the breakfast table in a shower of porcelain shards. "They did *what?!*"

"Catherine!" Lucy gasped in shock. She reached out to the mess of spilled tea and cream and sugar and plucked out the lizard handle, which had broken off from the bowl. The bowl itself was unsalvageable, its elegant curves now resting in several jagged pieces on the tea tray.

Catherine wanted to use them to slice all Mr. Hawley's precious flytraps into thin green ribbons. Which she would then brew into a noxious tea and pour down the treacherous throat of Mr. Wilby, who was at least as much to blame as the Society president. The shock of it made her light-headed. "An imposter?" she hissed. "Because you refused to let them scribble their names on a manuscript you did all the work of translating?"

Lucy set the poor lizard on a saucer. "Give me that before you break it, too," she said, and tugged the serpent teapot from the countess's tight-clenched fingers. While Catherine scowled and stewed, she added cream and sugar to another teacup and set it carefully in front of the countess. "It was cruel, but unsurprising. I was more hurt by Mr. Frampton's apparently joining in with them."

Catherine glared into her tea, wanting the scalding feel of it on her throat but not yet feeling civilized enough to pick up the delicate cup. "I shall have some choice words for him when next he dares show his face."

"He claims he has a plan." Lucy sipped thirstily at her tea, steam curling dragonish around her.

"I'm sure he does. But will it work?"

Lucy shrugged. "I have to assume it won't, and brace myself for the worst." She outlined the preparations she would undertake, all the reading she would do in advance of the Symposium. Catherine listened with half an ear as her mind raced a million miles ahead.

The crux was this: she didn't just want to help Lucy through a single crisis, howsoever significant it was. She wanted to offer Lucy something that would last for the rest of their lives.

This, Catherine thought, was why brides came with dowries: it was something concrete and immediate to offer a spouse, something more than beauty or bloodlines or the ephemeral possibility of an heir. You couldn't eat bloodlines, after all. Children might never result, either—or they might all be daughters, unable to inherit or to carry on a family name.

Money, though—money was practical. You could do a lot with it. You could even do nothing, and it would still be useful: having ready wealth was never a bad guard against the vagaries of chance and crisis. Lucy had some money, now—what if

Catherine offered her more of that? As something like a dowry, to connect them for the future?

No. That wasn't quite right. Lucy didn't want money from Catherine; she'd reacted badly the last time Catherine had offered it. What Lucy wanted was marriage: a permanent connection, something legal and public and celebratory . . .

After breakfast, Lucy decamped to the library and set to work. So, in rather a different way, did Catherine. Since there was nothing Catherine could do to help Lucy with the Symposium itself, she would help with absolutely everything else.

First thing was to write to Aunt Kelmarsh and invite her to stay for Christmas. It looked to be a particularly frigid one. Catherine would feel more at ease if her aunt were close and cozy during the coming months. She also had some questions to pose to her aunt about women naturalists from her mother's generation . . .

Then, since she was already at her writing desk, she composed a letter to Miss Annabelle Barber of Sussex. Who may or may not still reside at the same address. Who may or may not have married or died or otherwise vanished from reach in the decades since her letter was published in *Polite Philosophies*.

But at least it was somewhere to start.

That day set the tempo for the autumn and early winter: Lucy finished reading the rest of Oléron's oeuvre, and Catherine turned George's bedroom into a proper guest suite for Aunt Kelmarsh. Lucy invited Mr. Edwards to instruct her about electrochemistry, and Catherine refined her embroidery designs for publication while Mrs. Edwards read aloud from her latest novel. Word came that the Society had voted overwhelmingly in favor of admitting Oléron as a Foreign Member. Lucy and Mr. Frampton went out and bought a whole shelf's worth of new mathematical texts, while Catherine snuck (rather guiltily) into the library and combed the archives of *Polite Philosophies* for more women's names and addresses.

Eventually the replies began trickling in: who had died, who had married, who had given up science at the demands of family and friends, who were still pursuing experiments and lines of inquiry and collecting specimens. An astonishing number of these last women had taken to writing children's schoolbooks on their chosen subject. Catherine began to keep files on what she learned, and as the weeks passed, an idea began to take shape, a great and glorious Something that she initially categorized as an auxiliary in case the Symposium brought disaster for Lucy, but that soon came to loom even larger in Catherine's strategic mind. Larger than anything she'd done before.

Something that would take a lifetime to accomplish.

This almost-plan helped Catherine not to fret herself to pieces as she watched the dark circles flower beneath Lucy's eyes, or the worried twist to her mouth that became more and more habitual as the weeks spun by. The closer the Symposium came, the later Lucy stayed in the library each day. Her restlessness proved contagious, and Catherine cast about for ways to keep her hands busy and her mind from going over the same unchanging fears time and time again. She found comfort where she always had: in needle and thread and the careful process of stitching into fabric, one tiny bit at a time.

She couldn't help Lucy in the actual battle—but she could make sure she didn't go unarmored into the field.

Chapter Sixteen

The day of the Symposium dawned clear and cold, with a frost sheening over everything in the garden. Lucy stared out at silver-edged leaves and icy wrought iron and resonated with the frozen fixity of it all. Her anxiety had crystallized overnight into something hard and clear and seemingly calm, but that smooth facade was a thin and brittle shell overlying a universe of panic.

She feared it would only take one blow to shatter her completely.

Catherine slipped up behind to embrace her, nuzzling her face into Lucy's shoulder. Lucy grasped the arms that twined around her waist and leaned cravingly back into the countess's warmth. "Good morning." Catherine yawned.

"Morning," Lucy echoed, unthawed.

"Time to get dressed—unless you want to sleep longer?"

"Sleep is for the comfortable. I am anything but." A horrid revelation struck Lucy, a sidelong slap in the face that she'd have seen coming if she hadn't had her gaze so focused on the goal ahead. "Oh, lord, Catherine—what am I going to wear?" The gold gown was her finest, but entirely wrong for the occasion: it was too decadent, too luxurious to wear to address a group of motley and indifferently garbed scholars. She'd look like a brothel mistress among a collection of churchmen.

Catherine's laugh was sleep-tinged and knowing; Lucy melted a little to hear it, and turned in the countess's arms. The shorter woman grinned up at her, all slyness and soft flesh and tousled curls. "Don't fret about that," she said. "I've been working on something."

She led Lucy over to the wardrobe and pulled out a dress wrapped in tissue, which Lucy in her fixation had managed not to notice before. Slowly, Catherine laid the bundle on the chaise and peeled the paper away.

A velvet gown in rich blue-green, with accents of soft gold. Simpler than many of Catherine's other designs—but the more Lucy looked at it, the more she liked it. The heavy velvet gave weight to the skirt, while a spray of delicate rays stitched in gold thread fanned out around the bodice. They looked like the lines of illumination you'd see in an engraving surrounding a candle: slim, dotted beams of light that winked within the high pile of the velvet. The shimmering pattern caught the gaze and directed attention inexorably upward, toward the wearer's face.

Lucy knew exactly how she'd feel as soon as she put it on: feminine, warm, and elegant. Strong, but not forbidding, not aggressive. It was a design that spoke of precision without being in the least cold. It was absolutely, beautifully the right thing for a lady astronomer to wear if she planned to dazzle a roomful of suspicious men.

"Do you like it?" Catherine asked, still standing beside the chaise, her hands clasped anxiously behind her.

"It is perfect. You are perfect." Lucy turned and kissed her, as a tiny light like a candle flame flickered into life within her icy heart. Catherine sighed into Lucy's mouth and the countess's whole body relaxed. She had been more tense than Lucy realized.

Regret assailed her: she'd been so focused on what this night meant for her, that she'd quite ignored how Catherine had been feeling about all of this. Lucy gripped the countess's shoulders as her anxiousness shifted focus. "Are you worried about tonight?"

"Not at all." Catherine's rosebud smile bloomed fully, and as always Lucy's breath caught to see it. "I have every faith in you."

So simple a thing to say, and so powerful when said in earnest. Lucy's heart sounded like a bell, setting her whole body ringing. She rested her forehead against Catherine's and simply stood there, breathing her in.

No matter what happened tonight, at the end of it she would have this beautiful, stalwart, thoughtful, fierce woman by her side.

Tonight could still ruin her reputation among men of science, but it would not take Catherine from her. She would be left with something after all of this was through. And the mathematics were clear: something was infinitely more than nothing.

Her hands might still shake and her head might still be spinning, but for the first time in months she could glimpse a future beyond this evening's events.

She managed a good breakfast and buttered toast at tea, but by the time Narayan helped button up the blue-green velvet, she was feeling chilled through again. Her appetite had given way to a hollow, twisting feeling that made her feel skittish as a bird on the verge of startling. Long white gloves and a thick cream shawl did nothing to banish the shivers, but she had expected nothing less. She tried to take deep breaths and calm herself. This was just a more intensified version of the nerves she'd suffered from every exam period at Cramlington, she told herself. She always fretted right up until she started answering questions. This would be no different.

If she repeated it often enough, maybe it would prove prophetic.

The carriage was brought round in due course. Catherine and Aunt Kelmarsh conspired to hold a restful silence the whole way to Somerset House. Lucy clenched her hands in her lap until the knuckles creaked, and concentrated on not being sick out the carriage window.

The Polite Science Society had the use of a set of offices in Somerset House, and the Symposium was always held in the portico rooms overlooking the terrace on the riverside. The three made their way across the courtyard—the same route Lucy and Catherine had walked six short months ago for the Summer Exhibition. But there were no daylight throngs of visitors now, no chattering artists or painted glory or vivid sunset scenes. There was only one or two hurrying figures in the lamplight, muffled up against the cold, and above it all the tall, glacial face of the building, its classical columns looming like prison bars, or the teeth of some prim but ravenous predator.

Catherine tucked her hand into the crook of Lucy's arm and squeezed for support. Lucy, grateful and somewhat beyond speech, squeezed back.

They found Mr. Frampton waiting at the base of the sinuous stairs—and he wasn't alone.

His face lit up when he saw them approach, and he straightened his shoulders with evident excitement and pride. "I am so glad you are prompt," he said, and turned to his companion. "Madame la marquise, may I introduce Lady Moth, Mrs. Kelmarsh, and Miss Muchelney? My lady, Mrs. Kelmarsh, Miss Muchelney—I am honored to present you to Gervaise Marie Oléron, Marquise de Lantier."

Aunt Kelmarsh's head snapped up in surprise. Catherine let out the tiniest of gasps, barely more than a breath. The lady being introduced stepped forward: she was clad in a rich blue gown that set off her brown skin to perfection, a turban of the same silk wound around the tight-curled locks of her hair, graced with comet-streaks of silver. Her shawl was deep gray and very fine where it looped about her neck and shoulders.

Lucy used the depth of her curtsy to cover for her amazement, and hoped her knees wouldn't give out and drop her in a heap to the floor. Oléron was a woman! A dark-skinned woman! As soon as the first shock had passed, she was flooded with chagrin at one simple, telling fact: the possibility of Oléron being anything other than a white-skinned man had quite simply not occurred to her.

What a mortifying realization for someone who prided herself on being keenly observant.

Well, astronomers did spend most of their time being wrong. What mattered was what they did when they realized the truth.

Lucy lifted her head and found herself the subject of an eye that twinkled sternly as a polar star. "So this is the translator of my work into English?" The marquise's accent was faint and charming, and when she smiled, laugh lines appeared at the corners of her mouth. "Our friend has sent me a copy—it was rather beautiful. Even the parts I did not write."

Lucy's blush could have melted all the ice in the world. "I tried to do justice to your work, madame."

"Do you plan to continue the project? There are five planned volumes in the *Méchanique céleste*. Two are out already."

Lucy bit her lip. "I have not thought that far ahead," she confessed. "Would you want me to continue?"

Her elegant eyebrow arched. "So long as you send me the manuscripts to critique before they are printed, it would please me very much to see more of your translating. There were, of course, a few phrases I should have liked to alter. Trifles, really, but I have spent fifty years trying to be precise about things and I am not about to change at so late a date as this."

Aunt Kelmarsh was laughing silently into her sleeve.

The marquise turned to Catherine and Mr. Frampton, who had watched this exchange with a mix of relish (his) and wonder (hers). "Now that your friends have arrived, monsieur, shall we go up?"

"Of course," he replied, and offered her his arm.

She waved him aside and grasped Lucy's elbow. "I should like to talk to this young lady a bit more, I think," she said.

She set a careful pace up the stairs, which Lucy took care to match.

"My ankle has not been the same this decade," the marquise explained. "The emperor's reign did not, it turns out, agree with me in every particular."

They walked a few steps in silence while Lucy's brain spun, placing new facts alongside the old ones and forging new connections and conclusions. The future had taken on a new but no less ominous cast—and not just for Lucy herself. She cleared her throat as they ascended to the first-floor landing. "I feel I ought to warn you, madame—the Polite Science Society has never admitted women to their membership before. When they realize you are not a man, they may rescind the invitation entirely. And . . ." she trailed off, took a breath, and plunged forward. "They may be cruelly insulting when they do it."

The marquise narrowed her dark eyes. "Yes, I noticed how graciously they worded their invitation for tonight's discussion. I also noticed how openly they questioned the legitimacy of your work. Such clever men, such logical arguments. Mr. Frampton sent me that paper, too. And told

me how shamefully they have treated him during this whole
business."

"He is a very prolific correspondent," Lucy said wryly.

The marquise chuckled. "But an earnest one. He reminds
me of my nephews—and a little of myself." She tossed her
head. "Do you know, my grandmother was friends with
Voltaire? So many clever men in that generation. I used to
sneak down to listen to them sharpen their wits on each
other in her salon. Once I was old enough to attend evening
parties myself, I learned how vicious things could get when
a dozen people are all trying to prove they are the cleverest
one in the room. This was long after the great man's death, of
course—but I dare say nobody has proved half as clever since
he left us." Her lips curved with a duelist's anticipation. "I
do hope these Society men have cause to regret all the errors
they'll soon learn they've made."

The lofty room at the top of the stairs was awash with
candlelight and cutlery. Windows looked out on the darkened Thames and reflected images of the guests back to
themselves. Botanists and chemists and astronomers and
naturalists greeted one another after the long year apart,
and immediately took up the thread of last year's arguments.
New debates sprouted up with each shift in the crowd, adding
to the cacophony. The din lessened briefly as the assembled
Fellows took note of Lucy's arrival, then redoubled itself with
vicious interest.

Lucy kept her chin high, though she still felt shaky. The
marquise preened like a bird of prey.

Mr. Frampton indicated the raised table at the head of

the room, with two podiums and places set to either side. "If you'll pardon me, ladies, I should present madame la marquise to our host."

Mr. Hawley was standing guard over one podium, his soft gray hair combed high. He'd chosen court dress for the evening, with breeches and buckles and a formal froth of lace. It made him look distinctly old-fashioned among the crowd, as though he'd stepped out of one of the last century's portraits where they hung in the gallery.

The marquise nodded to Lucy. "I look forward to our conversation after dinner," she said. With a touch of her hand, she allowed Mr. Frampton to lead her at a regal pace toward the front of the room.

Catherine asked a discreet question of a footman and learned that the other podium, and the place just beside it, had been reserved for Lucy. Catherine herself had been seated some ways apart with Aunt Kelmarsh. The countess grimaced to hear it, but quickly smoothed out her face and squeezed Lucy's hands. "It will all come right," she said. "Remember: you are brilliant." Her eyes flicked down to Lucy's mouth, and Lucy wished more than anything that she could steal a kiss for luck.

Afterward, she promised herself, then let go of Catherine's hands and turned toward her lonely seat.

She slowed and lingered: Mr. Frampton and the marquise were approaching Mr. Hawley, and if Lucy took her own chair she would not have quite such a good view on the encounter.

Mr. Frampton was making the introduction, his face

serene but for the fire in his eyes, and as he finished, the marquise held out one gloved hand, as graceful a gesture as Lucy could ever have expected of a French aristocrat. But Mr. Hawley . . .

Mr. Hawley went flat crimson as realization struck.

The marquise's hand hovered in midair.

Slowly, as the blood drained out of his face, Mr. Hawley reached out and grasped her hand, bowing over it. He said a few words, and the marquise responded, and allowed the visibly flustered gentleman to lead her over to her seat, beside his.

Mr. Frampton took up the place on Mr. Hawley's other side, and Lucy hurried forward to take her allotted seat beside the second podium.

For her sins, they'd seated Richard Wilby on her left. Dinner service began, and Lucy moved food around on her plate, put a little in her mouth to taste the sauce, and sipped only slightly at her wine.

Mr. Wilby, on the other hand, was in the highest of spirits, and tucked into his meat with an appetite. "Is the food always this good?" he asked, then immediately smirked and clucked his tongue. "Oh, I'm sorry, Miss Muchelney, I forgot—you've never been to a Symposium before."

"Perhaps I never will again," she replied, just to see him choke a little in surprise. She sipped her wine again, red as blood. "I can't imagine they are all as dramatic as this one will surely be."

He snickered. "That would be difficult, considering that we have never had an imposter as a guest before."

"Of course you have," Lucy contradicted breezily. Her fears were dissolving into bubbles that fizzed angrily in her thoughts. Not the wine, but the absurdity of it all had gone to her head. "Mr. Arbuthnot St. John in 1768 was found to have falsified several of his much-discussed experiments in magnetism. They struck him from the Fellowship rolls for his deception. That's only one instance, of course, but there are several others if you look back through the archives of *Polite Philosophies*. Not one of us is truly safe in this company, Mr. Wilby." She raised her glass in a mocking toast, letting the rim tilt pointedly in his direction.

It took him a long, long moment to swallow that bite of steak.

Lucy warmed to her theme and leaned in conspiratorially. "Tell me: Do you really think I stole my father's translation? Or did you just think it was a sound rhetorical tactic to increase your own standing in the Society?"

Mr. Wilby sputtered. "I think we have very little proof that the translation is yours, Miss Muchelney."

"Other than the fact that it exists and was published with my name on the title page? And that nobody else has stepped forward to claim credit—or a share in the royalties? Which, I should add, are not inconsiderable."

"People love a scandal," he sniffed.

"Oh yes," Lucy said with relish, "they very much do."

Mr. Hawley rose from his seat just then, and as he took the podium, the patchwork of arguments gave way to a single taut and very pregnant silence. "Gentlemen, Society Fellows, and honored guests," Mr. Hawley began. "I had prepared some few remarks with which to open tonight's discussion, but . . ." He glanced at the papers in his hand, and then uneasily at the marquise. He coughed slightly and allowed himself another gulp of wine. "Upon reflection, I think the most direct way is simply to begin. Ladies and gentlemen, please welcome Gervaise Marie Oléron, Marquise de Lantier."

Applause started up automatically, then scattered, and mixed with increasing murmurs of surprise as the marquise rose, thanked Mr. Hawley, and glided over to stand at the podium.

She cast her eye over the muttering assemblage of gentlemen like a general surveying the field. "So," she began, her voice ringing out to the very edges of the room.

Silence fell, almost in spite of itself. A few gentlemen who'd lurched to their feet slowly sat down again.

Lucy hid a smile. The marquise had grown up in the shadow of Voltaire, and survived both the Revolution and Napoleon's empire. Of course she would refuse to be quelled by a roomful of fractious academics.

She began again as soon as she had the room's attention. "My mother, Gabrièle Louise de Castagnère, Comtesse de Semur, was the first to translate Isaac Newton's great works into French for our astronomers, philosophers, and mathematicians. Her translations are still the primary editions used in my country to this day, nearly a century after she published her translation of the *Principia*. I grew up with Monsieur Newton's *Opticks* instead of bedtime stories, and my life's work has been to build upon the truths he discovered and the calculations his work made possible. He claimed he had only seen further because he stood on the shoulders of his predecessors. So, too, does our age seek to look ever farther—and higher— the better to comprehend our place in the universe.

"It is a jostling business, this climb. We must take care that what we set our feet upon is sound, and that it can support us as we move higher. We have to trust one another, that we don't end up pulling one another down in the scramble to succeed. And all of us, even the most brilliant, even Newton himself, must yield pride of place to the generations who come after us." She paused, and her eye pinned every member of the audience in place. "Your English astronomers now can begin to evaluate how sturdy my own conclusions are. You have invited me into your Society as an honor—but also to test the one who has framed my words in English, and added explanations of her own. It is of the utmost importance that we understand one another clearly. So I would like to ask her to stand, while I put a few questions to her."

The crowd hummed like a hive of bees ready to swarm.

Lucy gulped and rose to her feet. The wood of the podium was old and well polished by a hundred years of sweaty hands. She clutched it as she'd clutch a ship's wheel in the midst of rising wind and waves.

Two hundred faces bent an avid light upon her—but if she looked at the crowd, she would lose all her nerve. Instead she looked steadily at Gervaise Oléron, whose slight nod of approval gave Lucy some relief.

"Miss Muchelney," the marquise began, "please tell these assembled gentlemen why you chose to expand my *Méchanique celeste*, rather than translate it plain."

Lucy's mouth went slack with surprise, before she caught it. Judging by the murmurs in the crowd, this was just as unexpected a tack for them as it was for her.

She cleared her throat and managed not to let her voice shake as she answered. "I admired the work extremely—but one of the reasons I admired it was that it synthesized so many ideas from so many other places. Newton, obviously, but also Lavoisier, Euler, Lagrange. Probably others I have not yet read. There are not many of us—especially among English astronomers—who have read all these authors either in the original or in a reliable translation. In your book it was . . . it was as if you'd built a ship and were sailing somewhere new. And important. I didn't want anyone to be left behind."

Lucy turned her head, and her gaze found Catherine out there in the crowd, haloed in candlelight, her eyes tender as morning stars.

Lucy smiled, unable to help herself. "I didn't want *anyone* to be left behind," she repeated, "whether or not they'd had the chance to study astronomy before picking up your book. It seemed natural to add explanations, to make it more clear what the text was putting into practice. The section on Saturn, for instance, makes good use of several recent advances, and is particularly worth being widely disseminated. The more minds we have working on a problem, the faster it will surely be solved."

"And has the reception been what you hoped?" the marquise asked. "Do you feel you have claimed more minds for science?"

Lucy's eyes found Catherine again. "I would not compel anyone to choose the subject if they were not of themselves inclined to pursue it. Science is not the only noble endeavor in this world." She raised her voice to cover the affronted murmur that bubbled up at this. "But anyone who yearns to discover more truths about the nature and order of our world—they ought to be encouraged, and not forced to re-discover what other people with better luck or more experience have already found out. Our energies are better spent if we work together than if we struggle separately—men and women of every nation and of every race."

"Hear hear!" This from Mr. Edwards, as the audience broke out again into restless murmurs.

The marquise raised her hand, and silence reigned again. The whole hall seemed to be holding its breath. "One final question, Miss Muchelney."

Lucy braced herself.

"What if I told you that in reading your translation, I discovered an error? A rather glaring one, in fact—fundamental to the section in which it appears."

Someone gasped. The marquise remained unruffled, her eyes stern, the slight curve of her lips warning Lucy to think carefully.

Lucy took a breath, as the silence lengthened. Denials rose up inside her—it was only natural to defend oneself against such a charge—but another moment's thought had her setting those instinctual denials aside. There were larger stakes here.

She faced the sea of avid scholars arrayed before her, and took a breath. "First, I would have to count myself in very good company: many of our greatest thinkers through history have been as famous for their mistakes as for their insights. Didn't Copernicus believe the sun revolved around the earth? And Newton's own work, though brilliant, has also been proven wrong in a dozen different ways." A few heads were nodding.

Lucy warmed to her theme. "Second, it would be vital to find out how the mistake came about. Was it an error in my assumptions, or in my data? Was it a mistake of imagination, or of deduction, or of hypothesis? Because unless we fix the way we think, we'll only be making the same kind of errors every time we try to solve the next problem."

"Would you publish an updated version of your translation?" the marquise asked, "or just let the mistake stand and move on to other work?"

"I would like to update my translation—but I should have to ask the publisher about that. There may be considerations I couldn't anticipate, as someone new to the trade. Can you . . ." she paused, then screwed her courage up. "Can you tell me what the error was?"

"Of course. It was in the section about tides and oscillation." Another hum of anticipation from the audience. "Your English indicates the tidal oscillations are a constant. As indeed they are, and must be. But it was in comparing your translation with my original that I realized my text had been not at all clear about this. It left open the possibility of the moon's gravity being a single action, rather than a continuous exertion. Which is absurd. So in reading your translation, I discovered my own error."

A roar went up from the surrounding Fellows.

The marquise chuckled at the consternation, and pitched her voice to soar over it. "I wrote to my publisher for a correction at once. As I told you before, I prefer to be precise."

For a moment everything in the world was chaos. Half-deafened by the hubbub of voices, Lucy once more sought out Catherine's face. The countess was laughing, but even from here Lucy could see the sparkle of tears in her eyes.

Relief, pure and sweet as ambrosia, poured over her. It was done. Oh, there would still be doubters to mutter quietly in the corner—but Lucy had stood up in front of the whole Society and proclaimed the truth about her work. Many of them had even accepted it: Mr. Edwards was applauding wildly and no few others were joining him.

The marquise lifted her hand—just a touch—and the hall went silent. She nodded at the President. "I believe I have fulfilled my role in this discussion. Mr. Hawley, I yield the floor to you."

More applause, though not without an undertone of uncertainty. The Society President bowed over the marquise's hand and stood before the podium. He looked shaken, winded, as though his whole world were spinning around him.

Lucy could sympathize, though not without a little vicious glee.

He cleared his throat twice before he managed to form words. "My esteemed Fellows of the Polite Science Society: tonight we invited one of the most brilliant scholars of our age to become the newest addition to our fellowship. Her words tonight have moved me greatly. They ring of the same keen insight that makes her astronomical work so substantial and significant." He deflated a bit, then pulled himself up again. "The Polite Science Society has never before admitted a woman into our lists. But tonight, let this tradition yield to a new and better one, even as we all must yield to the discoveries of those who follow in our footsteps. Please join me in welcoming our newest Fellow, Madame la Marquise de Lantier."

This time the applause thundered throughout the room, though Lucy saw one or two scowling faces slip out quietly into the hallway. Lucy herself clapped hard enough to make her palms burn, as the marquise rose to clasp Mr. Hawley's hand. Mr. Hawley then bid everyone a good night, though it was clear most of the assembled natural philosophers planned to linger and continue their beloved arguments with friends and nemeses alike.

Lucy rose, and Mr. Wilby was not so lost to politeness that he failed to rise with her. "Until next year, Mr. Wilby."

"Don't be certain, Miss Muchelney." His lips were pursed as though he'd swallowed an entire lemon since the discussion began, and with a nod that was barely polite enough to qualify, he scurried hastily away to a knot of red-faced and agitated young men in the corner.

Lucy turned—and found Mr. Hawley approaching. "My dear," he said, holding out his hands.

Lucy didn't take them. She only raised her head. "Mr. Hawley."

He dropped his hands after a moment, chagrin reddening his face like a sunrise. "I'm sure I owe you an apology."

"I'm sure you do—but there's someone else you might apologize to first, if you please."

He huffed a little. "I'm certain I have done nothing to offend madame la marquise—though really, someone ought to have warned me . . ."

"No." Lucy shook her head. "You ought to apologize to your sister."

"How did you . . ." Mr. Hawley trailed off, then heaved a lengthy sigh as if letting go a burden long carried. Lucy fancied she could see every year of his age fall over him, one at a time. "We have not spoken in some time."

"She wanted to become a Fellow," Lucy said. "I read her letter. You *published* her letter."

"Yes. Not because I doubted her ability, but because I wanted to gauge what the rest of the Society thought of the notion of including women of science." He shook his head. "They were almost entirely against it. The language in the letters they sent back! Those I refrained from publishing—but I never forgot them. They haunt my nightmares to this day."

"You could have supported her," Lucy said, her voice low and stern.

"Would that have stopped them? As a Fellow, she would have been far more open to attack. All her work would have been doubted, all her hypotheses resisted. It would have meant endless trouble for all of us, and I cared about her too much to subject her to such a gauntlet."

"Did she agree with your decision?"

Mr. Hawley sighed again. "I think you know she did not." He looked over at the marquise, who was laughing merrily at something Mrs. Edwards was saying to her, while the novelist's husband blushed furiously. "She might have been here tonight," he murmured, then clamped his mouth shut and drew himself up. "Do you intend to put your name forward for Fellowship in the Society?"

Lucy nodded, holding his gaze. "Will I have your support?"

"My dear girl," Mr. Hawley began in his usual chastising tone, then seemed to catch himself. "You will," he said instead. His lips twisted up, but when his eyes met hers again, his gaze was clear and steady. "Though I may argue against many of your conclusions."

"Have I ever demanded you shouldn't?" Lucy countered.

"No. You have only ever asked for the truth. Forgive an old, stout man for not bending as swiftly as he ought." With a bow and a flourish, he walked over to Sir Eldon and Mr. Chattenden, who were looking rather green around the gills.

Lucy was above all a creature of curiosity, and there was one question left unanswered. She made her way through all the handshakes and congratulations to where Mr. Frampton stood sipping cheerfully at his port in a corner. "How did you know?" she asked.

"About the marquise being—the marquise?" He leaned in close. "In one of her early letters, she used a phrase—a very distinctive French idiom—which I'd only ever heard from my grandmother and her sisters from Saint-Domingue. It felt like a wild supposition—but every instinct I trust told me it was true." He hid a smile behind the amber liquid in his glass. "All the same, I was very relieved to greet her tonight and discover for sure that I was right."

"And it won't hurt your career any, to be known as a friend of Oléron."

"A very welcome benefit, I assure you." His gaze over the top of the glass was untroubled. "She really is the great genius of our age."

"I know," Lucy said, and rested a hand on his arm. He stilled, surprised. "Thank you. I am greatly in your debt." She paused. "Have you put your name forward as a Fellow?"

"Not yet," he said. "The issues with Mr. Wilby rather put me off, as you can imagine."

"Would you consider trying now? You'd be assured of the marquise's support, of course, and Mr. Edwards, among others. And mine, if the vote goes my way."

He grinned. "Let's both put our names up, and race each other to the Fellowship. Or else confuse our enemies so much they let one of us slip through in the chaos."

"And then that one can nudge the door a little wider as they go through," Lucy laughed. She bid him good-night, and went to find Catherine and Aunt Kelmarsh.

It was time to make her exit, while things were still triumphant.

The journey across the courtyard of Somerset House was completely different this second time—though if anything, it had gotten colder and icier since the Symposium began. Lucy held tight to Catherine's arm, as Aunt Kelmarsh anchored the countess's other side.

Lucy raised her head and looked beyond the rooftops of the city—and there above her were the stars, shining only faintly in the London light but still gleaming, eternal and re-liable. For a moment she felt she was almost one of them, her heart a glorious, shimmering piece of silver in her breast.

Then Aunt Kelmarsh grumbled something about the food, and Catherine laughed gently, and Lucy found herself back on earth. But a different earth than the one she'd walked just a few hours before. A wider earth, with more space to expand and grow into the best version of herself.

She couldn't wait to begin.

Lucy's inner glow of satisfaction lasted nearly an entire day—which was quite long, in her experience. But, as always, the ethereal feelings faded as mundane reality reasserted itself. She was left with the itching, irrepressible question: What on earth was she going to do next?

Translate the next volume and send it to the marquise, obviously—but what had once seemed bold and challenging now felt . . . routine. Her energies were expanding to meet the scope of the work she chose—which was good, obviously, because it meant she was making progress. But it also meant Lucy had to cast about now for something new to aim for.

Catherine—beautiful, quiet, stalwart Catherine, whose pride and love shone out undimmed every time she looked at Lucy—turned out to have something already planned. She and Lucy left Aunt Kelmarsh dozing comfortably in the parlor—helped along no doubt by the splash of brandy she'd taken in her tea—and made their way to the library.

Lucy expected Catherine would take out her silks or her sketchbook, but instead she brought out a sheaf of papers from her writing desk and sat down on the sofa in a very formal, expectant kind of way. "I have a proposal to make to you."

Lucy's heart leaped before good sense reasserted itself. The countess couldn't have meant *that* kind of proposal, obviously. "Please," she said instead.

Catherine bit her lip, and Lucy realized with a small shock that the countess was nervous. More nervous than Lucy had seen her since perhaps that first kiss.

Lucy's spine straightened in anticipation, and she leaned forward in the stiff wooden library chair.

Finally, the countess spoke. "I've been writing to the women from *Polite Philosophies*."

"Which women?"

Catherine smiled. "All of them."

Lucy was thunderstruck.

"Well, all of the ones we could find, anyway. Many of them wrote back—some to tell me they were done with that part of their life, but others to tell me quite eagerly what they'd been working on since then. And there's so much work! Chemistry, astronomy, botany—a great deal of botany, it's astonishing— but every field of natural science is represented, more or less. And they often know other women who are doing similar things in small corners of the country. Writing books to educate children, running small experiments, collecting and cataloging samples, that kind of thing. I've compiled rather a long list of names in the past few months, and no doubt there are many more to be found . . ." She caught herself, coughed, and smiled wryly. "I may be straying from the topic."

"Yes," Lucy agreed, marveling. "What are you proposing, exactly?"

"A fund," Catherine said, and grinned a little at the way

Lucy's jaw dropped. "A rather substantial fund, administered by you and me, for the purposes of publishing women's writing on the natural sciences. We would partner with Griffin's, solicit women of science to be authors, and arrange to have them checked thoroughly for accuracy before offering them to the public."

"That . . ." Lucy had to swallow against a dry throat. "That sounds like an immense amount of work."

"Oh, it will be, I assure you. It will tie us together legally, and financially, and probably take us the rest of our lives to accomplish." She bit her lip again, looking down at the papers in her hand. "It is really a very long list of names."

Lucy slipped out of the hard chair and went to her knees on the library rug. Her hands closed over Catherine's, letters rustling a protest between their fingers. Lucy didn't care. She couldn't take her eyes off the countess's face—because Catherine was blushing, was laughing silently, her eyes sparkling with unshed tears.

For once, Lucy wasn't the one crying—because she was too blissfully, incredibly happy to cry. "Catherine," she breathed. "Ask me truly."

Catherine looked up, her face shining with hope and love and joy. "I am asking you to stay with me for the rest of our lives. I am asking you to join me in making this world a better place, insofar as we are able. We cannot stand up in a church and make vows—but we can stand up, publicly, and declare that we are important. Together." Lucy's breath caught in a hiccup, as Catherine raised one hand and cupped her cheek. "I love you, Lucy Muchelney. I always will."

How could Lucy not kiss her, at such a moment? Their lips were smiling too wide to melt together properly, and she could taste the salt from Catherine's tears as they finally slipped down her cheeks. "I love you, Catherine St. Day," she said. "I'm yours."

"So you'll do it?" Catherine's eagerness was half embarrassed. "You like the idea?"

"I think it's perfect," Lucy said, "with one emendation."

Catherine braced herself.

Lucy's voice turned sly. "We should include illustrations by women artists as well. Commissioned engravings, portraits, diagrams, historical scenes. Embroidery designs."

"Oh." It was just one soft syllable, barely more than a breath, but it rang in the air as though it contained the whole world.

Lucy had thought Catherine couldn't look any happier—but now she looked luminous, radiant. As though a new sun had burst into being somewhere inside her. "You are brilliant, Lucy Muchelney, and that's the truth."

Lucy allowed herself one more kiss, then pulled Catherine to her feet. Being at the beginning of a project brought a rush of elation, swelling within her like a tide. Time was short: no point in wasting it. With her beloved's hands still clasped in hers, Lucy asked: "Where do we start?"

Stay tuned for the next captivating romance

in the Feminine Pursuits series

Coming in 2020!